PRAISE FOR GEORGE PELECANOS'S
THE DOUBLE

"*The Double* lives up to its author's definition of 'a good story.'...Pelecanos is up there on the top shelf with Dennis Lehane and Michael Connelly...who have a great deal to tell us about that endlessly interesting subject, the way we live now....For me the most interesting character in his fiction is the District itself....From where I sit, Pelecanos gets it all just right, and that he tells a hell of a good story is just very nice icing on a very tasty cake."   —Jonathan Yardley, *Washington Post*

"The dude knows how to write a story—and *The Double* reinforces his role as a top-drawer tough-guy novelist. As always, Pelecanos's attention to telling details brilliantly evokes life in the darker corners."   —Adam Woog, *Seattle Times*

"It's astonishing all the good stuff Pelecanos can pack into one unpretentious book: meaty substance, multiple story lines, vital characters, choice dialogue, and all those descriptive details that make the story so rich. What really stays with you, though, are those visits Lucas makes to veterans' hospitals...and those quiet talks he has with the forgotten soldiers he calls brothers."

—Marilyn Stasio, *New York Times Book Review*

"Pelecanos is a restless talent, but his books share a goal in common, which is to offer 'a good story told with clean, efficient writing, a plot involving a problem to be solved or surmounted, and everyday characters the reader could relate to.' This too is part of the challenge, and the strength, of his writing—that he does all that while also managing to give us more...the inner life of the characters, their struggles and their failings, their small solaces and their mistakes.... *The Double* is terrific on those elements."
                                —David L. Ulin, *Los Angeles Times*

"Pungent, funny, outstanding... *The Double* is fast-paced, its villains feel fresh, and Spero Lucas has room to grow as a character.... Call me a hard-core Pelecanos junkie."
                                —Jocelyn McClurg, *USA Today*

"The author laces his story with vivid descriptions of Washington's changing urban landscape. The writing is taut, the violence is graphic, and the characters are so well-drawn that they step off the page and into your life. *The Double* is as good as it gets."   —Bruce DeSilva, Associated Press

"Pelecanos's work has antecedents in the books and films of Richard Stark (Donald Westlake), John D. MacDonald, Elmore Leonard, and Don Siegel, but also a spooky magic all his own—thanks to the utter believability he maintains."
                                —Tom Nolan, *Wall Street Journal*

"Spero Lucas brings almost an excess of zeal to his assignments."   —Sherryl Connelly, *New York Daily News*

"A straight-ahead, head-banging, yet still character-focused crime story....In a kind of homage not only to John D. MacDonald...but also to Charles Willeford and Don Carpenter...Pelecanos reinterprets and updates the theme of the charismatic sociopath who revels in draining the souls of his willing victims, bringing a heightened sensitivity and social consciousness to the story without losing the visceral terror that drives the narrative. Those who know their crime-fiction history will love the references to earlier masters, but, finally, it's Pelecanos with a new series up and running hard that's the real cause for celebration here."

—Bill Ott, *Booklist* (starred review)

"A shotgun ride with a guy who you know is bound to hit a wall, hard, at some point...built by the same smooth narrative machinery that Pelecanos has fine-tuned in recent years."

—Mark Athitakis, *Washington City Paper*

"Pelecanos has never been content to let his characters drift through a series of books....It is what elevates his fiction to literary achievement. His portrayal of the physical and emotional toll of war lends *The Cut* and *The Double* additional gravitas that few writers are able to convey."

—Robert Anglen, *Arizona Republic*

ALSO BY GEORGE PELECANOS

The Cut

What It Was

The Way Home

The Turnaround

The Night Gardener

Drama City

Hard Revolution

Soul Circus

Hell to Pay

Right as Rain

Shame the Devil

The Sweet Forever

King Suckerman

The Big Blowdown

Down by the River Where the Dead Men Go

Shoedog

Nick's Trip

A Firing Offense

THE DOUBLE

A NOVEL

GEORGE PELECANOS

BACK BAY BOOKS
LITTLE, BROWN AND COMPANY
NEW YORK BOSTON LONDON

Copyright © 2013 by George P. Pelecanos
Reading group guide copyright © 2014 by George P. Pelecanos and Little, Brown and Company
Excerpt from *The Martini Shot* copyright © 2014 by George P. Pelecanos

Back Bay Books / Little, Brown and Company
Hachette Book Group
237 Park Avenue, New York, NY 10021
littlebrown.com

Originally published in hardcover by Little, Brown and Company, October 2013
First Back Bay paperback edition, September 2014

Back Bay Books is an imprint of Little, Brown and Company. The Back Bay Books name and logo are trademarks of Hachette Book Group, Inc.

The publisher is not responsible for websites (or their content) that are not owned by the publisher.

Library of Congress Cataloging-in-Publication Data
Pelecanos, George P.
The double / George Pelecanos.
    p. cm.—(Spero Lucas)
  ISBN 978-0-316-07839-9 (hc) / 978-0-316-23989-9 (large print) /
978-0-316-07840-5 (pb)
1. Art thefts—Fiction. 2. Detective and mystery stories.
I. Title.
PS3566.E354D68 2013
813'.54—dc23   2013017709

10 9 8 7 6 5 4 3 2 1

RRD-C

Printed in the United States of America

Now some men like the fishin' and some men like the fowlin'
And some men like to hear a cannonball a roarin'.
                    —*"Whiskey in the Jar" (traditional)*

THE
DOUBLE

ONE

TOM PETERSEN sat tall behind his desk. He wore tailored jeans, zippered boots, an aquamarine Ben Sherman shirt, and an aquamarine tie bearing large white polka dots. His blond hair was carefully disheveled. His hands were folded in his lap.

Spero Lucas, seated in a chair before the desk, was dressed in slim-cut Dickies work pants, a plain white T-shirt, and Nike boots. Lucas, Petersen's investigator, took in the criminal attorney's outfit with curiosity and amusement.

"What is it?" said Petersen.

"Your getup," said Lucas. "There's somethin about it."

"I only wear a tie when I'm in court."

"Something else."

"Think of your father. It'll come to you." Petersen looked down at the contents of a manila file that was open on his desk. Beside it sat other files heaped inside a reinforced hanging folder. The package was thick as a phone book. "Let's get back to this."

They were discussing the case of Calvin Bates, a Petersen

client. Bates had been charged with first degree murder in the death of his mistress, Edwina Christian.

"Where was the body found?" said Lucas. He opened the pocket-sized Moleskine notebook he carried and readied his pen.

"I'll give you this short file when we're done."

"You know I like to take notes. The details help me work it out in my head."

"Edwina's body was discovered in Southern Maryland. A wooded spot in Charles County, off the Indian Head Highway. Are you familiar with that area?"

"I put my kayak in down there from time to time."

"Edwina had been missing for a week. Once the police actively began to look into her disappearance, Edwina's mother pointed them in the direction of her lover. Bates was a multiple offender who'd been having an off-and-on extramarital relationship with Edwina for years."

"Both of them were married?"

"Bates was married. Edwina was single."

"How'd the police find Edwina?"

"Bates led them to her in a roundabout way. He was in the High Intensity Supervision Program, run by Pre-trial Services."

"HISP. I'm familiar with it. Bates was already up on charges?"

"Drug charges. Nothing violent, but he'd been violated, and he was looking at return time."

"So he was wearing a GPS bracelet."

"On his ankle. The device records longitude and latitude coordinates every ten seconds and uploads them each minute to a database run by a private company under contract with HISP."

"What company?"

"It's called Satellite Tracking of People. Orwellian, don't you think?"

"*Touch of Evil* is one of my favorite movies."

"Spero, sometimes you work too hard at being an aw-shucks kind of guy."

"It serves me well. So, the company was called STOP."

"You ex-military do love your acronyms."

"And the law went to STOP to collect the data on Bates's whereabouts."

"Correct. The data was plotted onto a satellite-based map, progressed in real time in a video format. The results are accurate to within fifty feet. If the bracelet wearer is in a vehicle, its movement can be tracked as well."

"Let me guess," said Lucas. "The autopsy on Edwina Christian determined a general time of death. The coordinates on Bates put him down in Southern Maryland, where Edwina's body was found, at that same time. Right?"

"It gets more damning. Bates had reported his Jeep as being stolen around the time of Edwina's disappearance."

"Model and year of the Jeep?"

"Two thousand Cherokee. Same as yours."

Lucas drove a 2001, but there wasn't enough difference in the model years to mention. It was the boxy Jeep with the I-6 engine, still seen in great numbers on highways, beaches, and city streets, though the car had not been produced in eleven years.

"The Jeep was found in D.C.," said Petersen. "It had been

doused in an accelerant and lit on fire. The Mobile Crime Lab guys had little to work with. No shell casings were found. No prints, no hair follicles. They did find brush and debris lodged in the undercarriage, which suggested that the truck had been recently driven off-road."

"As they're engineered to do. How'd the police find Edwina's body?"

"The GPS coordinates led them to a farm alongside acreage that was heavily forested. They observed tire tracks on a dirt road leading into the woods. The imprints matched the tread patterns on the tires of the burned Jeep."

"How'd they find Edwina *exactly?*"

"Technology got them to the area. Nature led them to the body. The detectives saw buzzards circling over the treetops. They eyeballed the general location of the buzzards and walked into the woods. Edwina had been shot once behind the ear at close range, a small-caliber slug in her brainpan. She'd been picked over by the wildlife pretty thoroughly."

In the file, Petersen found several photographs, original size and blown up, and pushed them across the desk to Lucas. The photos were of the tire tracks found in Charles County. "Notice anything?" said Petersen. When Lucas did not reply, Petersen said, "The tires are kinda fat for that model Jeep, aren't they?"

"Doesn't mean anything. I have eighteens on mine. But I've seen twenty-twos mounted on those lifted Cherokees as well." Lucas stared at one of the photographs. There was something there, but the reveal was yet to come. "Can I walk with these?"

"I made this file for you. I've got the State's discovery material as well if you want to have a look at it here in the office. Three hundred and fifty pages' worth."

"I was gonna grab some lunch."

"Stay here and read some of the material. I'm going over to Carmine's on Seventh. I'll bring you something back."

"Calamari with red sauce, please."

Petersen waved his hand dismissively. "Peasant food."

"Don't sleep on squid," said Lucas. "It sounds like they've got your boy Bates dead to rights."

"Not yet," said Petersen. "But I'm playing an away game. The trial's in La Plata. I've never worked in that courtroom, and I don't know any of the black robes down there. I need your help. Anything you can give me."

"You think Bates murdered her?"

"That's irrelevant to me."

"What would be his motive?"

"Edwina's mother claimed that Edwina was trying to break up with him. That she decided she was done running around with a married man. Possible scenario? Bates couldn't deal with the breakup. If she didn't want to be with him, she wouldn't be with anyone else. Something like that."

Lucas stood. His back was beginning to feel the discomfort of sitting in one of the hard chairs on the uneven planked hardwood floors of Petersen's office. The attorney refused to modernize the rooms of the nineteenth-century row house, set on a corner of 5th and D, near the federal courts. He said he preferred to keep its "integrity" intact.

"*Between the Buttons,*" said Lucas, as it came to him, looking at Petersen's shirt and tie. At Petersen's suggestion, he'd been thinking of his late father, Van Lucas, who had owned an extensive Stones vinyl collection, from their first eponymous release through 1981's *Tattoo You*, which many, Lucas's father included, believed to be the last Rolling Stones record that mattered.

"Very good," said Petersen. "Charlie Watts is wearing an outfit like this in the cover photo. Of course, he's also wearing a double-breasted overcoat in the shot, but it's a bit hot for that today."

"But why are you dressed like him? Do you subscribe to *Teen Beat*, too?"

"I'm partial to *Tiger Beat*."

"Why that record?"

"Just having fun. It's a very cool cover, and an underrated album, especially the UK version. 'Backstreet Girl' is one of the most beautiful songs the lads ever cut. The Beatles never recorded a song so honest or so real."

Lucas had no skin in the Beatles versus Stones game, and offered no argument. In musical matters, particularly classic rock, he deferred to Petersen, who played no instrument but was a bona fide music freak. A few months back he had taken his annual trip to Jazz Fest, where he typically took in both weekends of the event and crawled back with sunburn, a headache, and ten extra pounds.

"Well, you look real spiffy," said Lucas. "Like a hairstylist on Carnaby Street. Or something."

"And you? Where did you buy that T-shirt? It's not Fruit of the Loom."

"American Apparel."

"And I'm guessing it's a medium, not a large. You're wearing it a size too small."

"For the fit. Your point?"

"Your look is just as studied as mine, in its own way."

"Don't include me in your club. I woke up this morning and threw this on."

At an inch under six feet, Lucas was not particularly tall, and at 175, his summer weight, he was not imposing. Nor was he a strutting peacock. His hair was black, kept short by a Nigerian barber at Afrikutz on Georgia Avenue, and he wore no jewelry, outside of his crucifix and *mati*. He was not stunningly handsome, certainly not in the manner of his brother Leo, who was one year older and looked like a young Denzel. But he had something. When he walked down the street or into a bar, women noticed him. Some of them got damp. He had recently turned thirty-one, and he was as lean, cut, and fit as the day he walked out of boot.

"Which reminds me," said Petersen. "While I'm out getting you lunch, no fraternizing with my interns."

"Right."

"Have you seen Constance lately?"

"No," said Lucas.

"I had planned on promoting her here."

"Guess she had other plans."

"Whatever happened between the two of you, she didn't want to cross paths with you anymore. That's why she left this office. When you have an opportunity to be with a quality young lady like Constance...A woman as choice as her doesn't fall into your hands every day, Spero."

"We had fun," said Lucas. "I liked Constance."

He knew that she was special. But he had been to bed with another woman while he'd been with her. He hadn't promised

Constance, directly or implicitly, that he would be faithful. He was a young man, making up for lost time. He was sorry that it hadn't worked out between them, but he had little remorse.

Petersen looked at Lucas, a marine veteran of Iraq who had fought in Fallujah, where the fiercest house-to-house combat of the war, perhaps any war, had occurred. A man who'd left his youth in the Middle East and come back looking for a replication of what he had experienced there every day: a sense of purpose and heightened sensation. Petersen sensed that there were night-black shadows beneath the surface of his investigator's cool facade. He was fond of Lucas, at times close to fatherly, but in personal matters, out of respect, Petersen didn't push him.

"On the Bates thing?" said Petersen. "Get me something."

Lucas said, "I will."

THAT EVENING, Lucas smoked a little weed, then grabbed his newest road bike, put it up on his shoulder, and walked it down the stairs of his crib. Summer nights were his favorite time to ride.

Lucas rented the top floor of a house on Emerson and Piney Branch Road, in Northwest, a four-square backed to a bucolic stretch of alley in 16th Street Heights. His landlord, an elderly fourth-generation Washingtonian named Miss Lee, lived on the first floor. His rent was reasonable and there was ample space for his bikes and kayak, which he hung from hooks on the back porch. When Miss Lee asked, he performed routine maintenance on the house and sometimes he did so unprompted. The setup, a country spot in the city, was perfect for him, though he suspected that his peace would soon be disrupted. A huge Mormon church had been erected across the alley in the past year and was due to open its doors. For now, though, all was quiet.

He had recently bought a used Greg LeMond bike from a friend who was about to leave the country for redeployment to Afghanistan. It was a righteous machine, but he didn't care for its rainbow of colors, and he wasn't into labels. Immediately he degreased, sanded, primed, and painted the tubes and forks a flat black. He kept the red wheels because he found them hot. It was a fast bike, significantly quicker than the one he had been riding for years.

Lucas swung onto his saddle, put his feet in the clips, and took 14th all the way downtown, then cut over into Northeast via K Street, and over to the 400 block of H, where he locked his bike to a post and entered Boundary Road, a restaurant on the edge of the thriving Atlas District. Unlike the riot corridors of U and 7th Streets, which had benefited more quickly from the construction of the Metro and its subway stations, H Street had taken forty years to be reborn after the '68 fires. Lit-up business establishments and the sounds of conversation and laughter on the street said that it was flourishing now.

Boundary Road was an airy two-story space: brick walls, a distinctive chandelier, low-key atmosphere. Lucas had a seat at the bar. The night manager, Dan, frequently played reggae and dub through the house system, an added attraction for Lucas. Plus, he could come as he was—tonight, black mountain-bike shorts and a plain white T-shirt—and not feel out of place. He ordered a Stella from the bartender, a friend named Amanda Brand, who had called and asked to see him. He had silent-bounced for Amanda in other establishments, so they had a history. She also knew of his side work and what he could do.

"You eating tonight, Spero?" said Amanda as she served him his beer.

"I'll have that flank steak, medium rare."

"We'll talk in a little bit, okay? I'm half in the weeds."

"I'm in no hurry," he said.

He listened to the Linton Kwesi Johnson coming through the system and drank from the neck of his cold beer. At the end of the full bar he noticed a nice-looking woman sitting alone. Their eyes met and hers did not cut away. It was he who blinked and lowered his gaze. He was typically a man of confidence, but her bold nature disturbed him. The next time he looked back at her she was getting up off her stool. He watched her walk toward him, heading for the restroom. She wore black jeans, a black tank top, and brown motorcycle boots with a T-strap and buckle. Her chestnut hair was shoulder length with cognac highlights. She had a strong, prominent nose and as she passed he saw her bright blue eyes, brilliant even in the low light of the room. She was tall, curvy, and full-breasted, built like a sixties movie star imported from Sweden or Italy. As she passed he studied her shoulders, her arms, and her back, and Lucas's mouth went dry. He had a long pull off his beer.

Amanda returned with his meal. The bar crowd thinned out somewhat.

"Eat," she said, nodding at his steak.

Lucas dug in and had his first taste. He swallowed and said, "What's up?"

"I have a friend, a woman named Grace. She's had a little trouble lately. I think you might be able to help her."

"What kind of trouble, exactly?"

"Man trouble. Not unusual for her, actually. Grace seems to attract a certain kind of guy. She's divorced, with a long line of cumsack boyfriends. They don't stick around long."

"Maybe it's her."

"If I didn't know her, I'd say the same thing. Thing is, she's a good person. She works for one of those feed-the-children nonprofits, even though she has a law degree and could be doing a lot better."

"So her flaw is her choice in men."

"This last guy she got tangled up with? If he's not a sociopath, he's in the next zip code."

"I'm no leg breaker."

"This is in your wheelhouse. He stole something from her, and she'd like to have it back. She suspects it wasn't the first time he took her off. But she can't prove it. The police won't do her any good. She needs some private help."

"What'd this gentleman take?"

"A painting. That's all I know. But I think he stole a lot more from her than that."

"Emotionally, you mean."

"You'll get it when you meet her."

"Is she aware of my cut?"

"I told her that you take forty percent."

"And if this turns into something, you'll get a piece of my recovery fee yourself, for the referral."

"Not on this one, Spero. Like I say, she's a friend."

"Give me her contact information," said Lucas. "And the contact information of that woman sitting down there on the end of the bar."

Amanda turned her head and saw the woman, still seated alone, a drink before her. "Does your periscope ever go down?"

"I like to live a full life. Do you know her name?"

"Grey Goose martini, rocks, three olives."

"Maybe I should buy her one."

"That's original."

"I never said I was clever. Just determined."

"Sure you wanna spring for the high shelf?"

"Please ask her if she'd like a drink, on me."

Amanda drifted. Lucas watched her make the pitch to the woman, and shortly thereafter the woman gathered her phone and shoulder bag. She left money and something else on the bar before she got up. Her eyes briefly found his as she passed by, and her lovely mouth turned up in a hint of a smile. And then she was gone.

Amanda returned. "She politely declined your offer."

Lucas spread his hands. "See? I don't always win."

"But the thing is, you pretty much do." Amanda placed a beverage napkin on the bar in front of Lucas. "She left her digits for you, handsome."

He looked at the name and phone number, folded the napkin, and stuffed it into a pocket of his shorts. "Sometimes a fella just gets lucky."

"What is it with you?"

"I don't know." And this was true. He was always somewhat surprised when a woman was interested in him. It wasn't like he was trying.

Lucas stood and reached for his wallet. He left twenty on thirty. If Amanda wasn't going to take a bite of his fee, at least he could treat her right.

"Thanks, Marine."

"My pleasure."

"Do me a favor. I'm going to give you Grace's contact information. Call her."

"I'll hit her up."

On the bike ride uptown, Lucas thought of the woman at the end of the bar, the challenge of a new job, the comfort of a payday, the night of sleep that was to come. Sex, work, money, and a comfortable bed. Everything he dreamed of when he was overseas. A guy didn't need anything else. He shifted into a lower gear and found his groove. It had been a good night, filled with promise.

He couldn't know of the trouble yet to come.

TWO

THE NEXT morning, Lucas read the *Post* while sitting on the back porch of his apartment as a robin tended to her nest in the eaves and a pair of mockingbirds tormented a cat crossing the alley. In Metro an article detailed the noted drop in homicides and higher closure rate under the stewardship of Chief Cathy Lanier. A cultural shift, a civil servant–based economy mostly immune to the recession, and gentrification had played a role in the city's resurgence as well. Still, for many, tragedy was not a stranger, and several high-profile murders, both long ago and in the not-too-distant past, were on the mind of Washington's residents.

The vicious murder of Catherine Fuller, a ninety-nine-pound housewife and mother, in a Northeast alley in 1984 was perhaps the most brutal and senseless crime in D.C. history, emblematic of a decade gone wrong. Fuller had been beaten to death and sodomized with a metal pipe for fifty dollars and the cheap rings she wore on her fingers. Her ribs had been broken, her liver torn. Several young men went to prison for the crime, and those who were still alive were now being retried. Allegedly, confessions had been coerced, false testimony given, evidence suppressed. The retrial, for some, had reopened wounds.

The loved ones of Nori Amaya, found murdered in October 2009 in her apartment at the Woodner, her fingernails removed to erase DNA evidence, had yet to find justice or peace. Nori's killer was in the wind, and questions of investigative neglect persisted. Similarly, closure had not come to the friends and family of Lucki Pannell, eighteen, shot and killed in a drive-by. Racist reader comments in the *Washington Post* notwithstanding, Lucki was not a thug or corner girl, but a straight, vivacious high school student whose murder remained unsolved. District Councilman Jim Graham, when asked to comment, said that the victim was "in the wrong place at the wrong time." Lucas could only shake his head when he'd read the quote. Wrong place? Lucki had been on the porch of her own house when she was shot.

For Lucas, the most haunting murder of late had been that of Cherise Roberts, found in a Dumpster, strangled, with traces of semen on her face and in her rectum, blocks north of Cardozo High School, where Lucki Pannell had also been enrolled, in March. Cherise had been a student of Leo Lucas, an English teacher at the school. After her death, Leo had counseled many of the students who had been her friends and classmates. Spero, who had seen much death, had done the same for Leo over beers on many late nights, and he knew Leo remained deeply troubled by her murder. Cherise's killer still walked free.

Lucas ate some breakfast and packed a lunch. He lashed his

kayak to foam blocks fitted on the crossbars of his Cherokee, stowed his bike and paddling gear, and drove down to Charles County, Maryland, via Route 210, which most still called the Indian Head Highway. The trip was only thirty-some miles south of the Capital Beltway, but culturally much further. He saw fundamentalist churches, Harley-riders with Confederate flag decals on their helmets, barbecue joints whose smoke made his mouth water, and many liquor stores. Lucas turned on Mattingly, the last possible left before hitting the entrance to the Naval Surface Warfare Center.

Lucas unloaded his boat near Slavin's Launch, on Mattawoman Creek, and pulled the green Wilderness Systems fourteen-foot touring kayak down to the waterline. Fishermen, county locals, cast from the shore, while others used boats of various size and horsepower from the launch. Mattawoman was one of the richest fishing areas of all the Potomac River branches, home to largemouth bass, perch, river herring, and shad. It was a pristine area for paddlers as well.

Lucas approached a man who had just now pulled an aluminum V-hull out on his trailer. The man had a great belly and pants held up by camouflage suspenders showing geese in flight and shotgun barrels pointing out of tall grass.

"How was it out there?" said Lucas.

"This creek is a fickle bitch," said the man. "I caught twelve healthy bass in one day, just a week ago, but today, nary a one. I did get these bad boys, though. Come see."

Lucas went with the man to the side of the boat and watched as he reached over the gunwales and removed the cover on a Styrofoam cooler. In it were a half dozen long, fat fish whose bodies were scaled and marked in the manner of pythons. Lucas had not seen anything quite like them.

"Snakeheads," said the man, grabbing one firmly with one hand and opening its mouth with a set of pliers he had removed from a hip sheath. Lucas saw rows of sharp teeth.

"What the hell?" said Lucas.

"Don't know how they got introduced to these waters, but they're here to stay. They're predators, but nothin preys on them. And the females carry hundreds of eggs in their sacs, so it ain't like they're going away. Know what else? They got legs." The man smiled at Lucas's wide-eyed expression. "That's right. They can walk on land."

"What are you gonna do with them?"

"Oh, I'll grill 'em up. I don't take nothin from out the water that I don't eat." The man looked at Lucas's kayak and grinned. "Don't fall in. These suckers bite."

Lucas paddled out into the creek, going left, away from the Potomac, deep into the freshwater marsh, along bottomland forest, wetlands, and acres of American lotus. He powered through wet grass, his stroke even and sure, the sun hot on his shoulders and back. He saw bald eagles in their distinctive gliding flight, and many egrets, and turtles, and a water snake swimming in an S-curve across his bow. After forty-five minutes the veins had popped out on his forearms and biceps, and his back had a pleasant ache. He pulled in to a sand berm at the end of a small island and beached his boat. From a collapsible cooler in the stern bulkhead he retrieved a spicy salami sandwich and a cold bottle of beer. He sat on a blanket, which he'd spread over shells and goose poop, and ate and drank under the spotted shade of a sparsely leafed tree, looking out at the sun mirroring off the creek and the deep green forest of oak and pine on a nearby shore.

On the paddle back to the launch, Lucas saw three more snakes cutting through the water. This was unusual and disturbing. Once, when he was a kid, he had awakened from a nightmare to find his father sitting on his bed. He told his dad that, in his bad dream, he had been chased by a snake, and he could not seem to get away.

"Only one snake?" said Van Lucas.

"Yes," said Spero.

"Then you got nothin to worry about, boy. The Greeks say that when you dream of one snake, it's your friend. More than one, it means something else."

"What does it mean when you see more than one snake, *Baba?*"

"Something bad's about to happen," said his father. "But not to you. Now, you go back to sleep."

"Don't leave me, okay? Stay here."

"I'm not goin anywhere, son."

Twenty years later, while in the desert in Iraq, Spero saw two horned vipers sidewinding up a dune at dusk, and felt a melancholy drop in his stomach. Van Lucas died the next day, in Washington, of the cancer that had slowly eaten his brain.

BY THE time he had loaded his boat and gear, and taken a bike ride on a railroad trail, it was late afternoon. Lucas drove back up the Indian Head Highway and, with the help of his GPS system, found the wooded area where Edwina Christian had been discovered. The forest was set back from acres of farmland, currently yielding a crop of soybean. The road that led into the woods was not a road exactly, but a cut-through in the field, worn down to dirt by years of use.

Lucas put his Jeep in 4WD and drove onto the road. Using the photographs he had brought with him, he found the approximate spot where Calvin Bates had allegedly left tracks from his Cherokee. Lucas parked his own Cherokee there. He got out and used his iPhone to take photographs of his vehicle in position. He studied the blown-up photographs of the Bates tracks, and compared them to the images on his phone. He then retrieved a twenty-five-foot Craftsman tape measure from his vehicle and took the width of the road, and the distance-width between his tires. He entered the numbers into the Notes app of his phone.

He had something now.

WHEN LUCAS got back to his place, he did some research on his laptop, then called Petersen and told him what he'd found.

"You're talking about the wheelbase," said Petersen.

"No," said Lucas. "The wheelbase is the distance between the center of the front wheel and the center of the rear wheel. I'm talking about the axle track: the distance between the centerline of two tires on the same axle."

"The width."

"Basically. Just from eyeballing the photos of the tracks, and putting my truck in the same spot, it looks to me that the tracks laid down on that road were wider than a Jeep Cherokee would leave."

"It looks to you."

"Go to the discovery and check it out. The police report will have the recorded distance between the tracks. Compare that distance to the axle-track specs on a 2000 Cherokee. I can damn near guarantee that the two measurements will differ. We're talking about a bigger vehicle, a heavy-duty truck or one of those oversized SUVs that nobody actually needs."

"You're saying what?"

"I don't know that Calvin Bates didn't kill that woman. Maybe he did, and maybe he took her down to those woods in his truck. But the tracks they found were not consistent with tracks from a Jeep of that year and model."

"What about the tire tread?"

"Any specific tire can be mounted on thousands, tens of thousands of different cars. Right? If you bring that up to a jury…"

"Thank you, Jack McCoy."

"Just sayin."

"It's something," said Petersen.

"I'm not done," said Lucas. "I'll talk to Edwina Christian's mother next. The transcripts of her interviews were a little off. You notice that?"

"She's had problems. She was once a police officer in PG County, but she left the force under a cloud. Something to do with a credit card scam."

"I'll get on it."

"Tonight?"

"No, not tonight. I've got an appointment with a woman."

"I should have known."

"Not like that. Business."

"One of your side jobs?"

"I'll talk to you soon."

Lucas ended the call and sat down in his favorite chair, set next to a side table holding books. He watched the dim light of dusk outside his windows, and felt a familiar stirring inside him. He looked again at his phone, scrolled through his contacts, and found the name and number he had entered the night before. He touched the number on the screen and waited.

"Charlotte Rivers," said the voice on the other end of the line.

"It's Spero Lucas. The guy at the bar of Boundary Road. White T-shirt, black shorts. You know, *GQ*'s Man of the Year?"

"I remember you."

"And I you."

"Hold on." He waited, and soon after that he heard the closing of a door.

"Hello?" said Lucas.

"I'm here."

"Thank you for, you know, being so nice last night. Giving me a chance, I mean. I should have come over and introduced myself."

"You tried to buy me a drink instead."

"I admit, that was clumsy. I was a little intimidated, to tell you the truth."

"By me?"

"You're a beautiful woman. I was sweaty from a bike ride, not properly dressed. I wasn't exactly at my best."

"But I left you my phone number anyway."

"I know. Why?"

"I'm not sure myself."

"Listen…"

"What?"

"Can I meet you sometime, for coffee, or whatever you'd like? I promise I'll come correct."

"I have some time tomorrow evening," she said. No hesitation. She suggested a time and place. Lucas wrote it down and they ended the call.

He stared stupidly at his cell. He thought of her walking past the bar, black tank top, black jeans, brown motorcycle boots, exquisitely built, those brilliant blue eyes, that up-turned mouth with the hint of a smile. Lucas had swelled and he felt flushed. The last time he'd gotten an erection while talking to a girl on the phone, he'd been a teenager. But this was a full-blown woman, not a girl. There was something about Charlotte Rivers that heated him. Maybe she was just another challenge, and he was hot with the thrill of the new.

He had an appointment with Grace Kinkaid. He took a shower and began to think of Charlotte and her throaty voice. He tried not to fall in love with a bar of soap while he was in the stall.

THREE

GRACE KINKAID lived on the 2300 block of Champlain Street, in Adams Morgan, in a newish condo building set on the slope between Columbia Road and Florida Avenue. Her place was orderly, gender neutral at first glance, and minimally furnished. The walls were painted in pale shades of green and gold.

Lucas and Grace sat on her balcony in fold-out chairs, a small black table between them. Below them, in the light of a streetlamp, a father and son kicked a soccer ball back and forth.

On the table lay a manila folder. Grace was drinking Chardonnay from a large glass meant for red wine. Lucas had gone with ice water. From inside her living room, music played through her open sliding glass doors. Her stereo dial was set to 89.3, WPFW, the jazz station broadcasting from a building on Champlain, a half block north of where they sat.

"The painting," said Lucas. "Can you describe it?"

"Take a look at it," said Grace, opening the folder and

pushing it across the table. The top sheet, one of many papers in the file, was a photograph of a framed oil painting mounted on a wall painted light green. Lucas supposed it had been taken while it hung in her condo.

"It's nice," said Lucas, to move the conversation along.

The painting was of two men, one middle-aged, one young, shown from the bare shoulders up, both of them looking directly into the eyes of the viewer. The middle-aged man had a gaunt face, a receding hairline, and a beard. The young man was clean shaven with a full head of black hair. The artist had painted a black backdrop for the older man and a brown backdrop for the younger one, giving the effect of separation within the frame. The portions of their chest and arms that showed were creamy white, while their necks and faces were burnished from the sun. Workers, thought Lucas. That, and the vaguely east-of-Europe features of the men, brought to mind one of those Russian proletariat posters...or something. He liked the painting, but he had no idea what he was looking at. Lucas didn't "know" art.

"It's called *The Double*," said Grace. "The artist is Loretta Browning. Born in nineteenth-century America, studied in New York and Chicago, moved to Paris after the First World War. Known for her portraitures, landscapes, and still-life paintings. Died in California, mid-twentieth century."

"You say she was known."

"Not *well* known. Up until recently, that is. Some scholarly reassessments and a few key gallery showings have elevated her reputation to the general public in the past ten years."

"And elevated the worth of her paintings."

"Considerably. I got the painting fifteen years ago."

"So you bought it relatively cheaply."

"I didn't buy it at all," said Grace. "It was a gift from my uncle Ron before he died. He said, 'Take good care of this, honey. It's going to be worth a lot of money someday.' He was right."

"How much is it worth?" said Lucas.

"I had it assessed before it was stolen. The man who came here and looked at it said it was worth somewhere in the neighborhood of two hundred thousand dollars."

"That's a pretty exclusive neighborhood."

"I know."

"And your uncle just gave you the painting? Why?"

"After my parents passed, my uncle became the father figure for me and my brothers. Then he came out as a gay man, officially, and my brothers, who weren't the most enlightened guys at the time, sort of rejected him. My uncle was a fair guy and he offered the painting to all of us. But my brothers looked at it, connected the images to Uncle Ron, and saw a picture of two gay guys. They felt that it promoted a lifestyle, and they didn't want it in their homes, what with their babies and all. Like a painting could corrupt their kids. Me, I just liked the way it looked, so I took it. Of course my brothers' feelings on the issue have evolved, just like our president's, but it's too late."

"It's too late for them to cash in because you own it."

"I used to own it."

"What happened?"

"I believe it was stolen by a man I was in a relationship with. A guy named Billy Hunter."

"Like it sounds, I assume," said Lucas, scribbling the name in his Moleskine notebook.

"Yes," said Grace. "I'm gonna have another glass of wine. Would you like something besides water?"

"I don't think so."

"You don't drink?"

"Not when I'm working."

"Please don't let me drink alone. I have some things to tell you that are somewhat difficult for me to talk about."

"Okay. I'll take a beer if you have it."

"I have a variety."

"Anything that's not light."

He watched her get out of her chair and, because he was that kind of man, watched her behind as she walked, somewhat unsteadily, into her apartment. She was a woman nearing her forties, or already there. Black hair undone, olive green slacks, a short-sleeve tangerine peasant shirt, simple sandals. Grace was attractive, with green eyes and an aquiline nose, but the eyes were needy, and her arms were too thin for her frame. Grace was untoned, with the spent look of a woman whose weight loss had come from stress.

She returned with a bottle of Dogfish Head and her own glass, refilled to the rim. Lucas guessed that Grace, on her third wine since he'd arrived, had a drinking problem. He'd seen the pattern in his mother, who had developed a dependency on alcohol after his father died.

Grace retook her seat and crossed one leg over the other.

Lucas sipped from his bottle. "That's good. Thanks."

"So," she said.

"Tell me about Billy Hunter."

"Where to start? I met him at the Safeway up on Columbia Road, by the vegetable and fruit bins. He asked me how to buy a ripe avocado, and the secret to a good guacamole. I thought it was a chance encounter. I now think it was a setup."

"He followed you there?"

"I was a mark."

"How so?"

"I'll get to that later. Billy asked me out for coffee or a drink. I accepted. He was funny, he seemed to be a gentleman, he was handsome in a marina rat sort of way: tan, blond, blue-eyed, and fit. He was my body type, too. Strong legs, low center of gravity, powerfully built." She paused.

Lucas nodded awkwardly. "Go on."

"The next night, we met down at Cashion's."

"Columbia, off Eighteenth. I know the spot."

"I guess I had one too many glasses of wine. I don't normally take a man home with me on the first date, but I did. We made love that night and frankly it was wonderful. He was good in bed, with staying power. Tender when it was called for and rough when I wanted it to be."

She watched Lucas, whose eyes had gone down to the pages of his open notebook.

"Am I making you uncomfortable?" she said.

"I'm fine."

"What I'm telling you is pertinent to the story. You'll see where I'm going with this by the time I'm done."

"Go on."

"I started seeing him regularly. After that first night at Cashion's, we never went out. Billy always came to my place and it was always the same thing. We were in the bedroom minutes after he walked through the door. And we stayed in there for hours. Whatever tenderness he'd shown that first time was gone. He knew what he was doing. When he was in bed the light that I had seen in his eyes initially, the playfulness, was gone. He enjoyed wearing me out. There wasn't any lovemaking involved. He took me like an animal, and I liked it."

Lucas reached for the bottle of beer and took a pull.

"I'm forty-two years old," said Grace. "I've been with my share of men, but never anyone like him. When I wasn't with him, I was thinking of him. *Obsessing* is a better word. Preparing for the next time he'd come over, debating what to wear, how to fix my hair, all of that. I wanted to please him. All my planning and preparation, and he didn't even notice. He'd walk in, point to my outfit, and say, 'Take that shit off.' He'd put me right on my back. He'd put me on all fours, sit me on the bathroom sink, stand me up against a wall. I climaxed repeatedly, and every time I did, he laughed. It was like he'd won. For his part, he could only get there if I put him in my mouth. Then he'd get dressed without so much as a word and leave. You'd think I wouldn't allow myself to be treated that way, but I found myself desperate for him to come back. And also dreading it. Because I was aware what he was doing to me. I ate very little. I drank more than I ever did before. I began to lose weight. I knew that I was just a receptacle to him. I knew it and I didn't care."

"You never went to where he lived?" said Lucas, just to say something.

"No. He said he had a housemate he was trying to get rid of, that the atmosphere wouldn't be right."

"So you don't know his address."

"I don't."

"Or where he worked."

"All he said was that he was in finance."

"You communicated by cell?"

"Yes, we texted back and forth and sometimes I called him."

"You still have that number?"

"Yes, I have it."

"Give it to me."

Lucas wrote it down. "Did you see a credit card of his? A driver's license?"

Grace shook her head. "The one time we went out, he paid the tab in cash."

"So you don't know if his name is actually Billy Hunter."

"I can't be sure," said Grace. She picked up her glass and stood abruptly. There was sweat beaded on her face. Lucas's shirt was also damp. "I'm ready for another glass of wine. Would you like another beer?"

"I would."

"Meet me inside. It's cooler in there. Bring the file with you, okay?"

She disappeared into her condo. Lucas sat for a few minutes, digesting their conversation, then followed her inside. The volume on the stereo had been turned down very low. She was on a couch set before a glass table, where she had placed a fresh glass of wine and a new bottle of beer. Lucas dropped the file on the table and sat beside her. He noticed that Grace had run a brush through her hair.

"Are you shocked?" she said.

"Not at all," said Lucas, telling a lie. "How did this all end?"

"I came home one day to find that I'd been burgled."

"The painting was gone."

"Yes."

"Just the painting?"

"Yes."

"Was your condo broken into?"

"Nothing was broken. He had a key. I suppose he could have made an imprint of mine in putty, like thieves do. Or had one made off an original, then returned it discreetly. I keep an extra in a bowl by the door. "

"He, meaning Hunter."

"Of course."

"You're certain?"

Grace shrugged. "I haven't heard from him since the burglary. Stealing that painting was his way of screwing me again, one last time. It's in character for him, don't you think?"

"You tried texting or calling him?"

"I did, and I got dead air."

"He was probably using a burner," said Lucas.

"What?"

"A disposable cell. Let me ask you something: did you and Hunter ever discuss the value of the painting?"

"We never talked about the painting at all."

Lucas thought this over. "You said that you now think this was all a setup. That you were a mark. How so?"

"There are additional papers in that file. Take a look."

Lucas opened the file and withdrew a set of pages paper-clipped together, a series of printed e-mails between Grace and someone named Grant Summers. The earliest dated e-mail, from Summers to Grace, read:

> *Hello,*
> *I am selling this beautiful, well-maintained forest-green 2003 Mini Cooper S because my brigade will deploy for 14 months to*

Afghanistan. I'm under enormous time pressure cause I need to sell it fast, that is the reason I sell it so low. It is immaculate condition, non-smoker, well maintained, and hasn't been involved in accident...I have the title, free and clear, under my name. It is gently used with only 69,320 miles!!

It is still for sale if you are interested, price as stated in the ad: $2,990. The car is in Troy, NY, and in case it gets sold to you I'll take care of shipping. Let me know if your interest, e-mail me back!!

I've attached 90 photos.

Thank you,

> *Grant Summers*
> *4th Combat Engineer Battalion*
> *United States Marine Corps*
> *One team, one fight*

Below the name and battalion designation, the sender had included a replication of the Marine Corps insignia. Lucas felt his eyes narrow.

"I was looking for a Mini Cooper," said Grace. "My pre-midlife crisis. I could have bought a new one, but I'm a bit of a bargain hunter. I found an ad for one on Craigslist that looked like a great deal. It was the exact color I wanted, too."

"That's how they rope you in," said Lucas. He knew the rest but he allowed her to tell it.

"I e-mailed him back," said Grace. "I asked if we could speak over the phone, but he returned with a message saying that deploying marines aren't allowed to use a phone. He suggested we use an authorized third party for the escrow; I think it was Google Checkout."

"I suppose he took the liberty of opening an account."

"Right. Said he'd give me a five-day period to inspect and test-drive the car before the escrow account would release my payment to him. In that way, I would be protected…No disappointments, he said. He'd ship it free of charge with the title and two sets of keys. The money would have to be wired via Western Union. I was wary, but it was the car I really wanted at a very good price."

"Did you do it?"

"I tried. Drove over to my bank, withdrew the cash, and went to the nearest Western Union office. I was all set to wire the money when the lady behind the counter, nice Pakistani woman, talked me out of it. She'd seen this scam worked before. When I came home, I called the FBI and reported the whole thing. The guy on the other end of the line took my name and number but he never called me back. "

"The Feds don't have the time or manpower to chase a couple of thousand dollars down a rabbit hole."

"Is this a common crime?"

"It's the Nigerian four-one-nine scam," said Lucas. "So named for that country's four-one-nine code, after this type of Internet crime. Shame the Nigerians get tarred for the car thing too, but there it is. Why do you think Hunter was connected to this?"

"One night we were talking," said Grace. "One of those pointless conversations about what we'd do if we hit the lottery. Billy said, 'You could buy that Mini S you've always wanted.' And then he got a weird look on his face, like he knew he'd messed up. How would he know I had my eyes on a Mini Cooper S? I never told him. But Grant Summers knew, and I had given him my home address for the shipping of the car. Later on it made me think, maybe Billy Hunter and Grant Summers were the same man. That he saw me as an easy mark after the car thing and followed me from here to the Safeway that first night."

"Did Hunter have a foreign accent?"

"No."

"Most of the guys who pull these car scams are foreigners. Just by reading this top e-mail, there are several mistakes in the tenses and verbiage. That tells me that English was a second language for Grant Summers."

"You don't think the two events are connected?"

"I don't know. It's a stretch. But I'll look into it. That is, if you decide to hire me."

"Amanda said you get forty percent."

"I take it in cash. In this case, that equals eighty thousand dollars, based on the assessed value of the painting. It's a lot of money, Grace."

"I'm aware of that."

"Frankly, I find it odd that you would spend eighty grand getting back a painting that you got for free."

"Actually, I don't have the eighty yet. But I do have a buyer for the painting. Assuming you retrieve it for me."

"A buyer," said Lucas, trying to keep the skepticism from his voice.

"A serious collector has given me a pledge, in writing, that he'll purchase it for two hundred thousand dollars. When I sell *The Double*, I'll cut your eighty thousand out of the payment."

"This is real?"

"Yes."

"Okay. But you could take that money and buy a fleet of Minis, brand new and loaded, and pay retail this time."

"It's got nothing to do with money," said Grace. "I want to see that painting on my wall again, if only for a little while. In a way, he raped me, and he won. I need to take something back from him. When the painting is hanging on my wall, I can get started with my life again."

Lucas wasn't so sure. Grace Kinkaid's washed-out eyes, her pencil-thin arms, her increasingly slurred speech all told him she had a long way to go before she'd ever be right. "You want me to provide some references?"

"Not necessary. Amanda says you're competent and straight."

"So I'm hired?"

"Yes."

He touched his finger to the file. "Can I have this?"

"It's for you," said Grace, and she looked him over. "I hope you're as advertised. Billy's all kinds of twisted."

"Thanks for the work, and your confidence." Lucas picked up the file and stood. "I'll be in touch."

FOUR

THE FOLLOWING morning, Lucas worked at home. On his laptop, he typed in the names William Hunter and Bill Hunter and searched for them via his premium People Finder program. He came up with several hits in the District/Montgomery County, PG County, Maryland/Northern Virginia area, which folks now called the DMV. He recorded the most recent addresses of all the listings and, where available, the phone numbers, and made some calls.

Lucas reached a couple of men, discounted them due to age and their responses, and made a note to follow up on those William Hunters he couldn't reach. But he was not encouraged or particularly hopeful. Billy Hunter was most likely a fake name the predator had created. It had come to Lucas at the tail end of the previous night, when he had returned from Grace Kinkaid's apartment, smoked some herb, and sat thinking, expansively, in his living room chair.

Billy Hunter = Pussy Hunter.

A sociopath would create a name like that deliberately, and laugh about it.

Lucas opened the file Grace Kinkaid had given him. He looked at the e-mail from Grant Summers regarding the sale of the Mini Cooper S. Lucas figured that Summers's e-mail address, ending with @msn.com, had been set up as a throw-away, as scammers tended to use companies like MSN, Yahoo!, and Hotmail, which required no verification for the setup. Without a subpoena, which he had no chance of obtaining, tracing the address back to a specific computer or person would be impossible.

Lucas Googled and Bing-searched the address, and came up with nothing. He took the next step: e-mail tracking. Using three of his investigative database searches, IRBsearch, Lex-isNexis/Accurint, and Tracers, he attempted to identify the owner of the Grant Summers e-mail address. Again, nothing.

He was pretty sure the message had been sent from an Internet café in Paris, London, or Amsterdam, but for shits and grins Lucas highlighted the Grant Summers e-mail address and clicked on Options. A dialogue box opened, and at the bottom of the box there appeared a section, displayed in very small letters, called Internet Headers. There he found a series of numbers: the originating IP address of the Grant Summers e-mail. Using Melissa Data, he was able to locate the city, state, country, and zip code of origin, as well as the latitudinal and longitudinal coordinates of the e-mail's origin. Looking at the information, he felt both high and caffeinated. He Google-Mapped the coordinates and came up with a row house on a local street. The location lookup was not an exact science, and there was a chance that this was not the house he was looking for, but it put him on a block, enough for a neigh-borhood canvass. Grant Summers, whoever he was, might well have been a foreigner, but he was operating his car scam out of D.C.

Lucas saved the data.

He did four sets of forty push-ups on rotating stands, and two hundred crunches, his prison workout and daily ritual. He took a shower, dressed in utilitarian clothing, and drove his Jeep over to Prince George's County, where he had arranged an interview with the mother of Edwina Christian.

Lucas made a low hourly wage working for Tom Petersen, and he was looking at an eighty-thousand-dollar payoff on the Kinkaid job. A smart guy might have prioritized the work. But Lucas liked to honor his commitments, and he had promised Petersen he'd get him something useful before the trial. Also, he was curious.

VIRGINIA CHRISTIAN lived in a boxy brick apartment building in Hyattsville, off Ager Road, near the Northwest Branch of the Anacostia River. Lucas sometimes passed through this area on his long bike rides out to Lake Artemesia, and while pedal-ing through the partially wooded area of the neighborhood he always took care. Gang signs were sometimes spray-painted on the paved trail, and often he came across groups of young and not-so-young men smoking weed and drinking beer in the middle of the day. It wasn't the marijuana or the alcohol use that bothered him, as he partook himself. There had been several rapes and assaults on this stretch of the bike trail the past few years.

Virginia Christian let him in to her apartment, which

smelled of nicotine and fried food, and led him to a breakfast table. She was in her midforties, heavily made-up, large of leg and back, large-featured, with treated, tinted hair worn in waves and touching her shoulders. Rolls of excess weight showed beneath the lower portion of her deep red blouse.

Over the phone, Lucas had simply identified himself as an investigator, as he always did, which implied authority without detail or explanation, and Virginia had immediately said, "For who?" Lucas gave up the fact that he was working for Tom Petersen, the attorney defending Calvin Bates, who was charged with her daughter's murder. Surprisingly, she said he could come on over and talk. She had been a police officer at one time, she explained, and she understood the process, adding, "And the game."

The stale smell of alcohol came off Virginia Christian as they talked across the table. It was early, and the scent could have been a remnant of the night before. If so, it had been a long night of drink.

"You mind?" said Virginia, pausing before lighting a Newport that she had extracted from a deck.

"Not at all."

Lucas opened his notebook and uncapped a pen. Virginia used a blue butane lighter to put fire to her cigarette.

"So y'all trying to get Bates off?"

"Yes, ma'am. I'm an investigator working for the defense. And I'm very sorry for your loss."

"So am I."

"I mean you no disrespect."

"I was in law enforcement myself. You're just doin your job."

Lucas wondered if she had been good police, and where

and why she had gone off the path. Petersen had mentioned something about a credit card scam. The indiscretion had gotten her booted off the Prince George's County force, but she remained in the same line of work: Lucas had noticed a shirt with a security-company patch on a coat tree by the front door.

"Thank you for your consideration," said Lucas. "I'll make this brief."

"Go ahead."

"Edwina had been dating Calvin for how long?"

"Years, on and off. She was straight, had a steady job as a receptionist at an orthopedist's office in Greenbelt. Went to church regular. Smoked a little get-high and hit the clubs now and again, but that was all. Like a lot of women, she made poor decisions with regards to men."

"With Calvin, you mean."

"Bates was married, and he was in the life. Boy dealt chips. She knew it was wrong to be with a dude like him. I told her to leave that man and find someone who was right. She was trying. Started to see someone else, but Bates wouldn't leave her alone. He must have had somethin I couldn't see with my naked eye, 'cause she always went back to him."

Lucas stopped writing in his notebook. "I read something in the transcripts. In your interview, you indicated that at one point Edwina said she wanted to take care of Calvin. Is that right?"

"Edwina felt sorry for him, I guess. Looked at him like some kind of project. On Sundays, the preacher at our church blew her up with all that redemption stuff. How we got to support our men, through the good and the bad, do the Lord's work in our relationships. All that." Virginia dragged on her Newport and exhaled smoke. "For her trouble Bates shot her in the head and dumped her like a dog in those woods."

Lucas looked at his notes. "You said she was seeing someone else. Was this at the time of her death?"

Virginia nodded. "Man named Brian Dodson. Auto mechanic, works in a shop over by Cottage City, on Bladensburg Road."

"What's the name of the shop?"

"Handy's."

Lucas took down the information. "Like handyman, right?"

"Yes. Dodson's a quiet man, goes to work every day. Owns his own house in Colmar Manor. She met him at church, where he went regular. Edwina was too young to see the value in all of that. She liked the idea of runnin with a dangerous type, I guess. I remember what that was like. I liked 'em dangerous when I was young, too."

"I don't remember you talking about another man in the transcripts."

"I learned from my own years in law enforcement, when the lawyers do their interviews, you don't offer up any information 'less they ask for it specific. Besides, that detail isn't pertinent. I know who killed my daughter, and so do you. I don't hold it against you for trying to earn your pay, but please. That GPS device Bates wore put him down at the site of the murder, close to her time of death. Why would a city boy like him drive down to the woods of Charles County, at *night?* Why would he burn up his car? He was trying to destroy evidence is why. Like a lot of these fools who take their criminal cues from TV, he saw that shit on *CSI.*"

Lucas agreed with her about Bates. It looked like he was right as rain for the murder of Edwina Christian.

"Anything else?" said Lucas. "Something you didn't tell the police or prosecutors?"

"Nothing comes to mind," said Virginia, a hint of warmth in her eyes. "I'll answer anything you ask, if you care to get particular. But don't expect me to do your job for you, Lucas."

"Call me Spero."

"What kind of name is that?"

"Greek."

Virginia ashed her Newport. "Hmph."

Lucas closed his notebook and stood. "I appreciate your time. And again, my sympathies to you and your family."

"Bates killed my baby," said Virginia. "Bank that."

FIVE

Lucas drove over to the Walter Reed National Military Medical Center in Bethesda, Maryland. The longtime Washington hospital and attendant facilities, close to his apartment, had been recently shuttered, its wooded acreage between Georgia Avenue and 16th Street, just a handful of miles from the White House, too valuable to sit on any longer. It was a hump and inconvenience for Lucas to visit the hospital in the traffic-plagued city, but he continued to make the effort.

He drove through the security post without a hitch. He had been given a pass from his friend Gail Moore, an army public affairs officer who had previously been with AW2—the Army Wounded Warrior Program—and now worked for the army's chief of public affairs. Lucas lifted a box of books from the cargo area of his Jeep and took it into the building and down to the library.

Lucas had too many books in his apartment and he liked to pass them on to the wounded soldiers and marines who had little to do beyond their rehab. Some of the books were biography and history, and some were considered literary fiction, whatever that was. But like most people, the recovering veterans enjoyed a good story told with clean, efficient writing, a plot involving a problem to be solved or surmounted, and everyday characters the reader could relate to. Today Lucas had crime novels by Elmore Leonard, James Lee Burke, Lawrence Block, and James Crumley, and Westerns by Leonard, Jack Schaefer, Tom Franklin, Ron Hansen, and A. B. Guthrie. He had purchased a complete used Steinbeck paperback collection, all with the penguin on the spine, from Silver Spring Books the previous week, and had brought that along as well.

He slipped one of the paperbacks into his back pocket, left the others, and walked to the building housing Therapy Services. There he found Winston Dupree, here at his scheduled time in a large room crowded with patients, doctors, free weights, weight machines, treadmills, mats, medicine balls, and tennis balls. A golden retriever wandered the room, stopping occasionally to be petted, scratched, and talked to. Wounded veterans were working out or receiving PT, or road testing their recently installed prosthetic limbs. A young man in a harness, bearing new shin poles for legs, was gamely attempting his first steps, steadied by a therapist holding a leash.

Dupree sat on a raised stool, his thick right forearm resting on a padded table. Several adhesive electrodes, their cords attached to a nearby machine, had been stuck to the area around his elbow. Dupree was a tall, wide-shouldered man whose size was somewhat undercut by his wire-rim glasses and soft-spoken nature. He wore his hair in an unfashionable fade. Lucas removed the paperback from his pocket and pulled up a chair beside him.

"Luke," said Dupree, his pronounced overbite triggered by his smile.

"Got this for you." Lucas handed him the book. "Thought you'd like it."

Dupree inspected the cover. "Is this one of those with the white protagonist and his black sidekick?"

"It's not one of those."

"'Cause I read that one. The black dude is suspicious of the white dude at first. He's one of those angry black men who's been feeling the brunt of racial injustice his whole life."

"You mean, like a black militant."

"He's not wearing a beret or nothin like that. Got an attitude, is all. But the black dude comes around in the end, when he figures out that the white dude's all right. He's not like all those other insensitive white dudes that the black dude's known in the past. And it makes the black dude think: maybe not all white people are bad. There's hope for humanity, after all."

"The black guy likes women," said Lucas, getting into it, "but he doesn't like them too much. He's more into helping the white people solve their problems than he is nailing ass."

"Yeah, we never actually see him in the act. Thereby subverting the stereotype of the oversexed black man with the extra large Johnson." Dupree grinned. "Me, I'm quite the stereotype."

"Minus the extra large Johnson."

"I do like trim, though."

"You like thinking about it." Lucas nodded at Dupree's bum arm. "What happened, were you pulling on your rod so hard that you hurt yourself?"

"No, I was pullin on *yours*. Don't you remember?"

"That was you?"

"Actually, I was pulling a suitcase out of the trunk of a car, and I tore some shit around my elbow. Acute tendonitis, the doc says. Now they got me doing this ultrasound. It's a stubborn injury. I bounced back from my combat wound quicker than I did this."

Dupree had been an ace SAW gunner serving in the Second Battalion of the First Marine Regiment. He was fierce, dependable, and a key component of Lucas's unit. Near the Jolan graveyard, in Fallujah, an AK round had passed through his calf and shredded its primary muscle. Dupree would walk with a slight limp for the rest of his life.

"I can't even type on a laptop with this gimp-ass arm of mine," said Dupree.

"They'll fix you up," said Lucas.

"Hard to find a job if you can't work on a computer."

"But you're still looking, right? Anything going on?"

"With my leg, it's tough. Wasn't worth my time to put in an application with the police. Even rent-a-cop work's pretty much out of the question. Not qualified for an office and I don't want to be in one. I'm not about to stand up all day in some procurement center or factory. I guess I could apply to Bed, Bath, and motherfuckin Beyond or sumshit, but I doubt they'd want my broke-down self, either."

The golden retriever appeared and rested his nose on Dupree's thigh. With his right hand he scratched behind its ear. The frown that had come to Dupree's face faded. "That's a girl."

"Maybe you should work with animals," said Lucas.

"I do," said Dupree. "There's this organization, Paws4Vets, they get wounded soldiers like me to train service dogs for disabled veterans who are worse off than I am. You know, men and women who been blinded or generally can't get around. I did a program with the Warrior Transition Battalion at Winn Army Hospital. Now I got a pretty chocolate Lab mix I been training, living with me in my crib. I'm gonna have to give her up when they find the right match for her. That's the hard part, man."

"So you're working."

"Volunteer work," said Dupree. "Ain't the same as getting paid. A man only feels like a man when he gets a paycheck."

"And some pie."

"No doubt."

The dog lay down at Dupree's side and rested his head on one of his feet.

"I need something to do," said Dupree, looking directly into Lucas's eyes.

"I'll keep it in mind."

"I mean it, Luke."

"I won't forget." Lucas stood and bumped Dupree's fist. "Two-One, partner."

"Two-One," said Dupree.

LUCAS WALKED over to Building 8 and took the elevator up to the third floor. There he knocked on the door of Olivia O'Leary, a psychiatric therapist who counseled wounded soldiers and their families. Dr. O'Leary, a pushing-fifty brunette with the bright eyes of an optimist, told him to come in and have a seat.

"I can't stay long," said Lucas.

"I have a few minutes," said O'Leary. "Sit down."

Lucas took a chair across from her desk, crowded with paperwork, AW2 lapel pins, and American flag memorabilia. The office itself was cramped, bordering on claustrophobic. She had been told that this was her temporary space since the move, but had seen no evidence that a bigger office was in her future.

"I brought some books over for the troops," said Lucas. "Stopped by and saw Winston Dupree, down in therapy."

"He's having issues with his arm," said O'Leary.

"So you've spoken with him."

"Yes." Olivia O'Leary said nothing else.

Lucas said, "How did you find him?"

"You mean, what's his state of mind? Spero, you know I can't discuss that with you."

"I'm worried about him."

"How so?"

"He seems a little, you know, melancholy. I don't know what the professional term for that is. Depressed? We joked around some, but it was tired on his part, like he was forcing himself to be in a good mood. Winston's a little lost, you ask me. He hasn't been able to find any meaningful work. He has no…"

"Purpose."

"Yeah."

"A relative few are as fortunate as you've been, Spero. You've found work that approximates the exhilaration of the experience you had in the Middle East. Most don't have that. Coming home can be a relief, peaceful even. But after a while, when things stateside don't turn out like they've imagined, soldiers often feel a disappointment, a kind of void. Those feelings turn to bitterness and hurt. I'm not telling you that this is what's going on with Winston, specifically. I'm speaking in generalities, of course."

"I understand."

"Unlike many others, Winston's not alone. He gets good care here, and he's got friends like you who look in on him from time to time."

"Right."

O'Leary crossed one leg over the other and sat back in her chair. "You still keep in touch with Marquis Rollins?"

"Yeah," said Lucas, feeling himself smile. "I see Marquis up at the American Legion in Silver Spring every so often. We talk on the phone."

"Is he getting around okay on that leg of his?"

"It's part of him now. It hasn't slowed him down much." Rollins had a plastic knee and a titanium shin pole for a left leg. It had replaced the leg that had been amputated after an RPG had sent a piece of shrapnel, large as a mobile phone circa 1990, into his thigh, and caused irreparable infection. "Marquis has a business, goes to car auctions up north and brings back luxury automobiles for clients down here in D.C. He also has God and his church. And he chases all kinds of women. With intent. As you would say, he has purpose."

"What about the other guys in your outfit? What's become of them?"

Some came back in caskets, thought Lucas. They're buried in Metairie, Louisiana. In Houston, and in Arlington, Virginia. Solomon King is a top car salesman at a Ford dealership in Overland, Kansas. Greg Evans works in Pennsylvania, filling orders for an Internet retailer. Rick McKenzie is in a federal prison somewhere out West, doing twenty years to life for stabbing a man to death in a Missoula bar. David Hess is unemployed, living in his parents' basement in Galveston. Last time Lucas talked to him, Lawson Cochrane had married a stripper after a long night of Milwaukee's Best and an ounce of crystal meth. Ronald Wilson reenlisted and is serving in Afghanistan. Alfred Turner went back to college for a law degree. Joey Fabiano hung himself from the rafters of a log cabin in Colorado.

"I don't know," said Lucas. "I guess I haven't been in touch with them lately. I should try."

O'Leary looked at him directly. "And how are you?"

"I'm fine. Everything's going well."

"That's good to hear."

"No worries," said Lucas.

I killed a man in a church parking lot on Georgia Avenue two years ago. Broke the hyoid bone of his neck as he writhed and struggled beneath me. I shot and killed three others in a Northeast warehouse not long after that. But they all had it coming. They were trying to kill me.

Dr. O'Leary picked up a book that was sitting on her desk and let Lucas see its cover. It was the popular, recently published memoir written by Chris Kyle, a celebrated Navy SEAL sniper who had served in Iraq. "Have you read this?"

Lucas shook his head. "Not yet. I know of it."

"It was given to me by a client. I saw the author interviewed on Bill O'Reilly's show."

"I met Chris Kyle when he was shooting in Fallujah."

"Apparently he had one hundred and fifty confirmed kills."

"Those are the confirmed. There were probably more."

"On O'Reilly he claimed to have no remorse for the lives he took, including women. Do you find that odd?"

"Not particularly. Kyle took out one hundred and fifty enemy combatants who would have killed countless American marines and soldiers if they had the chance. That Texan saved a lot of lives."

"By taking lives."

"Yes." Lucas gripped the arm of his chair.

"Spero, are you all right?"

I'm fine.

"Why?"

"You seem disturbed."

"Not at all, ma'am."

Olivia O'Leary cleared her throat. "You should make an appointment and come in."

"I'm straight. Anyway, I'm not exactly the type who, you know, sits in a room and discusses his feelings."

"Doesn't mean there's something wrong with you if you do. It's always beneficial to talk to someone."

A brief silence settled between them.

"You're a good person, Olivia."

"I think you are, too."

Lucas pushed himself up from his chair and stood to his height. "Take care, Doc."

"*You* take care."

On the way out of the building, Lucas passed a woman, early in her middle age, seated in a chair outside a room with a closed door. She had a towel wrapped around one bloodless hand and it was pressed against her face. Her eyes were pink and swollen, and there were mascara tracks on her cheeks. He had heard her deep sobs from far down the hall. He guessed she had been crying for some time. He had seen her kind here before. Another war-fucked soldier's mom.

Walking on, he thought of the woman he was about to meet for drinks. Sex took his mind off the stink of death.

SIX

LUCAS VALETED his Jeep outside a boutique hotel on the 1200 block of 16th Street, four blocks north of the White House. He wore a lightly textured powder-blue shirt, cream-colored 501s, and brown double-buckle monk straps made in Italy. He could clean up when he wanted to, and when it was appropriate. He'd heard about this hotel and its refurbishment in 2009. His brother Leo brought women to the bar here, if they and the occasion were special. Leo had said the place was first-class.

Lucas walked on a checkerboard marble floor through a lobby lit by lamps and dusk filtered through skylights. He passed a pedestaled bust of Thomas Jefferson and a library whose shelves held leather-bound books, and he walked on into the bar, clean and subtly lit, and saw her sitting at the stick. She was wearing a simple orange dress with a low neckline that clung to her nicely rather than cheaply. The orange lighting of the bar complemented her dress. He stepped up to her and reached out his hand. She smiled, took it, and gripped it firmly.

"I'm Charlotte."

"Spero Lucas. Now we're properly introduced."

"Have a seat. I saved it for you."

"I bet that wasn't easy. A buncha guys must've been trying to score this seat."

"Tons. I had to beat them off."

"Your hand must be awful tired."

Charlotte laughed charitably. "Please, sit down."

He took a seat beside her in a high black chair. They were by the turn in the bar, nearest the windows fronting 16th. There were others in the room, but Lucas took no notice.

"I'm having wine," said Charlotte. "Do you like Italian red?"

"Sure, why not."

"This Barolo's pretty nice." She offered him her glass to try it.

He took a sip and nodded. "That's good."

Charlotte looked him over. "Let's have a bottle. You want to?"

He stayed with her lovely blue eyes. "I'm game."

The bartender, a slender, quiet man, soon came with a bottle, showed its label to Charlotte, then uncorked it and poured a bit in a fresh glass. She tasted it and made a motion with her chin, and he poured her a full portion and some for Lucas.

"Shall I leave the bottle on the bar?" said the tender.

"Please," said Charlotte.

They tapped glasses. He watched her close her eyes as she drank. Now that he was close, he saw that she was older than him by several years. Late thirties if he had to guess. Her age was in her smile lines and the light imprints around her eyes, but it showed nowhere else. Her skin was smooth and her complexion was flawless. She smelled faintly of rainwater. He supposed it was her shampoo. For jewelry she wore a thin gold bracelet with a Grecian key inlay, and a strand of ice-blue crystals around her neck. A tan line showed on her ring finger.

"Work today?" she said.

"Yes. You?"

"Uh-huh."

"What do you do?"

"I'm a lobbyist over on K Street." She gave him a brief history of her career. She had been a Hill staffer for several years and eventually had served on the Senate Foreign Relations Committee and traveled extensively overseas. The natural progression and her Middle East and Near East connections led her to lobbying, and her current firm.

"Who are some of your clients?"

"Pakistan," she said.

"Wow."

"It's work. What did you do today?"

Lucas described his day. He said that the secret most investigators keep is that the bulk of their modern-day work is done via computer programs, but that he preferred to get out and talk to people when he could. He described the Virginia Christian conversation, that technically they were on opposite sides of the fence, but that he'd liked her, and he felt she'd liked him.

"I'm a marine," he said, keeping it in the present tense, as he tended to do. He told her where he had served. He told her about his visit to Walter Reed, something he normally wouldn't share with anyone but fellow veterans and family. It could come off as self-serving, but she seemed interested.

"You look like you came out of the war all right," said Charlotte.

"I'm ahead," said Lucas.

"Why'd you settle back in D.C.?"

"Home. Family." And again, he began to talk unguardedly.

He told her that he was the son of Greek-American parents, one of four siblings, three of whom had been adopted. His sister, Irene, was the biological product of the marriage, and was now an attorney in San Francisco. She was emotionally distant and largely absent from their lives. Dimitrius, the oldest brother, was a charming, degenerate criminal, and currently in the wind. Another brother, Leo, was a local high school teacher and a standout individual in every respect since childhood. A combination of rock star, athlete, do-gooder, and stud. Spero was the youngest of the bunch. High school wrestler, not particularly gifted academically, but a hard worker. Tried community college, then joined the Corps. His father passed while Lucas was serving in Iraq. He was still close to his mom.

"Do you ever wonder who your real parents are?" said Charlotte.

"I know who my parents are," said Lucas. "Van and Eleni Lucas."

"Stupid question."

"Not at all."

"I'm sorry."

"Forget it."

Charlotte leaned in toward him. "So what do you do for fun?"

"I ride a bicycle and I have a kayak," said Lucas. "I like to get out there."

"What else?"

"I'm into older movies and music. I read a lot of books."

"What kind of music?"

"Smart lyrics with guitars. Solos get me off. That takes away my punk credentials, but hey. I like stuff with a Southern bent or feel. Lucero, My Morning Jacket, DBT. The Hold Steady, Dinosaur Jr., Sonic Youth…guitar-heavy stuff. At home I'll listen to reggae."

"That means…"

"Yeah."

"I don't smoke marijuana," said Charlotte.

"I won't hold it against you."

"It makes me sleepy."

"We wouldn't want that."

"No, we wouldn't," said Charlotte.

Lucas studied the curve of her mouth as she poured him more wine. She poured a glass for herself.

"Why'd you leave me your phone number the other night?" said Lucas.

"I'm sure it's not the first time it's happened to you."

"They didn't look like you."

"Stop."

"You're a knockout," said Lucas.

"Thank you."

"I mean it."

"I liked what I saw in you, too," said Charlotte. "Even in a white T-shirt and a pair of shorts, you left an impression. And when you walked in tonight…"

"What?"

She looked directly into his eyes. "Don't act like you don't know."

"Huh," said Lucas, clumsily. He felt himself blush.

"Not that I'm all about that. Handsome alone doesn't close it for me. I went back to Boundary Road the next night and talked with the bartender. She said good things about you. So it wasn't much of a risk on my part to meet you here."

"Here we are."

"Yes." She reached over and laid her hand upon his, right on the bar. He felt a warm current.

"What now?"

"You like the wine?"

"Yes."

"I've got another bottle in my room."

"You have a room here?"

"Uh-huh. Why don't we go upstairs?"

Lucas finished the wine in his glass. His trousers were tight, and he could feel his heart in his chest. He reached for his wallet, but she said, "No." She paid the bartender in cash. Tan line on her ring finger, and she wasn't leaving a paper trail.

Charlotte Rivers was a bundle of dynamite in a dress. She was smart, accomplished, and funny. She was also married. For now, Lucas didn't care.

"You ready?" said Charlotte, getting down off her chair.

He was already standing. He stepped aside and let her lead the way.

HER ROOM was an elegant suite, tastefully decorated, and tomb-quiet, with a nearly soundless air-conditioning system keeping the space cool. The bed was a king dressed in custom linens and a down duvet, and at the foot of it sat a black velvet settee facing out. A bottle of the same Barolo they had drunk at the bar sat on a dresser.

"Why don't you take care of that?" said Charlotte, nodding to the bottle.

Lucas uncorked it and poured wine into two short water glasses, while Charlotte went around the suite, lighting votive candles. When she was done she turned off the lamps and overhead lights and returned to him in the bedroom. The suite glowed in candlelight and the flame-light flickered on its walls.

"You brought your own candles," said Lucas, incredulously, as he handed her a glass.

"The staff brought them up at my request," she said. "My firm puts our visiting clients and dignitaries in the deluxe suites on the top floors. We spend a lot of money here, and I'm treated well. And they're discreet."

Lucas sipped his wine and put the glass on the dresser. Charlotte set hers down as well.

"You could have been up here with your candles all alone," said Lucas.

"But I'm not alone."

"What if I wasn't what you expected?"

"You are," said Charlotte. "Stop talking."

They kissed. He touched her fingers and her hand. Her mouth fit his perfectly. He knew that it would.

Standing, they kissed for ten, fifteen minutes, more. Their tongues touched but just as often it was with crushed lips. They stayed fully dressed. This was enough for now.

Charlotte stepped out of her heels. He gathered her up in his arms, her breath warm on his face. She unbuttoned his shirt and he let her peel it off him and it fell to the floor. She ran her hands up his forearms and biceps and then put her hand under his wife beater and caressed his abs, driving her tongue deeply into his mouth. Both of them broke off and stepped back. They were sweating. Her hair had fallen about her face.

"Badass," said Lucas, with admiration.

She turned and he unzipped her dress. He kissed her warm, damp neck as he undressed her, and she faced him then and unbuttoned his 501s. He stepped out of them and kicked them aside. He pulled his T-shirt over his head and dropped it to the carpet.

She was wearing a thong and a lacy black bra and she was more than he had imagined. He had on only his boxer briefs. She reached out and stroked him through the fabric. He unfastened her bra at the front. When she was free, her breasts, full with dark, raised nipples, barely dropped, and the sight of her took his breath away. Lucas and Charlotte stayed standing in an embrace and kissed, and he set her breasts up high on his chest, and she said his name, and they kissed there and against the wall, and on the bed, and lost the rest of their clothing. Two hours passed with them simply, passionately making love with their mouths and hearts. Nothing like this had ever happened to Lucas before.

Naked on the bed and so hard it ached, he tried to move between her thighs, but she stopped him.

"Why not?" said Lucas.

"Kiss me down there."

She got up off the bed and went to the black velvet settee at its foot and sat upon it, and Lucas kneeled in front of her on the carpet. He used his mouth, thumb, and forefinger, and his face became wet with her. She climaxed quietly, and after she caught her breath in the hum of the room she looked down at him and said, "Now you." Back on the bed, she took him in her mouth, tongued his balls and shaft, and artfully, the head of his cock, and he felt himself panting, and his rapid heart rate, and he said, "Charlotte," and came like a cannonball in a long, hot surge.

Afterward they lay on the bed talking, laughing, drinking wine, and kissing. It wasn't too long before he grew hard once again.

"Impressive," said Charlotte, reaching out and touching him.

"It's you," said Lucas. "And I'm young."

They made love for a long time, and finished each other the same way. It was after midnight when she said it was time to go.

"I'll sleep here with you," said Lucas.

"I can't," she said.

"Can we…"

"Yes," said Charlotte. "We'll do this again."

HE WAS still sweating when he got into his own bed at two in the morning, wide awake. The smell of her, the image of her hair down around her face, her beautiful breasts, her voice, they were still there with him in the room.

Lucas got dressed and left his apartment. He went north on foot, through the dark alleys of 16th Street Heights. He was troubled and exhilarated, both at once.

He thought that a walk in the night might clear his head.

SEVEN

HANDY'S GARAGE was located on a service road behind a strip center on the Cottage City side of Bladensburg Road, not far from the Anacostia River, which stretched up into Prince George's County, Maryland. Lucas had ridden his bike along the river and paddled it many times, but this commercial section of fast-food, Chinese/steak-and-cheese, Laundromats, and check-cashing establishments was unfamiliar to him.

Lucas parked his Jeep in a small lot crowded with older vehicles, mostly GM products: Cutlasses, Caprice Classics, Regals, and Grand Nationals. The lot edged a set of open bay doors. Two men worked on cars in the bay. One was tall with gray hair. He was holding a crescent wrench and looking at the undercarriage of a cream-colored Deville that was up on lifts. The other man was heavyset with a moon-shaped face. He was gunning the lug nuts off a half-ton GMC truck that was the sister to the Chevy Silverado. It was a hot day and both wore long pants and long-sleeve shirts rolled back off the wrists, and they looked to be suffering in the heat. Lucas recalled his father's words: "That's why they call it work."

An old Kool and the Gang track circa *Wild and Peaceful* played trebly from a boom box that looked like it had been through a paintball fight. Lucas's brother Leo had called the group Kook and the Gang when he was a kid. Leo was a good English teacher but he had always mangled his words.

"Excuse me," said Lucas, staying outside the bay doors, observing mechanic's protocol. Walking into a garage unannounced was akin to boarding someone's boat without permission.

"What can I do for you?" said the gray-haired man.

"I was looking to talk to Brian Dodson," said Lucas. "He around?"

Eye contact passed between the gray-haired man and the moonfaced man, and Lucas caught it.

"I'm Handy," said the gray-haired man. "That Cherokee givin you any trouble?"

"I take good care of it."

"They get a little funny on the back end after a while. And I bet your check engine light is on, too."

"It is," said Lucas. "It stays on. That's just an issue with air getting into the gas cap. These years had that quirk."

"So you don't need repair work done?"

"No. I'm just looking to get up with Brian Dodson."

"I'm Dodson," said the moonfaced man, and he laid down the lug gun, picked up a shop rag, and walked out of the bay into the hot sunlight. He stood before Lucas and looked down on him. Dodson was a tall man with broad shoulders and back.

"I'm an investigator. My name's Spero Lucas."

Lucas put his hand out. Dodson wiped his hands on the shop rag and made no comment or movement to reciprocate. His eyes were flat and devoid of any emotion.

"I'm here regarding the death of Edwina Christian. I understand the two of you dated. Is that correct?"

"You're not with Homicide."

"No, I'm not."

"Homicide police don't dress like you," said Dodson, looking over Lucas's blue Dickies, white T, and Nike boots.

"I work for an attorney," said Lucas, leaving out the fact that Petersen was a defender. "Mr. Dodson, I'll only take a few minutes of your time."

"You ain't gonna take *no* minutes of my time," said Dodson, and he turned and walked back into the bay, where he dropped the greasy rag to the concrete and picked up his lug gun.

Lucas stood with his hands by his side.

"You might just want to get a new gas cap, on account of it'll give you a better seal," said Handy, helpfully and with good cheer. "That is if the check engine light bothers you."

"It doesn't," said Lucas. "Thanks for the tip."

"Don't cost nothin," said Handy.

Lucas went back to his Jeep and drove away.

HE PARKED in the strip center and let his truck idle. He called Marquis Rollins's cell and got him on the third ring.

"Marquis."

"It *is*. Semper Fi."

"Busy today?"

"I am right now. Hold on." Marquis took his phone into

another room and Lucas waited. "Had a date last night that turned into something good. Ethiopian lady. I'm about to take her to a late breakfast."

"I thought you couldn't get to first base with African women."

"I took this gal *around* the bases."

"She blind or something?"

"They say it heightens the other senses. Taste, touch, feel…and voice, too, if that's a sense. When I got her there, you shoulda heard her calling out, with that accent of hers."

"She was calling for help, most likely. Will you be available late in the afternoon?"

"What you got in mind?"

Lucas told him, where and when.

HE HAD time, so he drove back into D.C. and over to North Capitol Street, the dividing line between the Northeast and Northwest quadrants of the city. He parked above Florida Avenue, where the neighborhoods of Bloomingdale, Eckington, and LeDroit Park were in the midst of a turnaround that was unlikely and nearly unbelievable to seasoned observers of the District's renaissance. People with vision and money had been buying up row houses here in the past ten, fifteen years, putting down roots alongside longtime residents, and on North Capitol entrepreneurs both homegrown and immigrant had been opening up businesses and retail establishments that were not liquor stores, Chinese Plexiglas palaces, or check-cashing fleece operations. The area was moving in a forward direction, as was the city, a resurgence that started with the administration of Mayor Anthony Williams. Homicides were down, even in the poorer sections of town, and real estate values were up. More people were employed, making money, and issuing their children into the culture of work by example.

With this came negatives as well. Culturally, in Lucas's lifetime, Washington had been a black city with a Southern feel, but blacks would soon represent less than fifty percent of the population. Chocolate City was not coming back, and neither were generations of locals who had sold their homes, many for a large profit, and moved to PG, Charles, and Montgomery counties.

Coming in, Lucas noticed that his favorite mural in the city, on the side of a funeral home at Randolph Place and North Capitol, N.W., had been replaced. The old mural depicted Jesus reaching out to a man who was on the ground, with the words, "Don't look down on a man...unless you gonna pick him up." To Lucas the painting had always represented what was good about D.C. The new mural showed a vaguely spiritual figure carrying a depleted man in his arms on a beach as waves roll violently in toward the shore. It looked like an ad for suntan oil. The words read, "When it feels like you can't go on, the Lord will carry you through the storm." Same sentiment, different delivery. Lucas had asked a friend, a Bloomingdale resident, about the change. She said, "The man who owns the funeral home got pressure from the neighbors and a local nonprofit to get rid of the old mural. The paint *was* peeling. But them imposing their will and all, it didn't smell right to me. Some folks want this whole city to look like Georgetown. What you end up with is a clean town with no character or soul."

As E. Ethelbert Miller had written in the *Washington Post*, "Well, chocolate melts."

Lucas walked south toward Florida Avenue. He checked the longitudinal and latitudinal coordinates the Grant Summers e-mail address had supplied, and the attendant images on his phone that had come up on Google Maps. He passed a church and a used-furniture operation that put chairs, sofas, and tables out on the street to attract customers. On a strip that was both commercial and residential, he came upon two properties that were unoccupied, one with paper taped inside its windows. Both properties displayed a real estate sign showing the same broker's name and phone number. He was in the general vicinity of the coordinates. This IP address lookup wasn't on the nose, but it usually yielded fairly accurate results. The broker was a man named Abraham Woldu. Lucas recognized the surname as Ethiopian or Eritrean.

He rang up Woldu, told him his name, told him he'd like to speak to him about his vacant properties on North Capitol. Woldu agreed to meet Lucas there the next day.

Lucas swung around on North Capitol, went up Lincoln Road, and drove under the arches of Glenwood Cemetery, located several blocks north, in Northeast. He found his father's grave, near a drop-off to a short residential block of descending row homes on a street called Evarts, in the neighborhood of Stronghold. He no longer brought flowers to his *baba*'s resting place, preferring to give them to his mother when he saw her in Silver Spring. But he still came here often, even knowing it was an illogical act. The visits were for him, not his dad. He said a silent prayer, did his *stavro*, and got on his way.

Before meeting Marquis back in Cottage City, Lucas went

over to Fish in the Neighborhood, on the 3600 block of Georgia, in Park View, and got some takeout sandwiches. Formerly known as Fish in the Hood, the owner had recently altered the name to reflect the changing demographics of his customer base. But the product was the same. Lucas ordered fried catfish for Marquis, trout for himself, with tartar and extra hot sauce, and a side of their signature mac and cheese. He drove back across town and into Maryland.

MARQUIS WAS in his late-model Buick sedan, idling with the air-conditioning on, when Lucas found him in the strip center in Cottage City. He was wearing one of the pajama-style outfits he was fond of, the multicolored fabric falling loosely around the titanium pole that was his left leg. A New Balance sneaker was fitted on the end of the pole.

"Thanks for this," said Marquis, swallowing a mouthful of catfish, lettuce, tomato, and tarter. "I suppose you want a hug or something."

"And a piece of chocolate on my pillow," said Lucas.

"I'll smash your *face* into your pillow. How 'bout that?"

"You're so butch."

"Why you need me on this?"

"On account of this guy Dodson burned my Jeep."

"You just want me to tail him?"

"See where he goes when he gets off work."

"I can do that."

Lucas looked over Marquis's outfit. "What, was Hugh Hefner having a yard sale?"

"You just don't know how to dress. I bet you get your clothes at Sears and Roebucks, and shit."

"As matter of fact, I do."

"Looking like a custodian or something."

"That wasn't the idea," said Lucas. "But I'll take it."

They saw a Buick Grand National come around the corner of the service road. Lucas recognized the hulking Dodson behind the wheel.

"That's him," said Lucas.

"Those mechanics do love those GNs."

"Looks like an eighty-six or -seven."

"Got the intercooled engine, brah. We gonna need a rocket to catch up."

Marquis shoved the rest of his sandwich into its bag and pulled out of his space in the lot.

"Don't get too close," said Lucas.

"I don't need you to tell me that."

"I'm sayin, we look like police."

"*I* look like police," said Marquis. "You look like the dude who cleans my car."

EIGHT

BRIAN DODSON lived nearby in Colmar Manor, on the southern side of Bladensburg Road. His asbestos-shingled cottage
stood on a short block that was a court butting up against the
Colmar Manor Community Park, a large plot of forested land
bordering the Anacostia River. The neighborhood seemed
quiet and had a country feel.

Marquis drove past his street, avoiding the trap of the court.
He turned around and stopped on the cross street, where
they could get a look at Dodson's house. Marquis and Lucas
watched him park on the street and walk inside. There was a
maroon Ford Excursion, Ford's SUV version of a bus, in the
driveway. Lucas jotted that down in his notebook.

"What if he's in for the night?" said Marquis.

"Let's give him a half hour," said Lucas.

"I'll just go ahead and finish my sandwich."

As Marquis ate, Lucas dialed Charlotte Rivers, but got no
pickup. He left a voice message, did so quietly. He thanked her
for a wonderful night and asked when he could see her again.

"Thank you for a wonderful night," said Marquis, smiling at Lucas. And then he softly sang, "When will I see you...a-gain?"

"Fuck *you.*"

"The Three Degrees," said Marquis, feigning innocence. "My mother used to love that one when I was a kid."

"Yeah?"

"I'm sayin, that's a real good song."

Twenty minutes later Dodson emerged from the house with a daypack slung over his shoulder. He got into his black Grand National and fired it up. Marquis reversed his vehicle and deftly swung it into a more hidden spot.

"Nice move," said Lucas.

They stayed several car lengths back and followed him down Bladensburg Road, which cleaved the Fort Lincoln Cemetery and dropped into D.C., then turned onto Benning Road. They headed east and crossed the Anacostia River via the Benning Bridge.

Dodson took the Anacostia Freeway and made his way to Martin Luther King Avenue, the entranceway to Anacostia, and jumped off and went over to Firth Sterling Avenue, which took them along the Barry Farms Dwellings, two-story public housing structures set on weedy grounds. Dodson parked his car and Marquis drove on past.

"Go up the hill and turn around," said Lucas.

"What you suppose your man is doing in this part of town?"

"I don't know. Guy leaves his nice, neat little neighborhood to come down here? I reckon he's doing some kind of dirt."

They made a turnaround and parked up the hill. They could see young men, mothers, and girls, some who were also mothers, out around the dwellings. A group of men were throwing dice. It was late afternoon, and this time of year folks stayed outside. Dodson got out of his car with his daypack and walked by a group of young men who eye-fucked him but said nothing. He passed under an archway and entered a door to one of the units.

"The Farms," said Marquis. "This place was infamous when I was a youngster coming up in PG."

"I'm working a case for a woman got murdered down in Charles County," said Lucas. "The mother of the victim said her daughter was dating Dodson. Said he was a churchgoing type, steady worker, all that. Practically painted a halo over his head."

"We don't want to be sitting here too long, seeing as how we're a salt-and-pepper team. We look like law."

"*I* look like law," said Lucas. "You look like Sabu."

"Who's Sabu?"

Wasn't long before Dodson came out of the dwellings carrying his bag.

"What you think is in that bag?" said Marquis.

"Cash," said Lucas. "Drugs…a gun. Who knows? Something bad, for sure."

"Now you gonna tar all these people down here just 'cause they live in the Eights?"

"I'm not tarring anyone but Dodson. Tellin you, he's wrong."

"Want me to keep tailing him?"

"No," said Lucas. "I've seen enough."

AT HIS apartment, Lucas ran a statewide and nationwide criminal background check on Dodson using his Intelius program, and came up with some minor convictions and one major conviction for assault with a deadly weapon. There was nothing since 1999. Lucas picked up his phone and searched his contacts for Tim McCarthy's number.

Lucas had met McCarthy, a former 6D patrolman and Metropolitan Police Department investigator, through Tom Petersen. McCarthy had been in the Corps in peacetime and, in his fifties, had taken a leave of absence from the police force to return to Iraq to serve as a chaplain-with-an-M-16 for the marines. Now he was back, close to retirement. He would never give up police-business information to Lucas, but he could usually put him up with someone who could be more accommodating.

"Tim," said Lucas, when he got him on the line. "Spero Lucas."

"How's it going, Marine?"

"Copacetic. I'm working on something, need a little intel on a guy." Lucas gave him the name and address. "Also, any update on the Cherise Roberts murder would be much appreciated."

"That girl who was found in the Dumpster?"

"Her."

"You working murders now, Lucas?"

"I leave that to professionals. Just curious."

"I have your number," said McCarthy. "Someone will get back to you."

"Pete Gibson?" said Lucas, hopefully.

"Take care."

Lucas dressed, mindful of his brother Leo's inevitable comments, and drove over the District line to Silver Spring, where his mom lived in one of the many bungalows that lined her street. Hers had been refashioned and expanded by her builder husband as their family had grown. It no longer had the architectural integrity of a Sears bungalow, but it had successfully sheltered and warmed six humans and many dogs.

He went by Afrikutz to say hey to his barber and stopped at the Safeway on Fenton and Thayer to sign a card for his friend Mike Kingsbury, who had passed a year earlier. Lucas bought a bouquet of daisies while he was there and drove over to his mom's.

He entered the house and patted the dogs, Cheyenne and Yuma, short-haired Lab mixes from the Humane Society on Georgia at Geranium, who had greeted him with exuberant barks and swinging tails. He found his mother, Eleni, and his brother Leo back in the kitchen. His mother was working on a glass of white wine. It wasn't her first; she smelled sharply of it as he kissed her.

"How's it goin, Ma?" said Spero, handing her the daisies wrapped in damp paper.

"Thank you, honey. Leo?"

Leo fetched a vase from the top shelf of a cabinet, and she put the flowers in water.

Spero grabbed a couple of Stellas, which Eleni stocked for him, and popped the cap on one for himself and one for his brother. They tapped bottles and drank. Leo looked him over.

"You went for the fitted Polo," said Leo. "That's an upgrade for you."

"And you're like, what, a model for L.L.Bean now? You moving to Maine or sumshit?" Leo had on khakis with a green cloth belt and a neatly pressed blue chambray shirt.

"Brothers Brooks," said Leo, and for some reason he did the Heisman pose.

"You must be the only brother who shops at Brooks Brothers."

"See, you're wrong. But you wouldn't know 'cause you don't go to the higher-end spots. You just don't know fashion."

"I'm guessing they had to custom-make those pants to allow for your big caboose."

"Least I *got* one."

"Please," said Eleni, but she was half smiling.

"What's for dinner, Ma?" said Spero.

THEY ATE by candlelight on the screened-in porch out back. Eleni had grilled lamb skewered with vegetables out of her backyard garden, and served the kebabs over a bed of *pilafi* with a summer salad of tomatoes, onions, feta cheese, oregano, oil, and vinegar. Spero and Leo recalled stories about their father, discussed the latest news of their sister, Irene, noting her emotional and physical distance, and inevitably mentioned their wayward brother, Dimitrius, who hadn't been heard from in years.

"He'll turn up when he needs a loan," said Leo, who had no love for the brother he called the Degenerate. "Or bail money."

"Leonides," said Eleni. "He's got a sickness. You can't hate someone for being sick."

"I can come close to it."

"He needs help," said Eleni, her eyes increasingly unfocused, her speech a little slurred.

So do you, thought Spero. Leo would say to let her drink, if that's what makes her feel better. But it wasn't making her better. It was just aging her and ruining her health. Even in the forgiving candlelight, she was looking older than her sixty-plus years.

The sons cleared the table and returned to the porch. Eleni had insisted on doing the dishes herself.

"When I came in," said Leo, "she was in front of the TV, watching the Encore Western channel. I think she keeps it on 'cause Pop liked it so much. She'd sit with him through all those spaghetti Westerns he liked."

"Whenever they'd run *The Big Gundown*," said Spero, "during that final scene? With Van Cleef and Tomas Milian riding across the desert, the Morricone music on the soundtrack? *Baba* would be on his feet, giving praise to the director. 'Viva Sollima,' he'd say."

"It was his favorite Italian horse opera that wasn't directed by Leone."

"If they had a kung fu channel, Mom would be watching that, too."

"She did indulge him."

Leo watched as Spero checked his phone for messages. He'd been looking at his phone frequently throughout the night, but had not heard back from Charlotte Rivers. There was a text from Pete Gibson, though, telling Spero that he was available for a meet.

"What, you got a new girl?" said Leo.

"I think so."

"You been checking your phone like it's your first piece of ass. Stressin over a woman, that's not like you."

"She's special," said Spero.

"They're all special when they're new."

"I'm serious."

"So she's got that good stuff?"

"It's more than that. I opened up to her right away. I kissed her for what seemed like hours before I went any further."

"But you did go further."

"Yes."

"Was it good?"

"It was incredible."

"Careful. That oyster can make you light-headed. You might get dizzy and fall down."

"There's a big problem beyond that. She's married, Leo."

"Ho, shit." Leo shook his head. "I don't even know what to tell you about that. Except, step away."

"It's gonna be hard for me to do that. Haven't you ever found yourself in that situation?"

"You don't find yourself with a married woman. You make a choice."

Spero looked at his brother. "That math teacher you were dating, wasn't she married?"

"Separated," said Leo, shrugging sheepishly.

"Now you're splitting hairs."

"I split more than that."

"See?"

"I know."

Later, Leo asked Spero if there had been any progress in the murder case of Cherise Roberts, who had been his student.

"It would mean something to me, and to Cherise's family, if something got done on finding her killer," said Leo. "The kids at school are still messed up over her death. Tell you the truth, I am, too."

"I've got feelers out," said Spero. "All you got to do is find one person who knows something."

"And then get 'em to talk."

"If they're incarcerated, they generally won't talk to police. But they might talk to Petersen. Or me."

"And then what, you'd turn over the information to Homicide?"

"Yeah. I'd let the guys who do it for a living take over."

"I appreciate you looking into it," said Leo. "What else you working on?"

"I got a couple of cases, actually."

"Any progress?"

"You know how I do. I get out there and talk to people."

"And?"

"Things start to happen."

"Mind yourself with that woman of yours."

"I'll do my best."

Leo swigged his beer, set the bottle down gently on the glass table. "Don't fall in love with someone you can't have."

NINE

LUCAS MET Abraham Woldu, a well-dressed middle-aged man with curly black hair and an open smile, in front of his properties on North Capitol the next morning. Lucas had been honest about the fact that he was an investigator, though he declined to elaborate on the nature of the case, citing confidentiality. Nevertheless, Woldu appeared to be willing to talk. In the first few minutes of their conversation, Lucas learned that he was an immigrant from Eritrea, educated in Italy. He spoke several different languages, fluently. He had a wife and three sons who were now men. He owned the properties here and several others around town, served as his own broker, and had a license to do so.

"Are you Orthodox?" said Lucas.

"Yes."

"Me, too. We're brothers."

"Yes, we're brothers. But you don't need to grease me up. What is it you're looking for?"

"I'll get right to the point. I have reason to believe that

someone was running an Internet scam out of one of your properties this past year."

"What kind of scam?"

"It's not important. What's pertinent is that it was an unlawful operation. And if it was conducted under your roof, you're connected. I'd really like to have your help on this. I'd hate to have to go to the Feds."

"There's no need for threats," said Woldu.

"What I'm trying to say is, I'd appreciate your cooperation."

Woldu looked toward one of the two properties, a ground-level portion of a turreted row home fronted by a plate-glass window. "I had a Jamaican in there for a while. He sold CDs, incense, juices, and the like. Before that, there was a coffee shop run by a lady from my country. Neither of them made it. You want those types of businesses to do well in the neighborhood. It's good for property values, good for all of us eventually. But sometimes they just don't work."

"What about that one?" said Lucas, nodding to the first floor of the other Woldu property, the one with butcher paper taped over the window.

"That was a longtime hair and nail salon," said Woldu. "The owner-operator died suddenly. I had a man in there for four months after that, a short-term thing, off the books."

"What kind of business?"

"It was tax season. He said he was an accountant. He signed no lease. He paid me cash, well in advance, every month."

"Off the books," said Lucas.

"I reported the income to the IRS," said Woldu. "It wasn't me who asked for cash. He insisted."

"Did you ever go in there and see what he was up to?"

"Only to collect the rent. There were a couple of desks, computers…crated goods. No decorations of any kind. He had the blinds drawn all the time. Just as quickly as he was here, he was gone."

"Can I see the space?" said Lucas.

Woldu shrugged and pulled out a set of keys from his pocket. "Sure."

They went inside. It was an empty rectangular room painted white. Lucas looked in the restroom, which was surprisingly large, with exposed pipes in the ceiling and a full bath.

"The lady who had the hair salon enlarged the bathroom," said Woldu, seeing Lucas's inquisitive expression.

"So, this tenant. He must have given you a security deposit. If he did, you sent it to an address later on, right?"

"He did, in cash. But he came down here and met me for the refund. I returned his deposit, again in cash."

"For that meet, you must have communicated by phone."

"I have his number in my contacts, right here." Woldu produced a BlackBerry from his pocket. He scanned his contacts and said, "Serge Nikolai." He said the phone number, and Lucas wrote it down.

"You ever see his name on an ID?" said Lucas.

"No."

"Describe the guy."

"Medium height, black hair, pale skin. He spoke with an Eastern European or Russian accent."

That would be consistent with the mangled syntax of the e-mail message from Grant Summers to Grace Kinkaid, thought Lucas.

"Anyone else go in and out of the property while he was there?"

"Yes, there were people in there the few times I visited. Men in plain clothing."

"Can you describe those men?"

"There was a young man. I can barely picture him in my head. He had a beard, I think. Another, older man, too. Blond-haired, I believe." Woldu rubbed at a cluster of raised moles on his forehead. "When I saw them it was very briefly. I'd have to think about it."

"I have your number."

"And I have yours."

"I didn't mean to push," said Lucas. "I apologize."

"I have nothing to hide."

"Habesha," said Lucas.

They shook hands.

AT LUNCHTIME, Lucas walked into the Hitching Post, a soul food eat-house on Upshur, near the Old Soldier's Home. Owned and operated by Alvin and Adrienne Carter since 1967, it was one of D.C.'s hidden treasures that, like many other down-home Chocolate City legends, could not last. The decor was eclectic, with almost fifty years' worth of accumulation and whatever the liquor distributors had given the Carters. There was a full bar, several large booths covered in Naugahyde, and a patron-mix of races, classes, and generations. Folks came for the unusual ambience, the soul and funk jukebox, and the signature fried chicken.

Pete Gibson sat in one of the booths. Lucas made eye contact with him, then stopped to greet Mr. Carter, who had been a patrol cop in D.C. back when black police officers were in the minority.

"How's it goin, young fella?" said Al.

"Righteous," said Lucas. He smiled at Miss Adrienne, still working behind the counter. "Ma'am."

Lucas shook Pete Gibson's hand as he slid into the curve of the booth's seat. Gibson's hair was shaved close, his gray Vandyke so thin it was barely visible. He wore a neatly pressed checked shirt under a sport jacket, though it was a warm, humid day. In the chest pocket of the shirt was a hard deck of Marlboro Reds.

"Lucas," said Gibson, showing his white teeth.

With his blue eyes, strong jaw, and erect bearing, Gibson looked like an actor playing a marine: Richard Jaeckel in *The Dirty Dozen*. But Gibson had no military background. He had entered the MPD right out of high school, worked patrol, then K-9, and headed an investigative squad in 6 and 7D, the city's toughest districts. He ended his career as a lieutenant in the relatively soft Second. He lived out near Frederick now, like many former cops who had left the city for the exo-burbs or the mountains. But he had never really put the force behind him. In his head he was still a police officer, and he still craved the action.

Gibson had helped him on the Anwan Hawkins case, which had ended with a violent confrontation between Lucas, a man named Ricardo "Rooster" Holley, and others. Only Gibson knew of Lucas's actions and the bloody results.

"You look good, Pete. Trim."

Gibson patted his stomach. "Sit-ups, push-ups, and a chin-up bar. That's all a man needs. I want to be ready in case I get called up."

"For what?"

"You tell me. I wouldn't mind standing next to you if things got hot. I like how you resolved the Rooster Holley thing."

Lucas said nothing.

"Anyway, if you ever need any help beyond talk," said Gibson, "let me know. I can be more than just your bitch for information."

"I'll keep that in mind. You look at the menu yet?"

"I already ordered for both of us. Fried chicken sandwiches with sides of collard greens and mac and cheese. Is that all right?"

"Great."

"It takes a while in the place. You know what they say: if you're not hungry when you come to the Hitching Post, you will be by the time they serve your food."

"Cooked to order and worth the wait."

"Don't I know it."

A young waitress came by, and Lucas asked for iced tea.

When she walked away, Gibson said, "So, Tim McCarthy gave me the message. You're looking for something on a Brian Dodson."

"I have his criminal record, which ends in the nineties. Nothing since then on the books. By all accounts he's living a straight life. Works at a garage in Cottage City, has a little house in Colmar Manor. But yesterday I tailed him down to Barry Farms."

"That shithole?" said Gibson.

"It's not all that bad."

"No? I wouldn't live there if I *did* live there."

Lucas moved on. "Dodson walked into one of the dwellings with a bag over his shoulder, walked out with the same bag.

I'm guessing he was conducting some kind of business. Given his criminal record, and the neighborhood, I can assume he wasn't delivering Meals On Wheels."

"I had the pleasure of working those districts. In Six-D…I ever tell you about what we'd do to the dope fiends over there by Mayfair Gardens?"

"Yes," said Lucas, but that wasn't going to stop Gibson.

"We used to line up the junkies and crackheads, in the dead of winter, and have them take off all their clothes. Said we needed to search 'em, but we couldn't run the risk of pricking ourselves on dirty needles. So they'd get naked and put all their clothes on the hood of my squad car. And then I'd say to them, 'All right, now you got thirty seconds to get your shit off my car, 'cause I'm about to take off.' They'd panic and scramble. Put on whatever they could grab. Later, me and the guys in my unit, we'd see these pipers on the street, wearing mismatched outfits, a Nike and a Converse on each of their feet."

"Officer Friendly."

"I know." Gibson shook his head, his eyes bright with nostalgia. "It was wrong, I guess. But it *was* funnier than shit."

"Brian Dodson…"

"Right. Your boy isn't who you think he is."

"I already told you, I think he's dirty."

"It's worse than that. His name came up on a wiretap last year, a thing the Feds were working. Dude was talking, said he had a problem that needed to get solved, other dude suggests a guy named Brian Dodson. Said he'd put work in for a triple deuce. Meaning, he'd murder someone for six thousand dollars. These knotheads talk in code, think they're foolin someone. A retard could figure out the meaning of the words."

"He's…"

"Dodson's a mechanic."

"I know it."

"As in *The Mechanic,* with Charlie Bronson. He's an assassin."

"I *get* you, Pete. I'm just digesting it."

The waitress served Lucas his iced tea. He sipped it and waited for her to drift.

"Why didn't the law bring him in?" said Lucas.

"The dude who identified Dodson as a contract man is no longer available to elaborate on the subject."

"He skipped town?"

"He's Ten-Seven. That's police code for Out of Service, Lucas."

"I'm familiar with the codes."

"Someone put a bullet in his dome. But the Special Task Force is keeping an eye on Dodson. He's what they call a 'person of interest.'" Gibson grinned. "Good stuff, right?"

The waitress served their sides and chicken sandwiches, which were several pieces of bone-in fried chicken served on a piece of bread. How one could eat it as a sandwich was one of the pleasant mysteries of the Hitching Post. Lucas and Gibson commenced to getting down on their food.

They ate silently, ravenously.

A little while later, Lucas wiped a napkin across his face and said, "What about the Cherise Roberts murder? Anything on that?"

"No progress," said Gibson. "My guy in Homicide tells me that they turned up some interesting details on the victim, but they have nothing as of yet on a perpetrator."

"What about her?"

"A search of the history on her home computer indicated that she was running a little business on the side."

"What kind of business?"

"She was trickin."

"Cherise was a prostitute?"

"Not like the image you got in your head. She didn't walk the stroll or anything like that. You don't need to in this day and age. Teenage girls can retail their ass online if they're savvy. Any girl can be an entrepreneur with the help of the Internet. Cherise even had a prosti name."

"What was it?"

"I don't recall. Some kinda name designed to make the creeps get wood."

Lucas thought of Leo. His brother had expressed no suspicions about Cherise's character. Leo worked in a public school in the city—he was anything but naive. If this was true, Cherise had been discreet about her secret life. It would cut Leo deep if he were to hear about it.

"If they have the computer history," said Lucas, "then they have the names of some of her Johns."

"I'm sure they've conducted their interviews," said Gibson.

"Right."

"Let the real police do their jobs."

"I will," said Lucas. "Thanks for looking into all of this."

Gibson nodded. "Lunch is on you."

"If I need you again…"

"You've got my number," said Gibson.

Lucas signaled the waitress.

TEN

TOM PETERSEN sat behind his desk, reading the one-page report Lucas had typed and printed after his lunch at the Hitching Post. Lucas, seated before the desk in a wobbly chair, watched as Petersen dropped the sheet and folded his hands across his belly.

"I'm not sure what you're saying here," said Petersen. "Exactly."

"I'm giving you a scenario," said Lucas. "Edwina Christian was seeing a man named Brian Dodson at the same time she was seeing Calvin Bates. My source tells me that Dodson has been identified as a contract killer per Federal wiretaps."

"That's interesting."

"When I interviewed Virginia Christian, she explained a quote I read in the discovery material, something to the effect of her daughter wanting to 'take care' of Bates. Virginia said that this meant Edwina wanted to help Bates. That she was on a mission from her pastor at church. But what if Edwina Christian wanted to take care of Bates in a different way? As in, take him out permanently. He wouldn't leave her alone, and it had become a problem. She had a relationship with a low-rent hit man. Dodson would be the one she'd turn to."

"I'm getting a warm feeling now."

"What was the caliber of the slug found in Edwina's brainpan?" said Lucas.

"Twenty-two."

"Twenty-twos are used by professionals who like to work close-in."

"Now the blood is flowing to my pecker."

"And consider this: one of Dodson's vehicles is a Ford Excursion."

"I'm guessing it has a wide axle track."

"Look up the specs online. It could be that Dodson's Excursion is the vehicle that laid those tracks down near the woods in Southern Maryland."

"Yes, it could be. But why?"

"Because it's a heavy truck?"

"No, I'm asking, why would Brian Dodson murder Edwina Christian? What was the motive?"

"I don't know," said Lucas. "Maybe she paid him and he decided to do her instead of Bates. Maybe Dodson and Bates were in collusion."

"Don't stray too far into Candy Land."

"Okay, but let's stay with the theory that she paid Dodson to hit Bates. Go ahead and access her bank records. You might find a significant withdrawal before her murder."

"Okay, I'm still with you. But there's the matter of Bates's presence near those woods, right around her time of death. The GPS records from his ankle bracelet don't lie. What was he doing down there? And why would he torch his truck to cover up evidence if he was innocent?"

"Maybe someone else torched his truck and set him up."

"Candy Land."

"I'm only giving you some possibilities," said Lucas. "You asked me to find something, and I did."

Petersen stood. He paced the room, his cowboy boots clomping on the wood floor. "I'm going to trial in a couple of days."

"Then subpoena Dodson and put him on the stand," said Lucas. "At least you'll put a, you know, seed of doubt into the jury's mind."

"And cut to commercial break," said Petersen, with amusement.

Lucas got out of his chair. He stretched and picked up his notebook off the desk.

"You're leaving?" said Petersen.

"I've got plans tonight."

"A woman, I take it."

"I'm like that."

"'Gather ye rosebuds while ye may.'"

"I intend to," said Lucas. "By the way, I'm going to be out of commission for a while."

"Side job?"

Lucas didn't answer. He walked toward the door.

"Spero," said Petersen, and Lucas stopped and turned. "Nice work on this one. Real nice."

Lucas said, "I know."

*   *   *

ON THE way to Petersen's office, Lucas had gotten a call from Charlotte Rivers. She'd be at the hotel on 16th Street that evening, and was wondering if he wanted to stop by.

"I've been calling you," said Lucas.

"I don't leave that phone on much," said Charlotte. "Do you want to come or not?"

"I can meet you in the bar."

"Come straight up to my room," she said, and gave him the number on the door.

At his place, he heated up some thick spaghetti with meat sauce, cut a salad, got some food inside him, then showered, dressed, and drove over to the hotel, where he left his Jeep with the valet. The doorman recognized him and damn near winked as he ushered him through the entrance. Maybe Lucas imagined it. His mind was fuzzy. He was thinking of Charlotte up in that room.

She let him into a suite, identically furnished as the one before, and closed the door behind him. She had already lit candles and extinguished the lights. Music was playing from her phone, which was connected to a portable speaker she had brought with her. It was the Lee "Scratch" Perry compilation *Arkology,* which she had downloaded especially for him. Lucas liked that she had remembered.

Charlotte was dressed in a black tank top and black jeans, with brown T-strap boots, as she had been at Boundary Road, though tonight beneath the shirt she was free. He embraced her and ran his hands down her bare arms.

"We should talk," said Lucas.

"We will," she said.

She put her mouth to his and held the back of his neck as

they kissed. Her hair smelled of rainwater and her lips were butter. They kissed in the entranceway and against the wall, and soon found themselves lying on the thickly carpeted floor. An hour passed quickly, just like that, the two of them making out, sweating as if they had completed the act, though they'd not yet removed their clothes. They stopped so Lucas could uncork the bottle of Barolo that stood on the dresser. He poured it into two short glasses and they drank some, then put the glasses down and began to kiss some more. They made it to the bed and faced each other. She unbuttoned his jeans, released him, and stroked him lavishly.

"God," said Lucas.

"What do you like?" she said.

"This."

"Let me take my boots off."

"Let *me*," said Lucas.

He led her to the black velvet settee and sat her there. He put one of her boots up on his thigh and removed it, then the other. He lifted her tank top over her head, and she pushed her hips forward as he took off her jeans and peeled away her thong. Heat came off her.

"Lay down," he said, and he stretched her out on the settee and got on his knees. He kissed her mouth and shoulders, licked and bit at her nipples, and raised them. He moved his face to between her legs and pushed aside her hood and found her spot engorged with blood, and flicked his tongue there. Her breath grew short. He rubbed his forefinger down the strip, buried his thumb inside her, and kissed her pearl, then sucked on it. She said, "Spero," and grabbed his hair and came with abandon.

Afterward, she moved to put him in her mouth. But he shook his head, picked her up, and carried her to the bed, where he laid her down on her back atop the drawn sheets.

"Like this tonight," said Lucas. Her legs opened like a flower and he went to her in the flickering light.

"**HOW'D YOU** know I was married?" said Charlotte.

"A man knows," said Lucas. "That movie with the twist at the end, where Clooney finds out his girlfriend is married and it's supposed to be a shocker? That was bullshit. Good movie and all that. But bullshit."

They were finishing the wine in bed. Charlotte had a sip and said, "How do you feel about it? That I'm married."

"I came back," said Lucas. He knew what she was asking, but he was evading the question.

"I'm glad you did."

"Am I a first for you?" He nearly winced when he said it. He sounded like a boy.

"I came close once before. Made a date at the bar downstairs, in the same way that I asked to meet you the other night. Five minutes in, I knew he wasn't for me. He bragged about money. I had one drink and went home." She kissed him. "Let's not talk about that. Point is, I'm here with you."

"But why did you reach out to me? Why'd you reach out to that other guy?"

"That's pretty simple. There's something missing in my marriage."

"What?"

"This." She drew him close to her and kissed him softly.

"Thanks for bringing that reggae," said Lucas.

"It's good music to make love to."

"Yes." He looked into her eyes. "You're fucking amazing."

"Thank you, Spero."

"So how do you feel about it?" said Lucas. "Us, together like this."

"It's been incredible."

"*You* know what I mean."

"Am I torn up about the fact that I'm having an affair? No." Charlotte turned and put her empty glass on the nightstand. She lay back down on her side and faced him, ran her hand along his forearm. "I've been married for ten years. My husband is a good guy, very successful, a hard worker. Focused. We don't fight, and he's not abusive in any way. He's not even temperamental, really. But the passion isn't there. We make love a couple of times a month, and it's fine, but it's by the numbers, you know? I guess it's natural for it to be like that for two people after so many years. But it's not enough for me. I'm still young. If I was older, I suppose I could live with it, but I'm not willing to live with it yet. That's why I'm here."

"At your service," said Lucas. He didn't smile.

"Don't do that. You have no reason to be insecure. I haven't been able to get you out of my mind since the first time I saw you. It's not just the physical part of this that moves me."

"I feel the same way," said Lucas, and it was true.

"I brought another bottle of that Italian," said Charlotte. "Why don't you open it?"

Lucas left the bed naked, returned with the open bottle, poured some for her, poured more for himself. They had some more to drink, lying beside each other, kissed and whispered, and let the time pass that way.

"Spero?"

"Yeah."

"When you were in Iraq..."

He knew what was coming. The question was always the same.

"Yes?"

"Did you kill anyone?"

"Yes, I did."

What was it like?

"What was it like?" she said.

"The first time?" said Lucas. "I hesitated, I guess, but only for a few seconds. It wasn't a very tough decision to make. He would have killed me or my friends if he had the chance. That's really what the war was about for me. I was protecting my brothers. I was there to take out the enemy. I killed people who were trying to kill me. Morality and philosophy didn't enter into my thought process."

Lucas was surprised that he had said so much. He turned onto his back and stared at a ceiling lit by candle flames.

"Are you all right?" said Charlotte.

"Getting sleepy, I guess."

"That's not what I meant."

"I'm fine. Look, are we going to spend the night together this time?"

"I can't," said Charlotte. "I need to get home. My husband thinks I'm working a late dinner with Pakistani diplomats."

"Okay, then," said Lucas. He was annoyed, though he knew he had no right to be. "I gotta use the head."

He picked up his glass of wine from the nightstand, took it with him to the bathroom, and swigged the rest of it down

as he flicked on the bathroom light. He turned his head to
say something to Charlotte and tripped on the floor molding
that separated the carpeting from the marbled bathroom floor.
He dropped the glass and watched it shatter on the marble,
watched it as he was going down, put his left hand out to break
his fall, watched in slow motion as he landed in the glass, his
hand coming down on a large piece that was resting edge up,
feeling the sting of pain. He sat back against the vanity cabinet. He said, "Stupid," and he pulled the piece of glass out of
his palm. A great flap of skin lay open below his thumb and it
was white and quickly red with his blood.

"Oh, my God!" said Charlotte, who had come to the doorway and was staring with horror at his hand.

"Yeah, I know."

He rinsed it off in the sink, but the blood would not stop
coming. It was a deep cut in the shape of a crescent and
he knew he'd need stitches. Charlotte gave him a washcloth.
He wrapped his hand tightly, and the washcloth soon red-
dened.

"Get me my clothes, please," said Lucas. "I don't want to
bleed all over this suite. At least they can mop it up in here."

He dressed and gathered up the rest of the bathroom's
washcloths.

"You going to drive yourself?" said Charlotte.

"No sweat," said Lucas.

"I'll text you and see how you're doing."

"Yeah, okay. Hit me up."

He kissed her deeply and left the suite, got his Jeep without
too many questions from the doorman and the valet guy, and
drove out to Holy Cross in Silver Spring using only his right

hand. His left hand bled all over his jeans and the fabric of his seat.

He was in the waiting room of the ER for an hour or so, and he went through three more washcloths before they ushered him to a small room just inside the swinging doors, where an orderly took his vitals and applied a pressure bandage. He waited another hour, and finally a Dr. Eric Hernandez entered the room. The youngish bespectacled doctor had a look at his hand, and said, "Oh yeah, you did it," and he had Lucas take X-rays in another room. Later still, the doctor returned and said, "I can't guarantee that there's not more glass in there, but I'm gonna go ahead and stitch you up."

Lucas watched him prepare a needle of Novocain, or whatever they were using these days.

"I'm going to have to stick you in the center of your palm," said Dr. Hernandez.

"Just put the head in, okay, Doc? And be gentle with me. It's my first time."

"I'll wipe your tears away."

"Thank you."

"Now look, I'm not going to lie to you, this is going to hurt. If you jump, I'll have to stick you again."

Lucas turned his head and looked away.

It hurt like a motherfucker. But Lucas didn't jump.

DRIVING BACK to his apartment in the middle of the night, his hand stitched, throbbing, and covered in an antibiotic ointment and a sterile pad, Lucas checked his phone. Charlotte had texted him and asked if he was okay. Also, Abraham Woldu, the real estate broker on North Capitol, had left him a long text about the men who frequently occupied the office he had leased to Serge Nikolai. There was Nikolai, of course, and the young man who he was still barely able to describe, and a blond-haired, deeply tanned man with a strong build.

Woldu had described Billy Hunter. Hunter and Nikolai were together. The two of them had targeted Grace Kinkaid. Hunter, Nikolai, and one more.

There were three.

ELEVEN

THREE MEN sat in a white police-package Crown Victoria purchased at auction in Manassas, Virginia. They were in the lot of a Maryland rest area between Washington and Baltimore off Interstate 95. A middle-aged man approaching elderly had gotten out of a late-model Honda Accord and from its rear seat had retrieved a brown attaché case and a gym bag with padded handles. Now the man was walking, somewhat stoop-shouldered, toward the men's room. The men in the Ford were watching him.

"He is taking the goods inside with him," said Serge Bacalov from the backseat. He was dressed in tight jeans, a fitted T-shirt sporting a winged logo, and running shoes. His hair was curly and dark. He had thick lips, a simian-like muzzle, crooked teeth, and eyebrows that met above his nose.

In the passenger seat, Billy King made no comment. Bacalov tended to state the obvious and talked too much in general.

Billy was in his midthirties and wore khaki pants, leather

boat shoes without socks, and a sky-blue polo shirt stretched tight across his heavily muscled shoulders and chest. His thinning blond hair was combed to the side and some of it fell across his flat, tan forehead. His eyes were pale blue and lacked warmth. He was the type seen in beach towns and marinas in November, frayed shorts and brown Reef sandals, his sunglasses hanging on a leash, sitting at the bar next to an older divorcée, preparing to move in to her settlement-house for the winter.

Beside him, behind the wheel, was a younger man named Louis Smalls. He was tall, reedy, and quiet. His eyes were deep brown and could move quickly from needy to cool. He typically dressed in jeans, faded T-shirts, and Vans, wore his hair shaggy, and had a full beard in the manner of a singer-writer circa 1970 or a sensitive, hungry young poet. Of the three men, he was the only one carrying a criminal conviction. He had done time in Hagerstown for a series of convenience store robberies, which he'd committed using a ski mask and a snub-nosed .38. He had served out his full stretch deliberately, so as to avoid supervision. Despite his innocent looks, he was capable in complicated situations, ice when things got heated, and deft in the handling of cars.

King, Smalls, and Bacalov used different last names whenever the situation demanded it. They mostly used their real Christian names. Otherwise, a man could forget who he was and not respond when being spoken to. They all possessed multiple IDs. The IDs would not be passable to the eyes of trained law enforcement professionals, but for laymen they were fine. In the city, these were easy to obtain.

"I'll do it," said Bacalov, eagerly, reaching under the front seat and slipping something short and substantial under his shirt.

"Go with him, Louis," said King. "Abort if anything looks wrong."

Smalls nodded. He and Bacalov got out of the car and went where the old man had gone. King could not see much, as a row of hedges blocked his view of the facility, but he trusted Louis to make the right call. King sat calmly and waited.

Five minutes later, Bacalov and Smalls returned and took their spots in the car. Both were empty-handed.

"What happened?" said King.

"Fucking people," said Bacalov. The numerous tourists, truckers, and I-95 commuters milled around the facilities, some heading in and out of the bathrooms, others there for the Travel Information Center, or simply standing, smoking, walking their dogs by the picnic tables, or stretching in the lot.

"Too many," said Smalls. "And there's a camera mounted over the door to the men's room."

Smalls was particularly sensitive to the placement of surveillance cameras. He had been convicted based on the video obtained from a 7-Eleven he'd done in Burtonsville, Maryland. He had been wearing a mask, but his distinctive forearm tattoo, a skull cleaved by a dagger, had been visible in the shot. He'd rolled his sleeves up before he'd gone in, because he'd been hot. A mistake of youth, one he would not make again.

"He's in the bathroom?" said King.

"Serge followed him in," said Smalls.

"He is leaving shit," said Bacalov.

Taking a shit, you dumbass, thought King. But he made no comment.

Soon Rubin emerged from around the bank of hedges, goods in hand, and went to his Honda. He started the Accord, drove out of the lot onto the long exit road, and merged back on to 95 South. Smalls kept the Ford back and followed.

"He lives in Rockville," said King. "That's another half hour away. Old fuckers have weak bladders. Maybe he'll have to stop again."

"You hope," said Bacalov.

King grew doubtful as Rubin moved down the highway. They passed the exits for Route 216, then 198. They blew by an omnibus sign advertising lodging and fast food. Rubin hit his right turn signal at the next exit, Route 200, heading toward Calverton. Smalls let a Pathfinder get ahead of him, and as its driver put his car between the Crown Vic and the Accord, he too exited. On Powder Mill Road the Accord slowed down and turned into a lot of a McDonald's, and Smalls did the same, swinging into a spot far from where Rubin had parked. Rubin again got the attaché and gym bag out of his car and entered a side door of McDonald's.

"He saw the Golden Arches on the sign," said Bacalov. "Americans cannot resist."

"Why the side door if he's going to order food?" said Smalls.

"He's gonna wash his hands first," said King. "This could be our last chance. The next stop for Rubin is his house. I don't want to do an invasion. There's no need for that."

Ira Rubin was a coin dealer who had a retail storefront in the Wheaton Triangle. He was returning from a convention in Trenton, New Jersey, with many items he had bought in meetings held in private suites. While there he had successfully negotiated the purchase of a collection of uncirculated

1908-S twenty-dollar St. Gaudens gold pieces housed in thick plastic cases. Each could be resold for about nine thousand dollars, though Rubin had negotiated a far lower price. The collection, when sold together, was worth close to a hundred thousand dollars on the open market, and would soon be even more valuable, thanks to the recession and the attendant investment flight to gold. He had also purchased a rare, uncirculated 1926-D that was worth twelve thousand dollars.

King did not have knowledge of these transactions or details. But he knew that Ira Rubin was a large regional player in the coin world because he had read about him on several specialty Internet sites. He had also visited Rubin's shop. From message boards on those same sites, he had learned that Rubin would be attending the convention in Trenton and that he was "coming to buy." A story in the *Washington Post* about a coin dealer who was robbed in his own driveway in Arlington, Virginia, had further piqued King's interest. This was a job that could be easy and relatively safe.

King, Smalls, and Bacalov had once taken off a check-cashing store in a poor neighborhood of the District, but the monetary rewards had been paltry. With the cameras and the potential for armed employees, that type of thing carried too much risk. Only Bacalov seemed to enjoy the experience. In comparison to a retail job, hitting an old coin dealer seemed like a walk. Plus, gold was up to almost two thousand dollars an ounce. And, as always, Bacalov was game and had experience. He and his Russian friends had been involved in this kind of thing before. As for Smalls, he didn't object, which was like saying yes, for him. King thought, Why not?

It had cost them some seed money. They had tailed Rubin

from his house to New Jersey, had to spring for a couple of rooms at a Motel 6, fill their tanks many times with gas, buy meals and liquor. There had been no good opportunity for the takeoff up north.

Now they would see if the expense and time had been worthwhile. But it had to be now.

"You and me," said King, to Bacalov. "Let's go."

Smalls kept the motor running and watched King and Bacalov walk toward the fast-food house. King was talking, Bacalov nodding his head.

"I'll stand by the door," said King.

"Good."

"You have to do it fast, fella."

"Yes, of course." Bacalov smiled thinly. "I will give him a goodnight kiss."

They entered the side door of the McDonald's. It was not particularly full, some booths and two-tops occupied, many others empty. Bacalov went straight to the men's room door, pushed on it, and stepped inside. Billy King stood near the door, took his smartphone from his pocket, and studied its screen as if he were reading messages. From outside the door, he heard a thud, like laundry being dropped to the floor.

As soon as Bacalov entered the small men's room and saw the open stall door, he knew that he and Rubin were alone. Rubin had the attaché case and the gym bag wedged between his feet, and he was standing over the sink, splashing water on his face. He stood before a mirror but his eyes were closed, and Serge withdrew the sap he had wedged in his waistband. He raised it, stepped forward, and swung it with great force to the back of Rubin's head. Rubin said, "Ah," and his eyes rolled up as his knees buckled. His face hit the sink counter on the way down to the floor.

There was copious blood, a pool of it widening around the man's head. Bacalov did not check on him. He picked up the attaché and gym bag and went back toward the door. King had said not to dead the old man and he had not intended to, but there was only one way to get in and get out quickly, and that was to turn off Rubin's lights. Anyway, Bacalov had the goods.

Bacalov and King went through the side dining area, passing adults and their children busily eating their fast food. None of them looked up or seemed to notice anything at all.

"Did you hurt him?" said King, as they moved through the lot.

"Yes, I think so," said Bacalov.

Louis Smalls put the Ford in gear as they settled into their seats. He drove quickly out of the parking lot, careful not to leave rubber or make any significant noise, and soon the three of them were back on 95. There was a stony silence in the car, and Bacalov knew it was meant for him.

"I fucked up," said Bacalov, with a careless shrug. "Okay?"

"Serge hit the old man too hard," said King.

"You kill him?" said Smalls.

"No," said Bacalov. But he thought maybe he had.

THEY DROVE to a house they were renting in Croom, Maryland. It was not far from D.C., but it was straight country, west on 4, south on 301, in the hilly terrain near the Jug Bay Wetlands Sanctuary of the Patuxent River. King was pleased when he found it. He was most comfortable when he was near water.

The house was an old two-story colonial with a wraparound porch, clapboard siding, and thick plaster walls. It was reached by a gravel road, set back in the woods. King had seen a FOR RENT sign one day while driving to Chesapeake Beach, where he liked to troll for women, and he had come off the state highway, followed the sign to the house, and called the posted number. He made the deal right away, after he'd had a quick look inside. As always, he overpaid the owner, cash in advance.

The space on North Capitol had grown too small for the goods they were accumulating, and King did not like the fact that he and his partners lived apart. He trusted Smalls but not Bacalov. Serge was not treacherous but he was impulsive and careless, bordering on stupid.

In their living room, furnished in the manner of a biker/ stoner lair, complete with overstuffed furniture and a bong seated on a cable-spool table, they looked at what they had stolen from the old man. The coins were laid out on a dining room table illuminated from above by an old crystal chandelier. None of them had deep knowledge of the coin market, but a child could see that some were in better shape and more significant than others, and that the collection housed in plastic was clearly the prize. Certificates of authenticity, found in the gym bag, identified the coins. King used his personal laptop to discover that, indeed, the coins, if they matched the paperwork, had great value.

"Are we rich?" said Serge, seeing King's bright eyes.

"I'll take these to my man and find out what we've got," said King. "I'm guessing we did some good work today."

Bacalov went to a small table set up as a bar and poured himself a Luksusowa over ice. A decent potato vodka for the price: Polish, but what the hell. He went upstairs to one of the three bedrooms on the second floor, where he kept his cash, a pump-action Ithaca shotgun, and a Glock 17. Bacalov masturbated to some amateur porn he found on the RedTube website, then fell to sleep. He was a man of uncluttered needs.

Smalls had gone out to the porch to smoke a cigarette. He returned, filled the bowl of his bong with some good hydroponic, and fired it up. He let the smoke linger in his lungs before exhaling, then sat back on the couch, fitted the ear-buds of his smartphone to his head, and found some Mastodon he liked. He thought of an older man with one droopy eye coming to his bed at night, and he saw the man and smelled Lectric Shave and whiskey. The collision of that awful recollection and the violence of the music pleased him.

King walked into the kitchen past the dining room. It held a back door that opened to a small yard and the woods. He found a green bottle of beer in the fridge, uncapped it, and came back out to the living room. He pulled deeply from the bottle and looked around the room. Three framed paintings, wrapped in brown paper, leaned against one of the walls. One of them, *The Double*, was very valuable. The others, though of lesser value, were worth significant money as well. Stacks of laptops and other electronic goods, burgled from residences and commercial offices, lay heaped in a corner. The coin collection was on the table. Pistols had been strategically placed under the cushions of sofas and chairs.

They would sell their bounty to various buyers, mostly middlemen in the underworld who then moved the goods to private collectors and investors. King knew that what they'd get was very low compared to the actual value, and that he and his partners had incurred all of the physical risk, but he didn't care.

They were thrill seekers. Serge knew no other way of life. Louis used the jobs to fight off his demons. Billy King had come to the D.C. area to have fun, steal what he could, and fuck and use as many women as he could. No bosses, no rush hour, no line at Starbucks in the morning, no crowded Metro cars. No responsibilities.

It wasn't about money. It was about having enough to stay in the game.

TWELVE

IN THE next few days, after the accident in the hotel room, it seemed to Lucas that he had accomplished little. Later he'd know that he had done significant work in this period, but it would not come to him just yet. He was mainly frustrated and confused.

His hand was part of the problem. It bothered him to be a gimp. A man didn't like to walk down the street without the full ability to defend himself, and this was how it was for him now. He had sustained no significant injuries in Iraq outside of cuts, scrapes, and bruises, and had experienced the usual maladies, like dehydration, diarrhea, ingrown toenails, and athlete's foot, but he was not used to being hampered like this. He had once thought that Christ had been looking after him in the Middle East, but after witnessing many accidental deaths in the war, he knew he had been spared by virtue of dumb luck. Neither God nor luck had anything to do with this injury. Inattention had caused him to trip. Idiocy had put his hand out to break his fall on a floor of broken glass.

Underneath his bandage, his hand was heavily slathered in Neosporin. The crescent-shaped cut on the heel of his palm was stitched like a baseball. Still, he managed to maintain his exercise regimen. He could use the push-up stands if he didn't grip the handle too tightly and could ride his bike the same way. That left work.

He found it difficult to concentrate, but that wasn't because of his injury. It was Charlotte Rivers. His brother would say he was drunk on pussy, and that was part of it, but not all. He wanted her to be his girlfriend. He wanted to walk with her out in the world, as he would with any other woman. See her outside that suite, take her to a movie, hold her hand across the dinner table of a nice restaurant, Mourayo on Connecticut, or Petits Plats, the little French place he liked in Woodley Park. But Charlotte wasn't answering her phone or returning his texts. Of course she wasn't. She was married, and she owned a disposable cell for secretive purposes only. She turned on the burner only to contact him when she wanted to. Spero Lucas, her young lover. Her lover boy whom she summoned whenever *she* had the need.

"Fuck this," said Lucas, to no one, seated alone at his table, reading the morning *Post*.

He turned his attention to the Metro section of the newspaper. Among the usual violent deaths of blacks and Hispanics buried inside the section, one story got extra column inches and ink. An elderly coin dealer, Ira Rubin, well known in the area because of his longtime retail operation in Wheaton, had been severely injured and robbed of his goods inside a McDonald's bathroom in Beltsville. The man was listed in critical but stable condition, which typically meant he was going to recover. Rubin had been hit by a blunt object from behind, and the force of the blow had split his skull. *Bad Day at Black Rock*, thought Lucas. But at least he's alive.

Lucas got into shorts and a T, rode his bike up to Silver Spring, and locked it to a pole outside Kefa Cafe on Bonifant Street, his favorite coffee shop in his old neighborhood. Sitting at a table among the laptoppers and *City Paper* readers was John Starr, a private investigator who had garnered a rep around town in the past twenty years. Starr had been a guitarist and vocalist in one of the premiere bands recording for Dischord in the early nineties and, like many in the original Positive Force movement, had put his ideals to work as he moved along into his middle age. He mainly took cases or incidents when he thought that the defendant was being railroaded or wronged. Lucas had met him down at the federal courthouse one day while both of them were waiting to testify in separate trials. They'd hit it off.

"What'd you do, drop your wallet on your hand?" said Starr.

"Just garden-variety stupidity," said Lucas.

Starr was drinking coffee; Lucas, iced tea.

"So you want to draw this guy out?" said Starr.

"I think he's in town," said Lucas. "Him and another guy I'm looking at for something else. They're together."

"Together in what?"

"Criminal shit," said Lucas. "Scamming and thievery. At least one of them's a sociopath. There's a third guy, too, someone I know nothing about."

"But the one you're looking for first is the guy who ran the Nigerian four-one-nine thing?"

"I think he's going to be the easiest to find. The name on his

e-mails was Grant Summers, but his real name is Serge Nikolai. *If* that's his real name. I really don't know."

"After you called me, I contacted a Swiss friend who spe-
cializes in this type of fraud. He said that most of these guys
are organized and operate out of Internet cafés overseas."

"I don't know how organized they are. The other one, Billy
Hunter, he left my client a total wreck after he stole something out of her apartment. Used her till there was nothing
left of her and then walked away with a valuable piece of art.
They're leaving behind a trail of hurt, man. That makes them
sloppy."

"What's their motivation? Is it money?"

"In part, I would imagine."

"So tempt them with more. The Internet scammer first."
Starr sipped from his coffee cup. "I assume the ad for the Mini
Cooper has been taken down from Craigslist."

"Yes."

"But you still have the Grant Summers e-mail address. So
reach out to him. Try to ferret him out. Tell him you want that
particular car and will overpay to get it. Let him lick his chops
while you dig out pieces of information that you can use to
identify him. Basically, bait him. If he's about money, he'll surface."

"You think?"

"He's a lowlife," said Starr. "Dangle some dollars in front of
his face. He'll rear his ugly head."

LUCAS PEDALED back to his apartment and phoned Grace
Kinkaid. He had been looking through the notes of their first
meeting, and something had come to him.

"You said you had the painting assessed not long before you met Billy Hunter," said Lucas.

"That's right," said Grace.

"Who appraised it?"

"Charles Lumley."

"How did you get his name, originally?"

"I met him at a get-together here in the building. The Realtor sponsors these rooftop parties, open bar, ostensibly to let the residents mingle and get to know one another. But I think the real motive is to entice people who are thinking of buying and moving in here. There are always a few folks who show up who don't live in the building. That's where I met Charles."

"He was considering buying a unit?"

"No, I don't think so. He said he had a friend who owned a condo on one of the upper floors. Charles buys and sells art. He has a little place, a by-appointment thing, around Dupont Circle. We got to talking, and I told him about my painting, that I was curious about its value. He said he'd be happy to look at it. A couple of nights later he swung by and did the assessment. He was a nice man."

"You have his contact information?"

"Hold on." Lucas waited for her to find the phone number and address for Charles Lumley. He heard the rustle of a piece of paper as she got back on the line. "Ready?"

"That's great," said Lucas, after typing the data into his iPhone.

"Are you making any progress?"

"Yes," said Lucas, though it didn't feel that way to him. "I'll get back up with you soon."

*   *   *

AFTER LUNCH, Lucas opened his laptop and set up a Hotmail account under an assumed name. Using this account, he then typed a message to the Grant Summers e-mail address.

> *Hello, my name is Rick Bell. I am very interested in the 2003 Mini Cooper S you advertised months ago on Craigslist. I know you have taken the ad off the site but I'm wondering, is the car sold? I've been looking for this particular car for some time. Not to get into a long story, but my wife owned one just like it when we were dating, and it had tremendous sentimental value to her. We had to sell it after we got married for financial reasons, but those concerns are behind us now. I've been trying to find this Mini, this model, this year, and this color, to surprise her for our anniversary. Is the car still available? Assuming it is in good shape, I'd like to make you a generous offer.*
>
> *Please respond to the e-mail provided.*
>
> *Thank you,*
> *Rick Bell*

Lucas hit Send. He checked his laptop several times over the course of the afternoon but there was no reply to his query. Then he got a call from Charlotte Rivers's disposable. She was sorry she'd been out of touch, but she'd been very busy. She had a meeting in the dining room of the hotel on 16th Street, and then she had a few hours of free time, but only a few hours, because she had an obligation that night. Was he interested in stopping by the suite around four?

"Uh...," said Lucas.

"Don't you want to see me?"

Lucas hesitated, but only for a moment.

"I'll be there," he said.

THEY BEGAN to make love as soon as he entered the suite. She greeted him by the door wearing slacks with a silk blouse and camisole, and he undressed her there, in the entranceway, piece by piece. Soon she was nude, standing before him, curvy and full of breast, her hair about her face, and Lucas kissed her deeply and thought, This is what I fought for, to come back to someone like her. This is what every boy dreams of.

With the clumsiness of haste he removed his clothing as well, and they found themselves naked in the middle of the plush suite. Charlotte reached down and found his engorged pole and pulled him to her, rubbed his helmet on her lips. They broke apart suddenly and both of them laughed.

"What's wrong with us?" said Charlotte. Lucas knew what she meant. They couldn't keep their hands off each other.

"I missed you," said Lucas.

"I missed *you*," said Charlotte. "How's your hand?"

"It won't affect my performance, if that's what you mean. I've got a backup."

"Do what you do."

They moved to the bed. She had downloaded more music, *Soon Forward* by Gregory Isaacs, the perfect lovers' rock, and the insistent rhythm section of Sly Dunbar and Robbie Shakespeare gave Lucas a beat, and he became a machine. As she came he felt himself chuckle, and an image flashed of a smiling Billy Hunter on top of Grace Kinkaid, and Lucas shook that out of his mind and let himself go.

"What got into you?" said Charlotte, after they had separated and lay beside each other atop the sheets.

"Why?"

"I thought I lost you there for a while. You were, I don't know...a little focused. Workmanlike."

"You got there, didn't you?"

"I didn't say I wasn't pleased," she said. "It was different for us, is all."

Lucas got up, uncorked the Barolo that was on the dresser, then returned to the bed. "Next time, let me bring a good bottle of wine," said Lucas.

"I thought you liked this."

"I just want to contribute something," said Lucas. "You never let me pay for anything."

"I can afford it."

"So can *I*."

Charlotte brushed his short hair with her fingers. "Relax, honey. Enjoy this."

"Because it might not last?"

"Because it's good. Most people never get this, not even once in their lives."

"I don't want it to end."

"Don't be greedy." She kissed him. "Don't think past today."

A little while later, she got up off the bed and dressed. She was going to a neighbor's house with her husband for dinner, she said, and she had to get home.

"When will we see each other again?" said Lucas, watching her from the bed as she fixed a gold bracelet to her wrist.

"I'll call you, Spero."

Lucas thought, *When?*

HE RETURNED to his apartment. He should have been satiated, but instead he was lonely and a little bit empty. His mother had phoned him, and he returned the call. She asked him where he had been when she'd called, and he said, "Out," and when she pressed him he said, "I went to a movie," and when she asked him which one he thought of a title and said it. They talked some more and he told her he loved her, and when he hung up with her he winced, thinking, On top of everything else, I lied to Mom.

Lucas checked his laptop. Still no response from Grant Summers.

He ate some pasta and a salad and decided to watch a DVD. Lucas had intense interests in music, books, and film, and often homed in on a movie director and his work to the point of obsession. He had once watched a different film from the Robert Aldrich library every night for two straight weeks, and had done similar home film festivals for John Sturges, Peckinpah, and Don Siegel. Lately he had been checking out the work of John Flynn, an underrated director who had a spotty filmography that also included a couple of stone classics: *Rolling Thunder* and *The Outfit*. After many years out of circulation, *The Outfit,* based on a Parker novel by Donald Westlake writing as Richard Stark, had been rereleased. Lucas smoked down half a joint, got a Stella out of the refrigerator, and slid the disc into his player.

The movie had a plot that was familiar, but the execution was flawless and true to the no-nonsense spirit of the book.

Robert Duvall was Macklin, a stand-in name for Parker, teamed up with Joe Don Baker as Cody and Karen Black as Bett, Macklin's squeeze. In the penultimate scene, Macklin robs a mobbed-up card game in a hotel room, where at the table sits a vulgarian named Menner, played by the infamous character actor Timothy Carey. Menner explains the premise of the film to Macklin as he is being taken off: "You hit a bank. You and your brother and a guy called Cody before your stretch. Midwest National in Wichita. The Outfit owns it. So you know how it is: You hit us, we hit you." Menner previously used a cigarette to burn a hole in Bett's skin, in an attempt to get her to talk. Before he leaves, Macklin says to Menner, "You shouldn't use a girl's arm for an ashtray," and puts a close-range round through Menner's hand.

Lucas, high and transfixed, stared at the screen. *You hit us, we hit you.* He and his platoon had executed the same creed in the streets and houses of Fallujah.

The film ended. Lucas went to his laptop and checked his Hotmail account for messages, and found a response from Grant Summers:

Rick:

  The car is still available. You want to make generous offer? How generous?

> *Grant Summers*
> *4th Combat Engineer Battalion*
> *United States Marine Corps*
> *One Team, One Fight*

The Marine Corps insignia appeared below the text.

Lucas responded with an offer of five thousand dollars. He also wrote, *My father was a marine. I respect you guys and hope we can do business.* He waited, got nothing, and took a shower to pass some time. When he returned, Summers had sent him another message: *Ten thousand is the price.* Lucas immediately countered with an offer of eight thousand dollars. Summers sent another message that simply said, *Ten.* Lucas replied, *I will pay you ten thousand after I inspect the Mini. If I find it to be in top shape, I will give you the full payment. I do want the car.* Summers's response was, *Deal. I will contact you tomorrow with payment instructions.*

"Deal," said Lucas, and smiled grimly.

THIRTEEN

A MESSAGE from Grant Summers appeared on Lucas's laptop the next morning. In it were steps for setting up an escrow account and instructions for wiring the money. It was the identical system Summers had proposed for Grace Kinkaid, along with the identical guarantees, stating the money would be held in escrow for five days while Lucas drove the car, inspected it, and was fully satisfied with the vehicle.

Lucas replied: *As I told you, I need to inspect the Mini myself* before *I give you the money. I am not a tire kicker. I want this car. I am only protecting myself. I think you would do the same if you were in my position. Sincerely, Rick Bell.*

He got no response. Lucas changed into his bike shoes, lifted his LeMond onto his shoulder, and walked it downstairs. Out in the front yard, he used Miss Lee's garden hose to fill his water bottle, and saw his young neighbor Nick Simmons out in the street, detailing his beloved baby blue El-D with the gold spoke Vogue wheels, which he co-owned with his dad. Nick, his hair in full Rasta, his beard untrimmed per the

Old Testament he studied assiduously, deuced Lucas up with a two-finger salute.

Lucas swung onto his saddle and rode his bike north over the Maryland line, pedaling along the shoulder of the flat Sligo Creek Parkway, and into the hilly woods of Wheaton Regional Park. There he turned around and retraced his path. It was a solid twenty-mile ride.

When he got into his apartment, pleasantly sweaty and loose, he checked his laptop. Grant Summers had replied: *I cannot come to you with the car. I am about to deploy to Afghanistan. They do not allow us to leave base.*

Still deploying, thought Lucas, after all these months. Lucas hit him back with a phone number for one of several disposable cells he owned and said, *Call me so we can discuss.*

Immediately Summers replied, *I cannot use phone, it is against regulations for deploying soldiers.*

You mean, you cannot use *the* phone, thought Lucas. And you've forgotten, you're not in the army. Marines don't call themselves soldiers. They're marines.

Lucas wrote back: *I am willing to pay you seven thousand dollars over your original asking price, cash. If you want to make this deal, I need to see the car first. Respectfully, Rick Bell.*

Lucas waited and got no reply. He did some research on regional American painters on the Internet and found an artist who was neither nationally famous nor unknown, which made her suitable for his purposes. This took about an hour, and in that time he still had not received a response from Summers. It didn't seem fruitful to wait around the apartment any longer. He wondered if he had been too aggressive. Perhaps he had pushed too hard and scared Summers off. Anyway, he had sent the e-mails. He couldn't put the genie back in the bottle now.

Lucas had a shower, dressed in nice clothing, and drove over to the Fort Totten Metro Station, where he took the Red Line around to the Dupont Circle stop. He was hoping to talk to an art appraiser. Specifically, he was looking for Charles Lumley.

HE FOUND Lumley's small, unmarked storefront on the ground floor of a stone town house on 22nd, west of Connecticut Avenue, between R and S. The neighborhood north of the Circle was clean, pricey, with primarily white residents. In style and layout its streetscape was reminiscent of northern or northwestern Europe.

Lucas looked through curved plate glass. A man, turning the corner on forty, was inside the shop, seated behind a desk, working or trolling on an open Mac laptop. A couple of paintings, landscapes and portraits, were set up on easels, and a few were mounted on the white walls, but otherwise the store appeared to be low on saleable merchandise. Lucas tried the door and found it locked. He tapped on the window and got the man's attention. The man inspected Lucas, then put up one finger and buzzed him in. Lucas entered as the man stood.

"How can I help you?" said the man, now walking around the desk. He was trim and wore a nice chalk-stripe suit with flat-front pants, a jacket of narrow lapels, and a powder-blue shirt open at the neck. His eyeglasses had black frames and light-blue stems. The glasses barely clung to his small, pinched nose. His hair was thinning, cut short, and what there was of it was combed forward.

"I'm hoping you can," said Lucas, and he extended his hand. "My name is Bob."

"Charles Lumley."

They shook hands. Lucas thought, Soft.

"I have a painting," said Lucas. "It was willed to me from my grandparents. I think it might be valuable, but honestly, I don't know anything about art."

"Who is the artist? Do you know?"

"A woman named Emily Meyers. From what I read, she has quite a reputation up in Maine."

"Emily Meyers, yes," said Lumley, nodding his head. "I know of her. Lived in Deer Isle, painted scenes of local life up there, fishermen, houses, nets and traps, landscapes, and the like. Mostly worked in oil but there were some watercolors, I believe."

"This one's sorta like, you know, a scene of boats dry-docked in the winter. Like a wintry painting…"

"Do you have a photograph of it?"

"No, sorry. I guess I wasn't prepared to come see you today. I mean, I was in the neighborhood, and I remembered your shop was here. A lady I met told me about it, said you had worked with her before."

"What lady?"

"Her name was Grace Kinkaid."

Lumley's mouth twitched up into a smile. "Grace is lovely."

"I'm hoping to maybe sell the painting. I like it and all, but I move around a lot. Doesn't make sense for me to keep it at this point in my life. Trouble is, I have no idea how to go about making the sale."

"Well, I *could* help you," said Lumley. "What I'd need from you first are good clear photos of the front and back of the painting, size specs, and any interesting facts you can dig up regarding the personal relationship between your grandparents and the artist, if there was any such relationship. Gallery owners call this provenance. Of course, I'd have to see the painting myself, inspect it for authenticity."

"Okay..."

"Then I would appraise it for you, based on my experience and research. If you decided to go forward and attempt to make a sale, we would come to an agreement on a commission, and I'd get to work. I'd determine which geographic area was most relevant to the artist, and then I'd e-mail my network of galleries and collectors in that area with a brief description of the painting, along with photos."

"That'd be there in the Northeast, I guess," said Lucas, giving it his aw-shucks best. "Maine and all."

"New York to Maine, yes. Many well-off New Yorkers summer up in the Penobscot Bay area. They like to acquire the local art."

"This has been real helpful," said Lucas. "I'm completely in the dark when it comes to all this."

"That's what I'm here for," said Lumley cheerfully. "Hold on one second. Let me check on something before you go."

Lumley sat back down at his desk, pulled his laptop toward him, used his keyboard and mouse to search and scroll. Lucas watched his face go from eagerness to disappointment.

"I checked on some recent sales of Ms. Meyers's work. She is a talented artist. *Was*... She died in 2003—ninety-nine years old. But I have to tell you, in relative terms, her paintings are not very valuable."

"How not very?" said Lucas.

"Recent sales of her landscape oils have gone for between a thousand and fifteen hundred dollars."

"That's real money to me."

"But not to me, unfortunately. To be honest with you, it wouldn't be worth my time to represent you. However, I think I've given you enough information today to get you started on your own."

"You have. I appreciate it, too."

Lucas reached across the desk and once again shook Lumley's hand.

"I'll have to thank Grace for the referral," said Lumley. "Even though it didn't work out."

"Yeah, Grace seems like cool people."

"Where did you say you met her?"

"Didn't say. It was at Cashion's. I was at the bar and we struck up a conversation. She was with a blond-haired guy. I remember him because he seemed a little jealous that she was talking to me. Anyway, I heard her talking about a painting she owned, how she'd just gotten it appraised. I asked her who she'd worked with. That's how I got your name."

Lucas detected the flicker in Lumley's eyes. "I see."

"So long," said Lucas. "Thanks again."

"I didn't get your last name, Bob," said Lumley, to Lucas's back, but Lucas kept going and went out the door.

He walked down to the corner at R and approached a bicycle messenger who was wearing a knit hat over his dreads. Lucas had caught him in a rare moment of rest. He asked the guy to ride his bike by Lumley's shop, take a look inside, and tell him what Lumley was doing. He told him there'd be something in it for him when he returned.

The bike messenger did a quick recon and wheeled back to Lucas.

"He's on the phone."

"Cell or landline?" said Lucas, checking the messenger for verisimilitude.

"Landline."

"Thanks, brother." Lucas gave him a ten and the messenger sped off.

Grace Kinkaid said that she had never discussed her painting with Billy Hunter. This meant that he had gotten the information about its value from someone else. The logical conduit would have been Charles Lumley. Lumley, most likely, had an arrangement with Hunter. Lumley would identify the paintings first, contact Hunter, and Hunter would move in on his prey. If Lumley was in business with Hunter, he would now phone him and tell him that a young guy had just dropped his description in the shop. He'd tell him that the guy had claimed they'd met in Cashion's, and Hunter would know that they hadn't met, that it was a bullshit story, and that the young guy was not a bumpkin trying to sell a painting, but some sort of private heat hired by Grace Kinkaid.

Lucas wanted Hunter, or whatever his name was, to know that someone was looking for him. He wanted to draw him out. Either him or, if he came to ground first, Grant Summers.

Lucas knew this was reckless, but he felt he had no other way to get to them and complete the job. He had decided to be aggressive. He was tired of fucking around.

*   *   *

BACK IN his apartment, he phoned Grace Kinkaid and warned her that he'd probably exposed her in some way. She seemed unconcerned. She'd had the locks changed on her condo and always parked her car in the building's indoor garage. She felt that Billy Hunter would never reappear in her life. Grace thanked Lucas for the courtesy call and wished him luck in retrieving the painting.

All she's been through, thought Lucas, and she's still got a spine.

He checked his laptop and saw nothing from Summers. He then called Charlotte, not expecting her to pick up, and left a message telling her that he missed her.

He tried to get some reading done, but he couldn't focus. He didn't want to smoke any weed or drink alcohol, because he wasn't ready to relax. Lucas got back on the laptop and wrote Summers another message.

All right, Mr. Summers. As you know, you own the exact Mini I am looking for because of the year, color, features, etc. It's for my wife, and there can be no substitute. In other words, as much as I hate to admit it, you are dealing from a position of strength. So I am prepared to up my offer, but this will be my final offer. I will pay you $12,000 for the car, cash, provided it is in mint condition as described in your original ad, subject to my inspection before we make the deal. I realize it is difficult for you to leave base, so perhaps you can send someone down to the Washington area with the car as your representative. They or you should bring a clear title and two sets of

keys so we can complete the deal on-site. Please give me the
courtesy of a reply.

Sincerely,
Rick Bell

Lucas hit Send.

LUCAS HAD dinner alone at the bar of Cava Mezze, a Greek spot
on Capitol Hill. When he returned to his apartment he saw
that he'd received a message from Grant Summers.

You have wore me down, Mr. Bell. I will find a way to deliver
the car. Please give me a day so I can figure this out. Once I get
off base I will contact you and tell you where we can meet. Please
bring cash, as promised. I will have car, along with title and keys.
What is your contact number?

Lucas typed him the phone number to one of his disposables and asked, *What's yours?* Summers did not reply. It was
not surprising and also unimportant. Lucas was about to get
close to the one called Serge. Which would put Billy Hunter
in his field of fire, too.

"YOU THINK it's wise?" said Billy King.

"I think it's money," said Serge Bacalov.

They were in the living room of their rented house near Jug
Bay. Louis Smalls was on the couch, stoned, earbuds in, listening to something heavy and loud.

"You're gonna do what?" said King.

"*We* are going to rob him," said Bacalov.

"You gonna hit him on the head, too? You know you almost killed that old man."

"Almost is horseshoes and hand grenades."

"You got lucky."

"And I got your goods."

"Serge, you nearly always miss my point," said King. "I don't like sloppy. If there's a reason to kill, you do it all the way. That way they can't talk. I'm not about to go to prison 'cause you *almost* killed someone. I like my freedom."

"Do you like twelve thousand dollars?"

"Life's easier with money."

"Only if you can trade it. Cash is better than gold coins you cannot spend. Or paintings."

"I'm going to see the man tomorrow about the gold."

Bacalov smiled thinly. King would meet his middleman at a waterfront location. He'd then spend the night jackhammering some marina whore he'd meet in a bar.

"I'll come back with cash," said King.

"And with the smell of fish on you, no doubt," said Bacalov.

"What's it to you?" said King. He got up from his chair, tipped his bottle of Heineken to his lips, and finished it. Bacalov looked at King's drinking arm, the ripple in his massive forearms, thickly covered in blond hair like fur covers an animal. King was a beast. He should have had hooves for feet. It would complete his look.

"This will be easy," said Bacalov. "No worries. Louis will drive, you will back me up. I only need to pick the spot."

"So you're just gonna take his money."

"I will strong-arm him," said Bacalov. "It will be piece of cake."

King had gotten a call from Lumley about a man who had come into the art dealer's shop and described him as sitting at the bar of Cashion's with Grace Kinkaid. The man had said there'd been a conversation. But there had been no such man or conversation there that night. It bothered King that some-one was looking for him. Bothered him and excited him at the same time. But there was no reason to tell Bacalov about this man yet.

"What's this guy's name?" said King.

"He calls himself Rick Bell."

"How do you contact him?"

"By e-mail. My untrackable account. And I have a phone number for him if I need it."

"You ever stop to think this guy is baiting you?" said King.

"You think he is FBI, or something? They don't bother with these little potatoes."

"I don't know who he is. Neither do you. I'm saying, be careful."

"He wants car. For his wife. Can you imagine overpaying for present, for a woman you can have in bed anytime you want? He talks like *he* is the woman."

King had not wanted to double up with Bacalov on Grace Kinkaid. It seemed excessive, a bold move for bold's sake. And Bacalov had not even pulled his end off. King wondered, was the man in Lumley's shop after both of them? Lumley had de-scribed him as medium height, strong build, with short black hair. King could at least get a look at him when Bacalov tried to take him for the twelve.

"He is pussy," said Bacalov.

"Maybe."

"You come with me, eh?"

King said, "Yes."

FOURTEEN

THE NEXT day, Lucas met Marquis Rollins and Bobby Waldron at the bar of the American Legion, Cissel Saxon Post 41, on Sligo Avenue in Silver Spring. After he was buzzed through the security entrance, he slid onto a stool between Marquis and Waldron at the double-sided stick.

There were several solitary drinkers today and sets of two and three as well. The place was sparsely decorated in the manner of a school auditorium, and not well lit, but the draw wasn't the decor or the ambience. It was a second home to many veterans in the area and some who visited from out of state. People liked to drink with others who shared their experiences, and they liked to be with their own kind. Plus, the beer was cold and very cheap.

"What'd you do to that hand, lover?" said Marquis, nodding at Lucas's bandage.

"I fell down in some broken glass," said Lucas.

"Sure you didn't put your paw where it didn't belong?" said Waldron.

"There was a woman," said Lucas.

"Always is, with you," said Marquis.

The bartender put a Budweiser in front of Lucas. Here at the Legion he drank from brown bottles. He tapped his with Marquis's and Waldron's.

"Success," said Lucas.

"Hear, hear," said Marquis, looking smart in his matching outfit, a billowing print shirt and pants. His New Balance sneakers somewhat reduced the sartorial effect of his getup, but not entirely. Sneaks were the only kind of shoe he could comfortably wear on the end of his prosthetic leg.

"I'm for it," said Waldron, wearing a T-shirt with cutoff sleeves, the better to show off his guns and tiger-stripe tats. The "dots" on his forearm, small bits of shrapnel permanently embedded under his skin, were augmented with tiny dots inked in as well. "When I can get it."

"Still doing security work, Bobby?" said Lucas.

"The boss man's got me holding down an Urban Outfitters," said Waldron.

"It does have *urban* in the name," said Marquis. "So that means it must be dangerous."

"It's a jungle out there," said Waldron. "In Georgetown."

"Yeah, how's it feel to be back in uniform, Waldron?"

This came from Tom Kaniewski, seated on the other side of the bar, five beers deep into the afternoon. Kaniewski was in his late forties, a marine who had participated in an infamous Reagan-era military action. Waldron had been a PFC in the army, posted for recon at a firebase in the Korengol Valley of Afghanistan. The animosity between the branches of the service was real for some, almost a tradition, but Waldron plain didn't like Kaniewski, a decent guy ordinarily whose mouth overloaded his asshole when he drank. As for Lucas, he had nothing but respect for the guys in the army. They'd caught it in Fallujah, and dealt it back.

"Fuck you, *Tommy*," said Waldron.

"I'm just playing with you," said Kaniewski.

"Play with this," said Waldron. "I should be more understanding of you, I guess. You're still living with the posttraumatic stress of that Grenada invasion."

"That again."

"The climax of *Heartbreak Ridge* had me on the edge of my seat."

"Excuse me," said Kaniewski to the guy seated next to him, and clumsily got off his stool and headed toward the bathroom.

"Where you goin, Kaniewski?" said Waldron. "Is it time to change your tampon?"

A couple of the men at the bar smiled charitably. Then they kept drinking.

"I'm gonna catch a smoke," said Waldron, and he headed for the side door, which led out to a patio and yard.

"What's eating him?" said Lucas, after he was out of earshot.

"Bobby's just ornery like that," said Marquis. "You gonna hit him up for some iron?"

"I don't think so," said Lucas. "Not yet."

Waldron had an arsenal of firearms, ammunition, knives, combat gear, and body armor he sold and rented out to select people he could trust. He bought the hardware at gun shows and from private dealers. The ammo and armor had been easily purchased over the Internet.

"So this thing you called me about," said Marquis. "Should I be updating my will?"

"I don't know. We're dealing with three guys. One's an Internet scammer, the other's a thief and, when it comes to women, probably a sociopath. The third one, I've got nothing on him. But I'm not looking to bring a gun to this party. You pull a gun, you have to shoot it."

"What you gonna do if *they* have guns? Point your finger and go *bang?*"

"If it works out like I want, I'm just gonna piss this guy off enough for him to leave."

"And me?"

"We'll take two rentals. I'll go in for the meet, you hang outside the perimeter. When he leaves, tail him or his crew to wherever they go. I need to find out where these guys stay. Once I do that, I can figure out a way to get into their crib and steal back the painting."

"You make it sound like a picnic in Rock Creek Park."

Lucas shrugged. "It's what I do."

"What about the lay of the land?"

"The dude just gave me the location this morning. It's over there in Ward Nine."

After the increased migration of east-of-the-river residents from the 7th and 8th Wards of D.C. into Maryland, and the attendant rise in crime, some folks had been describing PG County as Ward 9. It was not a term of endearment.

"We Prince Georges County residents don't like it when you describe our home in that derogatory way."

"Sorry. The spot he picked used to be a strip mall in Oxon Hill. Now it's a bunch of empty stores with no tenants."

"A deserted strip mall."

"He wants me to meet him around back."

"Where it's even more deserted. This gets better the more you talk about it."

"We're gonna check it out first, of course."

"Of course."

Lucas drank some Bud and placed the bottle on the bar. He looked at Marquis's outfit and grinned. "Can't touch this."

"Huh?"

"MC Hammer's closet has some empty hangers in it today."

Marquis reached over and flicked the leg of Lucas's Dickies. "I used to have a pair of trousers like that."

"And then your father got a job."

"You should own *two* pairs."

"One to shit on, and one to cover it up with."

"You heard all those, huh? And here I was, thinking I was gonna make you smile."

"Let's finish these beers," said Lucas. "Go have a look at that mall."

BILLY KING sat in a window booth of Captain John's, overlooking a marina and sound. The restaurant was located on the mainland side of Cobb Island, Maryland, around fifty miles from D.C., down Route 5 and 254, where the Wicomico and Potomac Rivers meet.

Captain John's large, open dining room was crowded with locals, powerboaters, and day-trippers. King was eating steamed crabs spiced with Old Bay. A pitcher of beer, a mug, a paper cup holding vinegar, a wooden mallet, and a nutcracker sat on the table, which was covered in brown butcher paper. The attaché case and gym bag containing the coins were locked in the trunk of his black Monte Carlo SS, parked in the lot.

King pulled the claws off the crab, flipped it over, tore open the envelope, separated the top shell from the body, broke the body in half, discarded the "mustard" and intestines, and found the treasured back fin. He dipped this in vinegar and ate it. He'd get to the claws later. God, it was good. For a while he'd lived in Louisiana, where they boiled their crabs, and they were okay, but there was no comparison to steamed blue crabs from Maryland, properly spiced. He tossed the inedible stuff in a pile that was heaped in the middle of the table and wiped a paper towel across his face. All the beer he'd drank, he had to take a piss.

On the way to the head he walked by the bar and saw a woman seated alone. A lot of hair, midforties, nice ass in a white pair of jeans, a strong sit-up rack from what he could tell. She was drinking clear liquor in the afternoon. That was good.

On the way back he walked slow and easy, and waited for her to get a look at him in full. Some women were scared off by a guy his size, but just as many craved it. Her eyes nakedly appraised him, and he knew he was in. He got beside her and touched his forearm to hers as he leaned on the bar.

"'Scuse me," said King.

"That's all right," she said, with a smile. "No harm done."

Up close she looked closer to fifty. Long as she was on the wet side of menopause and her motor ran, that was all right by King.

To the bartender, King said, "A shot of Jamie. That would

be neat, professor. And please give my friend here whatever she's having, on me."

"That's kind of you," said the woman.

"My apologies for being so clumsy. I'm not the delicate type."

"I can see that, hon."

"Billy Hunter," he said, and extended his hand. She took it, and he squeezed it firmly. Now she'd know his strength.

"Lois Wilson. Pleased to meet you."

King smiled, showed her his white teeth. He brushed his blond hair back off his forehead. Women liked that move, too. "Pleased to meet *you*, darling."

She blushed. Lois the Ho-ess, thought King. I'm gonna peel you back and turn you inside out.

"What are you doing in these parts?" said Lois. "I know I haven't seen you here before."

"Meeting a man at the marina. I'm looking to buy a boat. It's a sickness."

"Don't do it," said Lois.

"I know," said King ruefully.

"I have a twenty-two-foot Whaler. It belonged to my ex. It's a money pit, Billy. The gas alone…"

"I just can't help myself," said King, liking the way the conversation was going. "Look, I was hoping to get a drink later on, maybe someplace, you know, more of a real bar than a restaurant. You know of any?"

"There's a little spot on Neale Sound Drive, on the island proper."

The bartender served Lois her vodka tonic and King his Jameson, straight up. King knocked his back at once and placed the empty shot glass on the bar.

"Maybe I'll see you over there tonight," said King, dropping cash on the stick.

"Maybe," said Lois coyly.

King walked back to his table to finish his crabs. Wasn't no maybe about it. She'd be at that bar, waiting on him. And soon after that, he'd look down and there she'd be. Hanging on the end of his dick, panting like a grateful dog.

ANOTHER CRAB house was set just across the road. King met a man named Arthur Spiegel in its lot. Spiegel wore gray slacks and a white short-sleeved button-down shirt with an oxford collar. His eyeglasses had bifocals and thick black stems. He looked like a math teacher. In fact he was a bridge man to black marketeers who dealt in coins and gold. King and Spiegel were in the front seat of Spiegel's Lincoln Town Car, facing the water. Spiegel was inspecting the goods in the open attaché set on the armrest between them.

"These Liberty five-dollar gold pieces are barely in the fine category," said Spiegel.

"And the Indian heads?" said King.

"Same. At retail, they'd go for four hundred and change. It's not even worth the risk for my buyer. I can have them melted down. With the price of gold right now, you're better off doing that. Just take the ounce value."

"What about the Saint Gaudens?" said King. "They're nineteen-o-eights, uncirculated. That's a sweet collection right there."

Spiegel picked up the set of coins, encased in hard plastic, from the attaché, and inspected it. "You did your homework."

"Yeah, and they've been authenticated. The papers are in that gym bag at your feet."

"Well…"

King smiled. "Don't try to put it in my dirt chute, Arthur."

Spiegel did not like to look King in the eye. It unsettled him. He stunk of alcohol and spices, and his bulky frame loomed in the car.

"I wouldn't," said Spiegel. "But the manner in which you obtained the goods, well, this wasn't an ordinary event. The newspapers and wire services have picked up the story. It's on the NCIC website."

"An old man got some stitches in his head. So what?"

"He detailed the missing goods to the press," said Spiegel. "It's going to make it hard to move the coins."

"How much?" said King, tiring of the game. "Roughly."

Spiegel removed his glasses. "Let's say…"

"Careful."

"Twenty thousand for everything."

"Fuck you."

"Inclusive of my cut."

"Fuck *you*. There's a nineteen twenty-six D in there, too. That's worth twelve grand all by itself."

"I was counting that."

"Maybe I'll shop around."

"That's up to you, Billy."

King looked down at his big hands, folded in his lap. He was powerful, crafty, and slick, but he wasn't smart. All his life, he'd managed to get by with the strong-arm and some degree of charm. But guys like Spiegel, physically inferior but with real

142 • George Pelecanos

brains, would always take him to school in the end. King knew
who he was.

"What do you think?" said Spiegel. "I've got the cash in the
trunk. We can do the deal right there."

"I bet you brought exactly twenty, too."

"I don't overspend, if that's what you mean. Do we have a
deal?"

Twenty thousand split three ways: six thousand three hundred and thirty-three each. Bacalov and the kid didn't need to
know what he'd got for the coin collection. So maybe he'd take
ten or twelve for himself. It wasn't much, but it was something.
And he still had the paintings. Once he moved the Loretta
Browning he'd be flush. Maybe buy himself a boat. A nice,
seaworthy Grady-White, or a sweet Bayliner. Or a Parker,
twinned-out with Yamahas.

"Gimme the money," said King.

By the time they finished, it was night.

KING DROVE over the bridge spanning Neale Sound and cruised
around the island until he found the bar Lois had mentioned.
It was a small place for locals, smelling of spilled beer, out-
fitted with a couple of televisions, Keno screens, a pool table,
and an electronic jukebox. She was there at the bar, talking to
a guy in a sleeveless shirt with arm tats. King crossed the bar-
room floor as a Jim Lauderdale cover of a Johnny Paycheck
song, "I Want You to Know," came from the juke. The pedal
steel landed pretty on King's ears.

"Did you buy that boat?" said Lois, as King sidled up to
her left and slid onto a wood stool. The guy with the tats
was seated to the right of Lois and stared straight ahead. He'd

worn the sleeveless shirt to show off his sculpted guns, but he had chicken legs. He needed to work on his beer hump, too.

"I'm gonna sleep on it," said King. He signaled the bartender and asked for a Heineken, which in this place was asking if it was all right to date the man's daughter. But the bartender served it without comment, along with a fresh vodka tonic for Lois, at King's instruction.

Lois thanked him and said she had to go to the "little girl's room," and when she was gone, King leaned over to the guy in the sleeveless shirt, who had uttered not one word, and said amiably, "I'd appreciate it you'd give us a little privacy."

"I'm not botherin anyone," he said weakly.

"Beat it, fella."

The guy got up off his stool, paid his tab, and left the bar.

Lois returned, smelling like she'd splashed something on. They had a couple of rounds and talked about what was going to happen without saying it. Lois was drunk by then, slurring what she thought were clever double entendres about "size" and "stamina." King thinking, Why do we need to talk? Though he smiled and nodded, and pretended he gave a shit. It was hard to act interested, but he had his needs.

They went to her spot back on the mainland, a creek-front colonial on Dyer Road that she'd snagged in her divorce settlement. Later, when he was putting his clothes back on, she was crying. She'd been begging him while he was fucking her, saying "please," over and over again. He complied in every which way he knew. At the end she was flopping all over the bed like a fish on a dock. Then, when *he* was ready to finish, he put it in her mouth. Her eyes had bugged, trying to take it in, King thrusting as hard as he would if he was plunging it into her hole. He really did wonder, Why did they always cry? He was only giving them what they wanted. What did Ho-ess think they were gonna do, back when she was talking all that funny stuff back at the bar? Exchange Hallmark cards?

"Will I see you again?" said Lois, just before he walked out the door.

King barked a laugh. "Count on it," he said.

He drove his Monte Carlo up 257, back toward the Washington area, the high beams on and the windows down, country music on the radio, twenty thousand dollars cash in the trunk of the car. His nuts were empty and he felt good. Also, he was somewhat high with anticipation, thinking of what came next. There was another twelve thousand waiting for them tomorrow. That is, if Serge didn't fuck things up. And maybe he'd get a look at the man who'd come into Charles Lumley's shop. He halfway hoped this supposed car-buyer and Lumley's visitor were one and the same. It had been a while since someone had showed him that kind of steel.

FIFTEEN

THE STRIP mall had been built in Oxon Hill, near the Henson Creek Golf Course and Henson Creek Park. The developers had hoped that the golfers and park users would generate sufficient traffic to support a small low-rise shopping center, with a Kmart as an anchor. But the Kmart went belly-up, and the satellite establishments—a video store, a dollar store, a hair and nail salon, a cut-rate furniture house, and a Chinese/steak-and-cheese house—soon followed. The center was scheduled to be demolished, but in the meantime it stood intact, albeit with an empty parking lot where weeds sprouted out of its cracked asphalt and concrete.

Behind the buildings was a smaller lot designed for truck and tractor trailer deliveries, and at its edge, a narrow but dense forest. This was where the meet would take place.

After the traditional pre-job breakfast at the Tastee Diner in Silver Spring, where Lucas had his cream chipped beef on toast and Marquis flirted with the Ethiopian waitresses, Lucas and Marquis went to a nearby car rental spot. Lucas, who had

a standing deal with the manager, chose a nondescript blue
Ford Fusion with a V-6 package. Marquis went with a black
Maxima that had more horses but also would not stand out
in traffic. There in the lot Lucas handed Marquis a business-
grade two-way Motorola radio and an earpiece with an in-line
voice-activated mic.

"You remember how to use that?" said Lucas.

"I know the drill," said Marquis, moving the black-framed
glasses he wore for distance to the crown of his head so he
could get a good look at the unit. "But I don't like wearing
this headset. I'm talking about all these cancer-causing radio
waves shooting into my ear."

"The waves go to the device."

"Yeah, but how do those waves know to go *directly* to the device? I'm sayin, do they make a shortcut and go through my
brain first to get there? Or do they enter through my *other* ear?
Radio waves can't think. They got no conscience."

"You survived the war, and you're worried about this?"

"Exactly. Life is precious, man. To go through all that and
then come back and let technology kill me? Uh-uh. There's
too many women out here, waitin on Marquis Rollins to service them. I check out early, they're gonna miss out."

"Oh, so now you're talking about yourself in the third person."

"It's just more dramatic like that. It makes my point."

"Let's go, LeBron. We got work to do."

They took 295 and picked up the Indian Head Highway,
keeping in contact via their radios as they made their way to
the strip mall. On Livingston Road they passed a fire house
and made other turnoffs and found the strip mall they had

studied the day before. Lucas saw no cars in the front lot, but he kept driving south, down a hill, and Marquis followed. They parked and idled on the shoulder of the road, about a half mile past the mall. Lucas got out of his vehicle and walked to the Maxima as the driver's side window slid down.

"There ain't nothin around that mall but weeds and trees," said Marquis. "Where can a handsome fellow like me be inconspicuous?"

"The meet time is in a half hour. You stay right here. I'm gonna go behind the mall and wait in my car. When he comes, I'll key the mic and you'll know it's on. Drive up the road and park on the shoulder near the entrance to the parking lot. When he or they come out, you follow as best you can. I'll be behind you. Stay in contact via your headset."

"Sounds foolproof."

"I know, it's fucked. The dude chose a spot to his advantage. What can we do?"

"I *am* getting paid for this, right?"

"You mean, money? I bought you breakfast."

"Monkey-lover." Marquis was a churchgoing type who tried not to curse.

Lucas got back in his Ford. He drove up the road and around back of the strip mall, behind the loading docks of the former Kmart. To his left the land sloped up into a forest of oak, maple, and pine. He sat in the driver's seat and listened to a mix he'd burned, guitar-driven Southern rock to keep his blood up. In the cup holder of the console rested the disposable cell that carried the number he'd given to Serge.

Lucas waited. There wasn't anything else to do.

*   *   *

LOUIS SMALLS, driving his police-package white Crown Vic, and Serge Bacalov, in the passenger seat, came up out of the south and headed for the strip mall. A half mile from the deserted mall, they both noticed a black Nissan Maxima parked on the side of the road.

"Slow down a little, Louis," said Bacalov. "Just a little bit, eh."

Smalls, wearing a bleached-out, holey red T-shirt, eased his foot off the accelerator so that Serge could get a quick look at the driver.

"Go," said Bacalov, and Smalls hit the gas.

"What's the problem?"

"Why he is parked there? There are no houses, no businesses. His flashers are not on, so he's not in trouble."

"Maybe he pulled over to text or make a call."

"Or maybe this Rick Bell has a partner."

"You get a good look at him?"

"He is *moulinyan*," said Bacalov, with a shrug.

Smalls made no comment. Bacalov had been born in Argentina, raised in Italy, seasoned in Russia, and eventually had washed up on American shores. On any given day, Bacalov might have called the Nissan's driver a *chornee, mayate,* nigger, or *moolie.* There was no reason for him to slur blacks, or anyone else, but he felt it in keeping with his self-image, which he'd obtained from the Golan-Globus films he'd seen as a child. Bacalov had cast himself as the villain in a Chuck Norris movie.

Bacalov looked in the side-view mirror at the black Nissan,

staying far back but approaching up the hill. "See? He is following."

"Maybe he's just getting on his way."

"I don't think so."

They pulled into the front lot of the strip mall and drove around back. There they saw a newish Ford sedan parked by the loading docks of the old Kmart. A man with short black hair, wearing a white T-shirt, was behind its wheel.

"Park near him," said Bacalov. "Angle your car so that he cannot drive around us. Leave it run."

Smalls did as instructed. He angled the Crown Victoria about twenty-five yards from the Fusion, palmed the transmission arm up into Park, and let the engine idle. Bacalov picked up a Glock 17 that rested on the floorboards at his feet and holstered it under the tail of his shirt, at the small of his back. He got out of the passenger-side door and closed it behind him. Smiling, he walked toward the man seated in the Ford.

LUCAS, UPON seeing the Crown Vic come around the corner and drive in his direction, keyed the mic of the two-way that he was holding beneath the windshield line.

"It's on," he said.

"Copy that," said Marquis.

Lucas put the radio in the glove box and shut it. He looked at the two men in the car. The driver was young and bearded, and had some sort of receiving device looped around his ear. He looked like a damaged folksinger. The one in the passenger seat was older yet somehow seemed more childish and primitive. That would be Serge.

Lucas lifted a cheap daypack he'd bought at a dollar store off the backseat and took it with him as he exited the car. He slung the pack over his shoulder. The man walking toward him was shorter than him by an inch or so, but stocky and strong. His mouth was chimplike, and he sported a unibrow and curly dark hair. Whether he was trying to hide his origin or not, his look said "not American." He was wearing a button-down shirt, tails out, which might have meant nothing. It could also mean that he was carrying a gun.

He's smiling, thought Lucas. I'll just go ahead and smile, too.

The man stopped twenty feet shy of him. Lucas stopped as well.

"Rick Bell?" said the man.

"Grant Summers?"

"Yes."

Lucas said, "Where's my car?"

MARQUIS FELT he had been burned by the men in the Crown Victoria. Further, there were two men in the car, and he didn't care for the odds. Luke wouldn't like that he'd disobeyed his instructions, but in his mind Marquis had little choice. He followed their car, staying back so that he could see them turn in to the strip small. He could only hope that he was far enough away that they wouldn't spot him. He drove up to the front lot of the mall and parked the Nissan on the right side of the former shops. He was out of sight from the back lot but close enough to pull around quickly and jump in, in the event that the meet flew apart. Wouldn't be the first time he'd pulled his boy out of trouble.

*　　*　　*

"**YOU HAVE** problem?" said Bacalov.

"I don't see a green Mini Cooper S," said Lucas.

"Show me the cash first. Then I take you to your car."

"That wasn't the deal," said Lucas pleasantly.

"You want the Mini? I need to see the cash."

"That wasn't the deal."

"So deal is off," said Bacalov.

"Then I guess you should leave," said Lucas.

"No. I don't think I'll leave yet."

Momentarily, Lucas and Bacalov said nothing. There was the sound of the Crown Vic idling and the shrill call of a flock of starlings that had lifted off the roof of the old Kmart. Lucas watched the black birds pass overhead and followed their path as they glided into the forest. As he peered into the trees, he saw a flash of light. Just as quickly it faded. He recognized this as sunlight flaring off a camera lens or binoculars. Or the lens of a scope.

"You brought backup," said Lucas.

Bacalov briefly looked over his shoulder in the direction of Smalls. "He is just a friend who drives the car."

"I don't mean him," said Lucas, and he began to walk forward. "I'm talking about the one in the woods."

"Stop," said Bacalov, but Lucas walked on.

Bacalov pulled the Glock from behind his back, flipped off its safety, and racked its slide. Lucas stopped walking.

"*Now* we have problem," said Bacalov.

Lucas stood at ease, his arms at his sides.

*　　*　　*

UP IN the woods, Billy King looked through a pair of 10x50 binoculars at Serge and the man who had come to meet him. Beside King lay a Bushmaster M4 with a sixteen-inch barrel and a Nikon scope, resting on a blanket at the base of an oak. He had brought the rifle along for insurance, but there was little likelihood that he would use it. He was more than one hundred yards away, and though it was well within range for this weapon, he was not a superior marksman. He wasn't about to shoot someone and bring in the law over a small botched deal. Also, the man who'd baited Serge had begun to interest him.

Obviously he was not who he claimed to be. He wasn't a young husband looking to make his wife happy with the purchase of a car. Short black hair, strong build…the man in the art shop, as Lumley had described him. Then there was his clothing: white T-shirt, blue work pants, lug-soled boots. He was working. Plus, his loose-limbed posture and athletic gait said "I don't give a fuck." And it said "private heat." Even now, after Serge had pulled his Glock, his face gone angry and heated, the man remained calm. King thinking, I'd like to meet this one myself.

He picked up the two-way radio that was on the blanket, keyed it, and got Smalls on his headset.

"Louis," said King. "Tell Serge to abort. It's over."

"Copy," said Smalls. "But we've got another problem. I think we got tailed into the lot. Could be this dude has a partner."

"Disable him," said King.

"Right."

King folded the stock of the Bushmaster and placed the rifle and the rest of his gear in a zippered nylon bag. He walked through the woods in the opposite direction of the mall to a clearing, and found the street where he'd parked his Monte Carlo. He stowed the bag in the trunk and drove off. He wasn't worried about Smalls. The kid was good, and he'd figure out his exit. As for Serge, the fuckup was on his own.

"NOW WHAT?" said Lucas.

"Is cash in the bag?" Bacalov, pointing the gun at Lucas, nodded at the backpack slung over his shoulder.

"I brought the paper," said Lucas.

"Give it to me."

"Okay."

Lucas raised one hand and with the other removed the backpack. He tossed it by its strap to the asphalt at Bacalov's feet. Still holding the gun on Lucas, Bacalov squatted and used his free hand to unzip the pack. He found the late edition of the *Washington Post* folded neatly inside. Bacalov stood and angrily kicked the backpack across the lot.

"I read it already," said Lucas. "You can keep it."

"Cock*suck*er."

"You can't do better than that?"

"Sosi hui," said Bacalov, repeating a variation of the vulgarity in one of his mother tongues. A vein had appeared on his forehead.

"What is that? Slovakian? Russian? *What?*"

"Let's go," said Smalls, calling out the open window of the Vic. "It's time."

It was over now. Defused. Lucas knew he should let Serge and his driver leave, give Marquis a chance to tail them and complete the task. But the boy in him couldn't let it go.

"You shouldn't impersonate a marine," said Lucas.

"What did you say?"

"Your e-mail claimed you were in the Fourth Combat Engineer Battalion. *Shit.* Those guys built and repaired bunkers and bridges under heavy enemy assault. They cleared land mines without fire support. You couldn't have a dream about wearing their uniform. A guy like you wouldn't even make it through boot."

"You..."

"What?"

"I should—"

"What?"

"Let's go," yelled Smalls from the car.

Bacalov, red-faced, turned and stalked back to the Crown Vic. He got in and slammed the door shut. Lucas watched them pull away, feeling a slight, satisfying shake in his hands. The car turned the corner and left his sight. He heard the big V-8 of the police-package sedan, and a growl of acceleration.

There was a sonic collision of metal to metal. Lucas sprinted across the lot.

AS SOON as they had turned the corner of the rear lot, Smalls saw the black Nissan Maxima parked to the side of the last building, facing them.

"Seat belt," said Smalls.

Bacalov clicked the belt into place as Smalls slammed his foot to the floor and flooded the Vic with gas. The car lifted and flew forward, accelerating wildly toward the Nissan's nose. The driver of the Nissan tried to back up, but his tires couldn't find purchase.

"Louis," said Bacalov, very quietly. The color had drained from his face.

There was a metallic explosion as the Crown Victoria plowed into the front of the Maxima. The Nissan's air bags blew out and the car was driven backward into a brick wall. The grille and front end were accordioned, and smoke poured from the crumpled hood. The driver had disappeared behind the bags that filled the windshield.

Smalls backed up, made a Y maneuver, then drove from the lot. There didn't seem to be much damage to his Ford.

"Awesome," said Smalls.

"You could have warned me you were going to do that."

"Billy said to disable him," said Smalls. "There wasn't time to ask your permission."

"How did you know we wouldn't be injured?"

"It's a police car. I figured the bumpers were fortified."

"You figured," said Bacalov. "Fucking idiot."

Smalls screwed a cigarette into his mouth and gave himself a light.

LUCAS OPENED the driver's side door of the mangled Maxima and found Marquis pinned against his seat behind the air bag, which had begun to deflate. Marquis was somewhat stunned but relatively intact. His glasses were askew on his face, and his earpiece had been knocked clean off.

"Help me out of here, brother."

"You all right?"

"My flesh-and-bone knee is a little sore. I think it came up on the wheel. And my face is burning some."

"That's the jet fuel from the bag. Come on." Lucas grabbed Marquis's forearm and gave him support.

Marquis began to move out of the seat, then stopped to rest. He looked up and shook his head. "I'm tired."

"Take your time."

"Hope you took the full comprehensive on this vehicle."

"I'll call my man, get a tow truck out here. He's not gonna be happy, but he's insured."

"I know you told me to hang back."

"Don't worry about it. You did right."

"I was just trying to cover you, man."

"I know it."

Lucas helped Marquis out of the car. Marquis leaned against the rear quarter panel and examined his eyeglasses. The left stem was bent.

"I'll take care of that," said Lucas.

"These are designer frames."

"Of course they are."

Marquis stood up straight. "Those boys were serious. What'd you do to set 'em off?"

"I talked too much."

Marquis was out. But Lucas was going to need some help.

SIXTEEN

LUCAS CALLED the rental car manager, a man he'd done business with many times before, and explained the situation. It wasn't a pleasant conversation, but it ended reasonably well and freed Lucas to find some medical attention for Marquis. Over Marquis's mild protests, Lucas drove him to the VA Medical Center on Irving Street in D.C.

Lucas sat in the waiting room with veterans of Korea, Vietnam, Kosovo, and various Middle East wars while Marquis saw the doctor. A WWII veteran in his late eighties, assisted by an oxygen tank and caregiver, sat waiting, too. Some of the patients had no visible ailments, some of them were amputees with prosthetics or no limb replacements at all, others were wheelchair bound, and one bore the unmistakable neurological damage of Agent Orange. Now middle-aged and elderly, they'd been treated in places like this one since they were young men and women. They'd continue to be under VA care for the rest of their lives. No one would ever film a Budweiser commercial here.

It was late afternoon when Marquis emerged from a treatment room. He had some ointment on his face from where the air-bag fuel had stung him, and he was walking a little more stiffly than usual.

"Everything in working order?" said Lucas.

"Doc said I'll be pretty sore tomorrow. But I'm fine."

"They give you anything good?"

"Vicodin. But you know I don't like pills."

"I've got some good smoke if you're interested. It'll take your mind off damn near everything."

"Much appreciated," said Marquis. "They had a fine nurse back in there, man. I was hoping she'd give me a thorough examination."

"They don't nut-check car accident victims."

"A man can dream."

Lucas had dropped Marquis off when they'd arrived. As they walked out the front doors of the hospital, he pointed across the lot. "There's the car."

"Can't you get it and pick me up?"

"Don't be a bitch."

Lucas stopped at his apartment for some weed, then drove Marquis to the rental car agency and dropped him off at his Buick.

"I'm real sorry about this," said Lucas.

"Ain't no thing," said Marquis.

They bumped fists.

BACK IN his apartment, Lucas checked his iPhone, which he'd left behind that morning in favor of a disposable. Charlotte Rivers had called to tell him that she was available in the early evening if he had the time. His heart pumped faster as he left a voice mail, telling her he'd be there. Tom Petersen had also called to give him an update on the Bates trial. Lucas hit him back. Reaching Petersen, he heard a car's engine, wind coming through open windows, and Led Zep.

"I'm on Route Five, headed back from La Plata," said Petersen.

"How's it going?"

"I put Brian Dodson on the stand today."

"The mechanic."

"Him. Truthfully, I've got nothing on Dodson. The tire tracks are inconclusive, of course. There's nothing else definitive that puts him down in Southern Maryland at the time of Edwina Christian's death."

"Did you ask him what kind of business he had that would take him to Barry Farms?"

"He said that his sister lives there. There was a present in that bag he was carrying into the units. A doll for his niece."

"I guess I was wrong on that one."

"Maybe she does live there. Doesn't mean he was visiting her that day. He was cagey. But I was able to bring up his old criminal record. The prosecutor objected, and the judge instructed the jury to disregard. But I think I got their attention."

"You planted a seed of doubt."

"Yes, Jack, I did. By the way, Calvin Bates would like to speak with you."

"What's he want?"

"Something about a card game. He wasn't making much sense, and frankly I wasn't really listening. I was busy trying to keep him out of prison for life. He's in the D.C. Jail until the trial ends."

"I'm tied up right now."

"It won't be right away. I'll get back to you on this and set up a meet."

"Right."

Lucas took a shower and dressed for his girl.

SHE WAS waiting for him in her suite, wearing a man's wife-beater and a black thong. He kissed her as the door shut behind him, and she kissed him back. It felt familiar and brand-new.

"What's that?" said Charlotte, reaching for the bottle of Barolo in his hand. He had bought it on the way over, but he didn't really know wine and was hoping he'd done well.

"I wanted to contribute something for a change."

"You're here. That's all I want."

"I'll put it on the dresser," he said, and he placed the bottle next to the one she had ordered up.

She followed him into the bedroom, and as he turned she came into his arms and they kissed again.

"Maybe we should talk first?" said Lucas.

"About what?" she said.

Soon they were on the bed, naked, joined and moving fluidly, damp with sweat. Their lovemaking was nearly violent, Charlotte's back arched, Lucas buried inside her. There had been little foreplay.

"God," said Charlotte, after they came.

"When worlds collide."

In bed, they drank some of the wine Lucas had brought. It

wasn't as good as the Barolo the hotel stocked, but neither of them mentioned it.

"They really take care of you here," said Lucas.

"It's nice."

"You have an arrangement with the manager?"

"I told you, my firm spends a lot of money here on visiting clients."

"What does the manager think you're doing in these rooms?"

"I don't know what he thinks. He's smart enough not to ask."

"You never sleep here…"

"I'd like to."

"With me?"

"I'd *love* to spend the night with you. But you know I can't. I have to go home at night."

"When you go home…when you leave me, I mean…"

"Don't."

"Do you ever fuck your husband right after you see me?"

"Stop it, Spero. Just stop."

"Sorry."

"I'm frustrated, too."

"I know you are." But he wasn't sure.

Charlotte put her glass on the nightstand, turned into him, and lay across his chest. She kissed him and held it for a long while.

"I'd watch you sleep," she said. "Are you a sound sleeper?"

"I guess."

"My grandfather was a marine in the Pacific. He fought in the Philippines. Grandma said he never had a good night's sleep for the rest of his life. He suffered from nightmares."

"It's not uncommon."

"Do you ever have nightmares?"

"Never," said Lucas, and then told another lie. "I don't even dream."

"Noises would set my grandfather off. Once I was with him when I was a little girl. We were walking across a parking lot, and he was holding my hand. A car backfired in the street, and he hit the ground. I didn't know what was wrong with him."

"Those guys caught hell over there," said Lucas. "Then they came home and quietly lived with whatever was crawling around in their heads. Only a few got treatment. There was no such thing as PTSD then. What I mean is, there wasn't a name for it."

"What about you? How do you deal with what you saw and did?"

Lucas, on his back, looked at her, her hair that smelled like rain, her lovely back, her breasts pressed against his chest.

"I deal with it like this," said Lucas. "Being with a woman like you puts me in the here and now."

"Thank you."

"I mean it."

"When you were over there..." Charlotte reached up and touched his face. "Did you kill many men?"

Not just men.

"Yes," said Lucas, staring up at the ceiling. "I told you I did."

"And you have no problem with that?"

"I was there to kill the enemy. They were trying to kill me. They would've killed my friends."

"All of them? Were they all shooting at you and your friends?"

"Combat's not an exact science," said Lucas. "You make a decision and you commit."

Lucas thought of the woman.

It had been a particularly brutal day of fighting on a residential street of Fallujah. They were all brutal days. The city was a fortress, the streets mined, the bunkerlike houses booby-trapped. Fortified buildings, some with walls several feet thick, many roofed with firing slits. Unlike other areas of combat in Iraq, Fallujah was loaded with experienced, fanatical insurgents, veterans of Afghanistan and Chechnya, Iranians, Europeans, and Asians, well-armed with AK-47s, RPGs, and PKM machine guns. Russian weapons, rifles from Iran, full-auto assault weapons manufactured in Germany. Enemy combatants wearing Kevlar helmets and full-body armor made in America. Some carrying the M-16s they'd taken off dead soldiers and marines. Their fighters were ready.

The woman. He'd observed her on her cell phone, running from house to house. He'd seen her raise two, three fingers as she talked. He supposed she was using the phone to observe and report the tactical positions of him and his fellow marines to the insurgents who had them pinned down. At least, that was Lucas's best guess. There was no opportunity or reason to ask her.

An hour earlier, he had lost his lieutenant, Randy Polanco, a man he'd admired and idolized, a thirty-two-year-old father of three who'd left his family in Houston and returned to active duty to be with his men. He'd been cut in half, parts of him vaporized, by an IED. The news of Lieutenant Polanco's death had energized and enraged Lucas and the men of his unit. There would be many enemy kills that day.

Lucas, peering over a tank-blown Texas barrier pocked with AK rounds, sighted the woman as she prepared to dash across the courtyard. Without hesitation or deliberation he shot her with a burst of his M-16. Feeling no emotion, he watched blood arc off her torso as she fell in a heap to the courtyard floor. Later, after the fighting had momentarily ceased, he went to where she lay, triggered his rifle, stitched her from groin to neck, and watched her body jump and come to rest. Lucas walked on, detached, because it meant nothing to him. *She* meant nothing in death.

"No regrets?" said Charlotte.

"None," said Lucas.

But he did dream.

"I SHOULDN'T have asked you so many questions," said Charlotte, later, as they had gotten off the bed. "What you did in the war is none of my business."

"It's okay," said Lucas. "I like talking to you."

She kissed him. "I should take a shower."

"I'll come in with you."

"If you come in the shower with me, only my tits will get clean."

"But they'll be *really* clean."

"I think I can manage myself. Besides, you don't want to get that hand wet."

"I think it's too late for that."

Charlotte smiled. "You know what I mean."

"My hand can get wet now. It's fine."

"Let me see it."

Lucas took off the bandage. The cut was no longer throbbing

or swelled, and beneath the stitches its crescent shape was more defined. Charlotte held his hand and looked at the wound.

"Does it still hurt?"

"Not really."

"Tough guy."

"Not really."

"You don't have to be so stoic all the time. You're much more complicated than you let on."

"No, I'm not."

"Still waters," she said.

"Maybe."

"I wish—"

"What?"

"I don't know how to help you."

"You *are*."

She kissed him and walked naked to the bathroom. She looked over her shoulder at him briefly, and in her eyes he saw pity, and maybe something like fear. He watched her, thinking, Please don't go. But he knew she'd soon be gone, back to her home, her husband, her life.

LUCAS DROVE home thinking of what came next. It seemed to him that now there was only one way to find Billy Hunter and the painting. This disturbed him, and excited him, too.

In his apartment, he smoked some herb, grabbed a green bottle of beer from the refrigerator, and put a classic Keith Hudson dub CD on the stereo. High and pensive, he sat down in his favorite chair and phoned his brother.

"What's that you got playin in the background?" said Leo. "Sounds nice."

"*Pick a Dub.*"

"*That* record. You must be up on something good."

"This smoke I've got is sweet. You could come over and burn some of this tree."

"You know I don't play that."

"'To each his reach…'"

"'And if I don't cop it ain't mine to have.' You quoting Parliament? Now I know you're high."

"*Baba* had that one on vinyl."

"I remember. Dad said it was gonna be worth something someday."

"Look, Leo…"

"What?"

"I'm in a fix. That woman I been seein…"

"I told you, man."

"I know."

"Get out of it. It can't come to any good."

"I don't know if I can. I'm in love with her. She's the only one I can talk to."

"You're talkin to me."

"It's not the same thing."

"Why, 'cause I don't have a lady-garden?"

Lucas chuckled. "Where'd you get that?"

"British friend of mine. They have the most creative names for pussy."

Lucas swigged his beer. "Leo?"

"What?"

"I think I'm about to go someplace bad."

"With this woman?"

"Work."

"So don't do it. Whatever it is, stop."

"It's not that simple. I took a job and I've got to see it through."

"Marine Corps must have loved you. High school wrestler, all those pins. They targeted guys like you."

"It's who I am," said Lucas.

"Nah. Don't talk that bullshit to me."

"Anyway…"

"Don't hang up."

"No, I need to go. I just wanted to say hey. It's good to hear your voice."

"Spero…"

"Talk to you soon. Love you."

"I love *you*."

Lucas ended the call. He sat for a while longer, listening to music, deliberating. Then he phoned Winston Dupree.

"Winston, it's Spero."

"What's up?"

"The sky is up. Birds are up, too."

"Oh, shit. You're high, boy."

"A little. How's that tendonitis?"

"Acute. Why you asking after my health?"

"I got some work for you. You interested?"

"Depends on what it is."

"Let's meet tomorrow," said Lucas.

"Come by my spot," said Dupree. "You can meet my dog."

SEVENTEEN

IN THE morning, Lucas made a couple of calls, packed a heavy-duty nylon bag, picked up a Buick Enclave SUV from his increasingly less-tolerant car rental agent, and drove over to North Capitol Street, where he met Abraham Woldu and traded a key in exchange for cash. Lucas then drove over to Winston Dupree's apartment, which took up the first floor of a 4th Street row house, just south of Missouri Avenue, in Manor Park.

On the street, Lucas parked the Enclave behind Dupree's truck, a Redskins-burgundy F-150 with a 'Skins headdress decal centered in the rear window. Two spots down, a similar half-ton truck sat parked with the Cowboys star decal on its bumper. Lucas had a sick feeling in his stomach whenever he saw the Star. He rooted for two teams: the Washington Redskins and whoever was playing the Dallas Cowboys.

A second door had been added to the row house when its owner had sectioned off the rental unit. Lucas, bag in hand, went through it when Dupree answered his knock, a chocolate-colored dog that was almost a Lab by his side. Dupree was wearing a Robert Griffin III jersey and black Nike shorts. Before his war injury, he'd been quick and athletic. He was still big enough to play on Sundays.

"Nice-looking dog," said Lucas.

"He got named Flash when he was a puppy," said Dupree. "But he's got too much ass on him to live up to it."

"Looks like he's carrying a little pit. His head's too squared off for full Lab."

"He couldn't hurt anybody."

"He would if they fucked with you." Lucas saw the way the dog was looking up at Dupree, listening to his voice with full devotion.

"This boy's gentle. Some lucky veteran's gonna get him soon. Come on in and sit."

They moved into a living room crowded with overstuffed furniture, passed down from Dupree's mother, a woman who'd recently died of complications related to her weight and diabetes. Dupree had grown up nearby, off Kennedy Street, in a time when drug-dealing and gangs were prevalent, in a neighborhood where some of his peers had been killed or shipped off to out-of-state prisons. Dupree's mother was a single parent to him and his brothers, with strength tempered by a strong belief in the Lord, and all of her boys had somehow managed to avoid the lure of the streets. Dupree had gone to DeMatha, the storied Catholic high school in Hyattsville, and had played safety for Coach Bill McGregor on the football squad. His brothers, who had gone on to professional careers, were DeMatha grads as well. Winston had Division I scholarship offers but, like Lucas, had elected to join the Marine Corps after September 11. Neither of them had enrolled in college after their tours. In this, in their love of the 'Skins, and in their shared combat experience overseas, they had bonded.

They sat on a couch, Flash lying at Dupree's feet, as Lucas explained the Grace Kinkaid job. He told Dupree what he had in mind for taking the task to the next level, and made him a monetary offer. When Lucas was done, Dupree took off his wire-rim glasses, fogged the lenses with his breath, and wiped them clean with his jersey.

"You sure about this?" said Dupree.

"The biggest risk is in taking him off the street. We do that without getting burned, we'll be all right."

"You got a place to take him?"

"We're set. I've got a one-day rental."

"That's all well and good. But what you're fixin to do to this man is…"

"A little extreme," said Lucas. "You in?"

Dupree nodded. "I got nothing else goin on."

"You're gonna need to change out of that RG-Three jersey."

"I wouldn't want to soil it." Dupree nodded at the nylon bag Lucas had set on the coffee table. "What you got in there?"

Lucas unzipped the bag. Dupree moved a small bolt cutter and a roll of duct tape aside and had a look at the rest of the contents.

"*Damn,* boy," said Dupree. "Where'd you get that stuff?"

"Amazon dot com."

"That piece right there, in that holster? It's illegal to receive it in D.C."

"I had it shipped to my mom's house in Silver Spring."

Dupree's teeth bucked as he smiled. "Do I get to be the good guy or the bad guy?"

"We're both gonna be bad," said Lucas. "Change into something less conspicuous and let's get going."

"I got a ninja suit hanging in my closet."

"Bring your throwing stars, too."

THEY PARKED the Buick on 22nd, between R and S, near Dupont Circle. There were many cars traveling on the roads but few pedestrians. Lucas was optimistic.

"Okay," said Lucas. "Go on up to his door and hit the buzzer. I want to make sure he's in, and I want you to get a look at him."

"That means he's gonna get a look at *me*," said Dupree.

"So? I'm gonna approach him when he comes out. Not you."

"What am I supposed to talk to him about when he lets me in?"

Dupree was a big black man wearing jeans and a gray Georgetown T-shirt. Lucas guessed that he wasn't going to be buzzed in. But he didn't want to break that to his friend.

"Improvise," said Lucas. "Ask for directions."

"All right, then. I'll be right back."

From the driver's seat, Lucas watched Dupree go to the door of the shop and push the buzzer. He watched Dupree mouth something to someone inside, and he watched his face go from hopeful to agitated. No one came to the door, and Dupree returned to the SUV and got into the passenger seat.

"Asshole," said Dupree.

"Describe him."

"Thin white dude, short hair, itty-bitty nose, wearing those artist-looking eyeglasses. Had on an expensive suit."

"That's Lumley."

"Man didn't let me in," said Dupree, shaking his head. "He mouthed the word *closed.*"

"He let *me* in."

"That's what I'm sayin."

"You could write your congressman."

"I live in D.C., so that doesn't work for me." Dupree took off his glasses. "People be hatin all over the world. You remember in Iraq, the hajjis would yell out to us from wherever they were hiding? They'd call us 'Dirty Stinking Jews.' Even after they had a look at me, they'd call me a Dirty Jew. Do I look Jewish to you?"

"Sammy Davis Jr. was a Jew."

"Do I look like Sammy Davis Jr. to you?"

"There was that night in the desert, when you drank all that beer? Your eye did look kind of glassy."

"Funny."

"You angry?"

"A little," said Dupree.

"Good," said Lucas. He wanted him to be.

THEY WERE ready when Lumley stepped out of his store about an hour later and walked down the sidewalk, along the space where the Buick was parked.

"Here we go," said Lucas, and he got out of the SUV. He waited for Lumley to come along the side of the Buick, then walked around the rear and met him on the sidewalk. A well-dressed elderly gentleman approached from the opposite direction. There was no time to stop this or try again.

Lumley recognized Lucas and stopped. He had little choice; Lucas was blocking his path.

"Charles," said Lucas. "Remember me?"

Dupree had come out of the passenger side of the Buick. He stepped quickly forward and placed a high-amperage stun gun directly on Lumley's upper back. He triggered the device and sent 150,000 volts into Lumley's body. Lumley made a short, high-pitched sound, spasmed, and collapsed, immobile and helpless, into Dupree's arms. Dupree dragged him backward, opened the back door of the Buick, sat on its seat, and pulled Lumley inside.

The elderly gentleman had come up on them and was staring at the scene. Lucas flipped open his wallet, which showed only his driver's license, and said, with authority, "Official business, sir. Please move along." The man complied. Lucas closed the passenger door, went around the Buick, and got behind the wheel of the SUV.

From the nylon bag Dupree had retrieved two sets of double-cuff disposable hand restraints. He had already bound Lumley's hands and was doing the same to his ankles. He next reached into the bag and brought out a roll of duct tape. He tore off a long strip for Lumley's mouth.

"We're good," said Dupree.

Lucas pulled away from the curb.

THEY WERE in the commercial space of the Woldu property on North Capitol, just above Florida Avenue. They had parked in the alley and walked Lumley in through the back door after removing his ankle restraints. Once inside, Dupree had used the bolt cutter to take the handcuffs off as well. Lumley himself ripped the duct tape from his mouth. Lucas told him to go into the bathroom, and he complied.

Lumley had said nothing. He was not being stoic. He had lost his color, and he seemed too afraid to talk.

The bathroom was large, with exposed pipes in the ceiling and a full tub. When Dupree entered, wearing the stun gun in a holster clipped to his belt, the space shrank.

"Take off your clothes, Charles," said Lucas.

"What for?" said Lumley, uttering his first words since they'd pulled him off the street.

"All of them," said Lucas. "Fold them neatly and hand them to me. I'll put them outside the door."

Lucas knew that there could be few things more humiliating for a man than to be naked in front of two fully clothed assailants. Lumley would now be submissive.

"Nice suit," said Dupree, as Lumley stepped out of his shoes and then removed his jacket and tie.

"Canali," said Lumley, trying to endear himself to his captors.

"Where'd you get it?"

"I have a salesman at Saks on Wisconsin Avenue."

"I bet he let *you* in when you came to the door."

Lumley kept his eyes downcast and finished undressing. When he was done he handed Lucas his clothing. Lucas, as promised, placed his folded clothing outside the door, along with his wallet and cell.

Lumley stood naked before them. He was a thin man with gym muscles on his chest and arms. He'd made the common mistake of not working his legs, so that the effect in total was artificial and incomplete. His penis wasn't small. Still, he crossed his hands over it as if he was ashamed.

"Relax, Charles," said Dupree.

Lumley let his hands rest at his sides.

"This is about Grace Kinkaid," said Lumley, to Lucas.

"Correct," said Lucas. "Answer our questions and I'll give you your clothing back and let you go."

"What do you want to know?"

"You're working with Billy Hunter," said Lucas. "What's Hunter's real name? Where does he stay?"

Lumley looked down at the checkerboard tiled floor.

Lucas glanced up at the pipes in the ceiling. He'd seen no chairs out in the main space, and Lumley wasn't tall enough to reach the pipes. If he had a chair, he could have Lumley stand on it, bind Lumley's hands behind his back, bind his hands to the pipes, and wait for him to fall forward. This would cause much pain and dislocation. The venerable Palestinian Crucifixion. But Lucas had no chair.

"Okay," said Lucas. "Go stand in the doorway, Charles. Raise your hands and grab the molding up top."

Lumley went to the doorway and did as he was told. "Like this?" he said, hopefully. It didn't seem like anything, yet.

"Just like that," said Lucas.

Lucas and Dupree had a seat on the edge of the tub as Lumley held his position.

"We shoulda brought a deck of cards," said Dupree.

"We've got our phones," said Lucas. "We could play Words with Friends."

"I don't want to play that game with you. You make words up, man."

"No, I don't."

"Last time, you played *dhole*. What is that?"

"It's a word," said Lucas.

LUMLEY BEGAN to feel some ache after fifteen minutes. It was hard to hold his arms up as the blood rushed to his lower body and he lost his strength. At the half-hour mark he experienced cramping and dizziness. He was sweating profusely. He made childish choking sounds.

"You recognize this place?" said Lucas. Lumley nodded weakly. "Billy Hunter, or whatever his name is, and a guy named Serge, and a third guy with a beard, they were renting this spot for a while. I imagine you came here when you were doing your dirt with Billy. Let's keep this simple: again, where are Billy and his partners now? Where do they stay, Charles?"

Lumley sharply shook his head. He briefly took his hands off the molding and began to lower them.

"Don't do that," said Lucas. "My friend will hit you with the stun gun again. This time he'll put it right on your testicles."

"God," said Lumley.

"Ain't no God in this room," said Dupree, though to him that was a lie. In his mind, the Lord was everywhere. Today, this disturbed him.

"Tell me where Billy Hunter stays right now," said Lucas. "Tell me where Grace Kinkaid's painting is."

Lumley shook his head.

"Hang there," said Lucas.

Twenty minutes later, Lumley fell like laundry to the tiled floor. Lying there in the fetal position, he shook and sobbed.

"Where's Billy Hunter?" said Lucas, after Lumley had composed himself.

"He'll kill me," said Lumley.

"Does that mean you're not going to tell us?" said Lucas.

"I *can't.*"

Tough guy, thought Lucas. He was surprised.

Lucas looked at Dupree and jerked his head toward the hot and cold taps. Both of them stood. Dupree opened the spigots and began to fill the tub.

"What are you doing?" said Lumley. "Are you two soldiers or something?"

They didn't answer.

"Are you going to waterboard me?"

Dupree chuckled. "We don't even know how to do that, Charles."

Lucas got two more pairs of restraints from his bag, turned Lumley over, and bound his hands and feet behind his back as the tub filled. He tore a long strip of duct tape off the roll. When he was done, the tub was sufficiently full.

"Is that water hot?" said Lumley. "Is it hot?"

Neither Lucas nor Dupree replied.

"One more chance," said Lucas.

Lumley winced and shook his head.

"All right," said Lucas. "This could have been easy. You made a choice."

"No," said Lumley. *"No."*

Lucas wrapped the duct tape around Lumley's mouth. Then he grabbed his biceps and hoisted him up to his knees. He scooted Lumley to the edge of the tub so that he was bent forward and looking into the water. Dupree, behind them, gripped Lumley's ankles. Lumley was wide-eyed and shaking.

"Blink if you're ready to talk," said Lucas.

Lumley did not blink, and with his hand firmly on the back of Lumley's head Lucas pushed his face down into the water. He held him there. At first, Lumley didn't move. Then he began to struggle.

"The tape wasn't a good idea," said Dupree. "He's gonna take water up in his nose."

Bubbles came to the surface of the water.

"Maybe you're right," said Lucas.

Lucas waited. He pulled Lumley's head up. His chest was heaving and he was trying to take in breath through his nose, but there was water in there, and he coughed, his breath outdenting the tape. Lucas ripped the tape away and let Lumley get his breath.

"Billy Hunter," said Lucas. "Where is he? Where's the painting?"

Lumley said nothing. Lucas pushed his head back down into the water and held it fast. Lumley writhed beneath his grip, his legs kicked out, and Dupree grasped his twisting ankles.

"Dude's stronger than he looks," said Dupree.

Lucas watched the water and studied the bubbles with a curious distance. Time passed. Lumley jerked violently and a great deal of bubbles burst on the surface. Lumley went lank and urinated on the floor.

"Luke," said Dupree.

Lucas's eyes regained their focus. He pulled Lumley from the water and put him facedown on the checkerboard tiles. Water spilled from his mouth. He began to heave, then cough, and then he began to breathe. Lucas and Dupree looked at each other. In Dupree's eyes Lucas saw relief.

Lumley, his face resting on its side, stared straight ahead.

"You ready now?" said Lucas.

"Cut off these fucking handcuffs," said Lumley, "and give me my clothes."

"I can do that," said Dupree.

LUMLEY SAT against a white wall in the main space of the property. He had put on his dress shirt and slacks and hand-combed his hair in a forward direction. His hair was still wet and there were wet spots under his shirt. His cell phone lay on the floor beside him. He limply held a bottle of blue sports drink that Lucas had packed in his nylon bag.

Winston Dupree sat nearby in a similar position. Lucas was standing.

"Repeat the location," said Lucas.

Lumley again gave him the location of the house in Croom, Maryland, and Lucas typed it into his iPhone.

"The painting is there?"

"Yes," said Lumley, his voice mechanical. "That one and others."

"Do they have weapons?"

"I've seen Serge handling a pistol. I don't know guns, so I can't be specific."

"What's Serge's last name?"

"Bacalov."

"Spell it." Lumley did so and Lucas said, "And Billy's?"

"Billy King."

"You have a phone number for King, right?"

Lumley read it off the contacts list of his own cell and Lucas made note.

"What about the young guy with the beard?" said Lucas.

"Louis. That's all I know."

"How'd you get mixed up in all of this?"

Lumley drank deeply from the plastic bottle and placed it on the wood floor by his side. He closed his eyes.

"Charles?" said Lucas. "I asked you a question."

"The recession," said Lumley. "I was underwater on my mortgage and I'd missed a couple of payments. I drive a Five Series BMW with a seven-year loan. I like expensive clothes. And my business has gone south. Billy walked into my store one day and caught me at the right time."

"Walked in and said what?"

"He was looking for an assessment on two paintings. He told me they were his. Later, after he'd gotten me caught up in all this, I found that they belonged to a woman he was sleeping with. An older divorcée who lived in the Wyoming."

"So this woman had money and the paintings were valuable. When you sold them, you got a piece of the action."

"Yes."

"Billy stole them how?"

"He had an apartment key made off of her spare. Same way he did with Grace. When he had used this woman up he simply walked in one day and took the paintings off her wall."

"You said you got caught up."

"Billy gets a look in his eye."

"You couldn't say no?"

"Look, I didn't like what I was doing."

"But you liked the money."

"It got me out of a jam. That's all it was to me. A solution."

"And you met Grace at her condo party and you saw that she was, what?"

"Vulnerable." Lumley looked away. "I knew Billy could take advantage of that. He's got a power over a certain kind of woman."

"Has Grace's painting been sold?"

"Not yet."

"So it's at the house in Croom?"

"Last time I was there, yes. I had to verify its authenticity." Lumley looked coolly at Lucas. "Can I go?"

"Not until we get a few things straight. First: if you tell Billy or his friends about this, I'll find you."

"I have no doubt you would."

"You're done in Washington. Close up your shop and leave town. I'll give you a couple weeks, and then I'm going to check up on you. If you're not gone, I'll turn all this information over to the police."

"Are you going to tell the police that you kidnapped and tortured me, too?"

"You can go," said Lucas.

"Aren't you going to drive me back to my shop?"

"You have your wallet. Walk down to Florida Avenue and get a cab."

Lumley stood, picked up his jacket and tie, rolled the tie into a ball, and stuffed it in a pocket. He didn't look at Lucas or Dupree. Straightening his posture, with the last bit of dignity he could muster, he walked out.

"You took everything that man had," said Dupree. "He ain't never gonna look at the world the same way. Those fancy clothes of his, that German automobile…They don't mean dick to him anymore. You robbed him of his manhood."

"He shouldn't have done what he did." Lucas reached out his hand and helped Dupree stand. "Let's clean this place up. I told Woldu I'd leave it as I found it."

"You do know that Charles peed on the floor in there."

"Can you get that?"

"*Screw* you, man."

LUCAS LOCKED the alley door. He and Dupree walked to the Buick.

"You still with me?" said Lucas.

"What's next?"

"A little recon. Then we go into that house."

"We're gonna need more than handcuffs and an electricity gun."

"That's not a problem."

"And I'll have to renegotiate my contract."

"So you're in?"

"Yeah," said Dupree. "I'm in."

In the car, driving uptown toward Manor Park, Dupree said, "*Dhole* is not a word."

"Yes, it is."

"What's it mean?"

"It's a wild dog native to Southeast Asia."

"You knew that?" said Dupree.

"I played the letters first, at random," said Lucas. "The game accepted the word. Then I looked up its meaning."

"You don't mind doin a little dirt, do you? Long as you come out on top."

Lucas nodded. "I like to win."

EIGHTEEN

IN **THE** morning, Lucas met Winston Dupree at his apartment on 4th and drove out to Rockville, Maryland. There, in a neighborhood of modest GI-Bill homes off Veirs Mill Road, they found the Waldron residence, a tidy rambler with a small, trimmed yard and an American flag hung above the front door. Bobby Waldron lived here with his parents, in the basement of the house in which he'd been raised.

They were greeted by Rosemary Waldron, a boisterous redhead, retired from a career-long slog in the cafeterias of the Montgomery County school system. Her husband, Bobby's father, was a master plumber and self-employed. When Bobby was a boy, his father had painted the words *Waldron and Son Plumbing* on the sides of his truck, but Bobby had expressed no desire to learn the trade. Instead, he enlisted in the army straight out of Richard Montgomery High.

Rosemary Waldron let Lucas and Dupree in and offered them a couple of Miller High Lifes. They declined. She knew Lucas but not Dupree and, assuming he was a veteran, asked

about his deployment and war experience. After Dupree detailed his military background to her in front of a fireplace
mantel holding photographs of Bobby in football and army
uniforms, he and Lucas excused themselves and met Bobby at
the foot of the basement stairs. He was wearing jeans and a
Champion jersey with cut-off sleeves, revealing his thick arms
and tiger-stripe tats.

Waldron had drunk beer with Dupree at the American Legion bar in Silver Spring many times, but they had not hit it
off. Waldron had a short-man complex, for one, and there was
the matter of Dupree's size. Also, Waldron liked to play that
Marine Corps versus army game, a dick-size contest that no
one could ever win. Lucas made it a point never to dip his toe,
or anything else, in those contaminated waters.

"Come with me," said Waldron.

They followed him to his dark, windowless room, which
smelled of Marlboros and Axe body spray. A dime would
bounce off Waldron's bed if tossed onto it; against the wall,
many pairs of sneakers were perfectly aligned. It was more
barracks than bedroom.

Waldron closed the door, locked it, then went to his closet
and retrieved a couple of duffel-sized ripstop bags. He
dropped the bags on his bed and unzipped them.

"Short notice," said Waldron. He looked up at Dupree and
shrugged elaborately. "If you'd given me some time, I could've
got you one of those SAWs."

"For real?" said Dupree, putting a little edge into his voice.
He doubted Waldron could have come up with an M249, a
machine gun capable of firing hundreds of rounds per minute.
But then again, they were in America.

"Yeah, for real," said Waldron.

"What do you have for us, Bobby?" said Lucas, hoping to cut the tension and move things along.

"Shotguns, to start," said Waldron. "Mossberg Five Hundreds." Waldron pulled a pump-action twelve-gauge from one of the bags. "I know you guys used Benellis…"

"We used anything we could get," said Lucas.

"The Mossberg will do," said Dupree.

"Military spec," said Waldron.

"Pistols," said Lucas.

"I got you a choice of revolvers, Luke. I know you like the no-jam insurance."

"Talk to me."

"S and W Combat Magnums. If you're looking for a hand cannon, I've got a three-fifty-seven."

"Too much."

"A thirty-eight, then."

"Let me see it."

Waldron handed Lucas a six-shot Smith & Wesson Special with a four-inch barrel and soft rubber grips.

Lucas hefted it in his hand. "I like this." He placed it on the bed.

"Now the semis," said Waldron. "You jarheads favor your Italian pieces. I came up with a couple of M-Nines in pristine condition."

Waldron handed a nine-millimeter semiautomatic pistol to Lucas. He ran his thumb over its black checkered grip. He turned the gun sideways and worked the slide. When it locked open, he inspected the chamber.

"Looks clean," said Lucas.

"I stripped and bored them myself," said Waldron.

"Military-issue mags?"

"Beretta, dad."

"Better," said Lucas. "We'll take 'em both. That okay by you, Winston?"

"Yep."

Waldron grinned. "The barrel on one of these was pre-threaded to accept a suppressor."

"You got it?" said Lucas.

"Right here," said Waldron, producing an SRT Arms silencer from the bag. Lucas took it and examined it with interest.

"What you need that for?" said Dupree.

"Need got nothin to do with it," said Lucas.

"All with holsters and bricks," said Waldron. "Shaved numbers on the pistols. You get popped, you're on your own."

Lucas nodded. "Understood. We're gonna need some goggles."

"Sure, I got NVGs."

"Throw those in."

"Kevlar?"

"Two vests," said Lucas.

"You need me to show you how to work the goggles?" said Waldron, looking at Dupree. "The Marine Corps only issued them to officers, right?"

"If you can figure it out, *we* damn sure can," said Dupree.

"Let me ask you somethin, Winston," said Waldron. "Why'd your mama name you after a cigarette?"

"Why do *you* look like that character on the Frosted Flakes box?"

They showed each other teeth.

"Put it all in one bag, Bobby," said Lucas. "We gotta get on our way."

Lucas gave him cash.

On the way out of the house, Lucas, carrying the long, heavy bag, stopped to say good-bye to Rosemary Waldron, now drinking a beer, seated in front of the living room television set.

"Sure you two don't want a couple of cold High Lifes?" she said.

"No, thank you," said Lucas.

"What you got in the bag, Spero?"

"Bobby loaned me his Xbox and some games."

"You boys have fun."

"Yes, ma'am," said Dupree. "We will."

They headed to the Jeep.

AT HIS apartment, Lucas packed the night vision goggles into his gear bag and found Dupree a pair of Leo's old gym shorts. Leo had size on him, but the shorts were still too small for Dupree.

"I'm supposed to wear these?" said Dupree.

"It's just for today."

"I'll look like John Stockton and shit. Why we got to pretend like we're sportsmen?"

"I'm not pretending," said Lucas. "You are."

Lucas and Dupree loaded the kayak onto the foam blocks atop the Jeep and fitted Lucas's old bike, a Trek hybrid, into the hitch-mounted rack. Dupree wound the rubber strap around the top tube of the Trek and snapped it over its male plug.

"Let me ask you somethin, man," said Dupree. "I've seen you riding your bike in your white T-shirt and plain-old shorts. Why you don't wear those outfits I see other dudes wearing, with the numbers and spandex?"

"When you throw a football around your yard, do you wear a full Redskins uniforms with pads?"

"Only in my head."

"I'm not in the Tour de France," said Lucas.

They drove downtown to Pennsylvania Avenue, which was Route 4, and took it out of the city to 301, in Prince George's County, Maryland. Turning off the highway, just twenty miles from D.C., they were suddenly in a sparsely populated, hilly terrain of forests and farmland, tobacco barns, old houses, and churches. The occasional liquor and bait store, and john-boats up on trailers, told them they were near water. Lucas wound up a rise on an asphalt road bleached by the sun, along wooded land, and as they came to a clearing on the high ground, they saw the ribbon of the Patuxent River below.

"Jug Bay," said Lucas.

They came upon another forest, and Lucas slowed down. He checked the Google Map he had printed out that morning, and pulled over on the shoulder. Up ahead was a driveway of gravel with a posted mailbox at its head.

"Could be it," said Lucas.

He drove on. A half mile or so up the road, at the end of the tree line, sat an old service station with plywood in its windows and a flat island that had once held two pumps. A two-toned Ford Lariat pickup with a FOR SALE sign in its window was parked in the small lot. Lucas pulled in and studied his map.

"All right," said Lucas. "If Lumley gave me the right information, King and them are staying in a house at the end of that gravel road."

"I don't see any other houses 'round here."

"There are, according to this map. But not too close by. That's good."

They drove down to the Jug Bay Wetlands Sanctuary and unloaded their recreational gear. Dupree grudgingly changed into Leo's shorts and took off on Lucas's bike.

Lucas put his kayak in at the boat ramp and headed out into a freshwater marsh carpeted in cattails, reed, and arrowhead. He had removed the bandage from his palm, and his hand on the paddle felt sure and strong. He saw a great blue heron, turtles, and a northern water snake. A front had taken away much of the humidity, and the sky was clear with full sun. It was one of those days that made Lucas believe in something higher. Whether or not there was an afterlife was irrelevant to him. When he witnessed this kind of natural beauty, he knew. This life was no cosmic accident.

LUCAS AND Dupree met up again in the late afternoon, changed clothes, and drove back over to Route 301, where they found a restaurant with wood-paneled walls that had salads, baked potatoes, and steaks. They ordered no alcohol and told the waitress to take her time. They were waiting for night.

"How'd you like that ride?" said Lucas.

"Your bike's a little small for me," said Dupree, cutting into a medium-rare New York strip. "Like those shorts you gave me."

"You'll sleep well tonight."

"How about you?" said Dupree. "How do you sleep?"

"Fine," said Lucas.

"I don't have a problem with that, either. You believe everything you read, all of us vets wake up in the middle of the night in a full sweat. But I never have nightmares, Luke."

"So you're normal, whatever that is. You're saying the war did nothing to you."

Dupree swallowed a mouthful of iceberg lettuce covered in blue cheese dressing. He placed his fork on the table. "You ever take those complimentary tickets they give out to veterans? You know, for Wizards and Nationals games?"

"Sure. I've sat behind home plate."

"Me, too. The announcer says the soldiers or marines are in the house tonight, and most everyone in the arena or stadium gets up and gives us a round of applause."

"They're paying tribute."

"They mean well. Then they sit back down in their seats, enjoy the game, and forget we're there. A lot of those dudes own businesses. Why don't they walk over to my seat and talk to me, see what I'm about? See if maybe they can find a spot on their payroll for a veteran who wants to put his back into it? Instead, they clap their hands and think they've done something."

"It's for them, not us. Those guys who stand up, with their golf shirts on? We did what they couldn't have done. And they know it."

"But they don't know *me*," said Dupree. "I'm not a cold-blooded murderer. I'm not a hero. I don't have PTSD."

"But you suffer from a touch of depression once in a while, Winston. Tell the truth."

"I'm just disappointed, man. I want to go to work every day

and get treated like everyone else. I don't need standing ovations. I don't want sympathy or a thank-you-for-your-service. Offer me a chance at a meaningful job so I can get my life going. Treat me like a man."

They ate silently for a while. Lucas looked like he was enjoying his meal, but he was thinking hard about his friend.

"This thing we're about to do," said Dupree.

"Uh-huh."

"All that hardware we got from Bobby…that's for show, right? I mean, we gonna go in strapped and scare the shit out of those boys, right?"

"That's the idea."

"I don't want to shoot anyone. I'm done with that."

"You won't have to," said Lucas. "You've got my word."

NIGHT FELL. They drove up to the shuttered gas station and parked the Jeep. From the cargo area they retrieved the NVGs and fitted them to their heads, temporarily leaving the lenses off their eyes. Lucas put his Moleskine notebook and a pen in his back pocket.

"We got a little moon," said Dupree. "That's good. We need the lume."

"I know. These thermals don't work for shit in absolute dark."

"You reckon we gotta hump, what, half a click?"

"That's my guess." Lucas showed Dupree his phone. "I got a compass on this thing."

"And Angry Birds."

"I figure the house is due southeast from where we are now. I'll shoot us an azimuth."

"Man, you don't know what the fuck you're doin, do you?"

"Let's just go. We'll find the house."

They activated the goggles, placed the lenses over their eyes, and walked into the woods.

BILLY KING came down the stairs of the colonial with a single piece of luggage in hand. In the soft bag was enough clothing for several days and nights, a couple of disposable cells, his portion of the cash he had skimmed from the coin deal, and the remaining cash from the previous jobs he had done with Bacalov and Smalls. He intended to return to the house in Croom, but he didn't want to leave any of his money behind. In the event that the house and its occupants became radioactive, and he could not come back, he had everything he needed in the bag. And he had wheels. If a man planned correctly, and traveled light, he could stay free.

Bacalov sat at the dining room table. He had field-stripped his Glock and was cleaning its barrel with a bore brush and solvent. Louis Smalls was sitting on the overstuffed couch. He had just done a bong hit of hydroponic and was now listening to an old Baroness album, *Blue Record*, through his earbuds, the psych-metal crunch of the music causing him to nod his head. He saw King come down the stairs, suitcase in hand, and his stomach dropped. Smalls pulled his buds out and stood.

"Where you go, eh?" said Bacalov.

"I'm going to visit a lady friend," said King.

"Always a woman with you."

"You should try it sometime. I'm talking about a real woman. Not one you've gotta blow up."

King had never seen Bacalov with a woman, though he'd

seen him watching them in strip joints and on the stroke sites he bookmarked on his laptop. First time they'd met, they'd been in that meat house on Connecticut Avenue, the one with the notoriously ugly dancers. Both of them at the bar, watching, though by rights King should have been home and satisfied. He'd just come from the Wyoming, where he'd banged his latest crinkle-bunny to within an inch of her life. King had struck up a conversation with Bacalov and found his chimplike face, his one eyebrow, and his mangling of the English language amusing. Also, he sensed that Bacalov had fire. They soon tired of their surroundings and moved together across the street to the bar of Russia House, a restaurant and lounge. Bacalov said he'd be more comfortable around his people. But the place was filled with Americans, and Bacalov didn't talk to any women there, either. Mainly, he boasted about his criminal past and what he was capable of. Told King about a local man he knew, a *moolie,* who would maim and kill for hire, even gave him the man's number so he could verify his claim. King thought that most of it was bullshit and alcohol talk. But not all. He saw potential.

"You put women over our business," said Bacalov.

"I sold the coins," said King. "I'm working on the paintings."

"The paintings just sit here."

"I left word with Lumley. He hasn't gotten back to me yet. He will."

"When are you coming back?"

"Couple, three days."

"Billy?" said Smalls. "Wait up, I'm coming out, too."

"Okay." To Bacalov, King said, "See you, monkey."

"Don't call me that."

"Monkey," said King, and smiled.

Smalls grabbed his deck of cigarettes and a matchbook and followed King outside to the wraparound porch. King dropped his suitcase to the gallery floor. A motion-sensitive light had come on when they'd stepped outside. It illuminated half the front yard, where the Crown Victoria and Monte Carlo SS were parked. The surrounding forest and gravel road were in darkness.

A branch snapped nearby. King turned his head toward the woods.

"Billy," said Smalls, redirecting King's attention.

"What did you want, Louis?"

"I just came out to have a smoke," said Smalls. "Serge doesn't like the smell of it in the house."

"Fuck what Serge doesn't like."

"He's our partner."

"I want a divorce."

Smalls lit his cigarette and exhaled smoke. "What about me?" He nearly winced at the desperation in his voice.

King looked him over. He knew what he was to the kid. But someday soon, King would have to cut him loose, too. King wasn't anyone's sidekick or father.

"What *about* you, Louis?"

"We're stayin together, right?"

"Sure. I'll see you soon."

Smalls eyed him warily. King picked up his bag, walked to his Monte Carlo, and opened its trunk.

LUCAS AND Dupree crouched at the edge of the woods in darkness, several yards in from the tree line. The curtains were drawn in the windows of the house and they couldn't see inside. Lucas had made a sketch of the colonial. He also drew a circle in the front of the house that estimated the size of the pool of light thrown out from the motion detector mounted above the gallery roof.

When the light had come on, Dupree had instinctively moved back a little, causing a branch to snap. The sudden illumination had surprised them when King and the one named Louis had walked out the front door. So had King's presence and size.

He was as Grace Kinkaid had described him: strong legs, low center of gravity, powerfully built. Blond and wrinkled by the sun. An aging beach stud, his thighs filling out his shorts, sockless feet in boat shoes, polo shirt stretched tight across his upper frame. Big as he was in the chest and shoulders, they paled in contrast to the massive muscle-and-bone structure below his waist.

Lucas studied him as he walked across the yard, suitcase in hand, leaving the lanky, bearded Louis behind, still smoking a cigarette on the porch. There was athleticism in King's step, and also a jaunty you-can't-fuck-with-me stride. King was something out of a painting hung in the dark corner of a museum, the kind that gives nightmares to a child. A goatish figure, more Minotaur than man.

Lucas looked at the nylon suitcase that King was dropping into the trunk of his Chevy. Its contents bulked out the bag's sides.

King had packed for more than one day. This was good.

In his head, Lucas made plans.

NINETEEN

LATE THAT night, Lucas dropped off Dupree at his apartment.

"So we gonna do this thing tomorrow night?" said Dupree.

"While King's out of town," said Lucas. "I'll call you in the morning and we'll firm it up."

Lucas had promised Dupree there would be no shooting. The only way to keep his word was to leave Dupree out of it. His friend had been a fierce and reliable brother on the battlefield, but clearly that part of him was done. Upon his return to the States, Lucas had continued to embrace his warrior nature, for reasons he himself didn't fully understand. Dupree had left his behind in the streets and deserts of Iraq.

Lucas felt that he'd been reckless to put his friend in harm's way for a money job, in the same way he'd been careless with Marquis. Lucas had made the decision over dinner, looking across the table at Dupree in the restaurant on Route 301. He'd compensate him for the work he'd already done, but Dupree was not going back with him to the house in Croom. Lucas would go in alone.

*   *   *

DUPREE PHONED him twice the next day. Lucas did not take the calls.

In the morning, he phoned Charlotte to see if they might meet for lunch. He wanted to talk to her in person, tell her how he felt about her before he made his move on the painting, in the event that things went wrong. He realized he'd never told her he loved her. In fact, he'd never said those words to any woman. But now he felt he could and should say it to her.

Outside of their initial meeting in the hotel bar, they'd never been together in public. In his mind he saw them at a nice, quiet restaurant, having a good meal, him looking into her eyes, reaching out, touching her hand. Practically speaking, and morally, he knew it was wrong. Charlotte was married. She'd never once expressed a desire to leave her husband. She wanted to maintain her status quo: successful career, marriage, a house in upper Northwest, and a young lover in her bed when she wanted it. A lunch with him out in the open was a ridiculous, dangerous proposition. It would threaten all that she had.

Still, he phoned her. Got the message box, as he knew he would. Told her that he needed to speak with her and asked her to call him back that day.

He waited around his apartment for an hour or so. His phone didn't ring.

Lucas changed into shorts and rode his bike down to Hains Point. He did the loop a couple of times, going along the Washington Channel and the Potomac River, passing fishermen at the rails, lovers on benches and blankets, golfers playing the public course, and fellow bikers on the road. The ride cleared his head.

Lucas locked his bike outside Jenny's on nearby Water Street, then had a hearty late-afternoon Chinese lunch at a table in the bar area, which gave to a view of the channel and marina. He glanced at the couples around him, sitting at two-tops, conversing, laughing. It occurred to him that most of his meals these days were eaten alone.

He pedaled from Jenny's up into Rock Creek Park, then up the gradual incline of Beach Drive, a good distance back to 16th Street Heights. When he returned to his apartment, he was energized rather than tired. He had been checking his phone, stashed in the small bag mounted beneath his saddle, during his trip. He phoned Charlotte again and left a message.

After a shower, Lucas grabbed Waldron's ripstop duffel bag from out of his closet, and his own personal bag, and laid his equipment out on the bed: flex-cuffs, a roll of duct tape, bolt cutters, a pair of night vision goggles, his Blackhawk Omega pistol vest, and a looped holster belt that would fit below it. He took out the silencer and the Kevlar vests and put them aside. Lucas then withdrew a Mossberg pump-action twelve-gauge and loaded it with rounds of buckshot. He put this on the bed alongside the NVGs. He took one of the Beretta M-9s and a magazine from out of the bag. He checked the top steel-jacketed round against the spring for tension, palmed the magazine into the grip, and slid the .9 into a Bianchi holster. He slipped a second fifteen-round mag into the pistol vest, then dropped several twelve-gauge shells into another compartment. Next, he found the S&W .38, released its cylinder, and loaded its chambers with hollow points. He snapped the cylinder back in place and put extra rounds into a third pouch. He slid his phone into the shoulder pouch designed for a radio; he was going to need the phone's compass to navigate the woods.

He mentally inventoried the weapons and gear on the bed, then placed them all back in the bag. He added his own tool, a short hollowed-out piece of hickory, filled with lead and wrapped in electrician's tape. Lucas felt that a man on a job should always have a sap.

He took a shower, dressed in a black T-shirt, dark-blue Dickies pants, a Timex Expedition digital watch, and lug-soled Nike boots. He picked up the bag, walked it downstairs and out to the street, and placed it in the cargo area of his Jeep.

Dusk had fallen on the streets. By the time Lucas had crossed the line from D.C. into Maryland, it was night.

LOUIS SMALLS sat in his room, Opeth coming from a speaker attached to his phone. The song was "Heir Apparent," a crushing track that always managed to take him somewhere outside of his tangled head. Mastodon, Opeth, Meshuggah...Smalls was into progressive metal in a big way. He had started with pre–Black Album Metallica, like many kids, but had graduated into the more complex, intense bands that delivered grooves, shifts of tone, growling vocals, laserlike drumming, and guitar fury. Music, drugs, his choice of peers, all of it was tied up in his attempt to run away.

His home life had been shit. He didn't have any memory of his father, who'd left when he was an infant. His mother worked behind the counter in an auto body shop during the day and was a wine alcoholic by night. Sometimes she never made it to her bed and fell asleep on the couch. Sometimes she peed there. She was unhealthy by anyone's measure, but she got by on genetic luck, a pretty face and a figure that resisted the damages of her prodigious alcohol consumption. Louis and Sharon Smalls had shared their apartment, a two-bedroom affair in an aged garden complex, with a succession of low-rent men.

One of them, a mattress salesman named Jim Ralston, moved in and stayed awhile when Louis was thirteen years old. His mother adored him. He too was a drinker: he had a thirst for blended whiskey. Ralston had slicked-back hair and one permanently droopy eye, the result of a sucker punch in a bar that had shattered his cheekbone. To a stranger it made him look gentle and somewhat kind, but to Louis he was anything but. He had no sexual interest in Louis's mother, though he dutifully climbed on top of her from time to time. He was there for the boy.

Night after night, after Sharon had passed out, he came into Louis's bedroom, smelling of Seagram's 7 and Lectric Shave. He'd pull a chair over to Louis's bed, talk to him softly, and reach into Louis's pajama bottoms and stroke him until he grew hard. He'd tell Louis to do the same kind of favor for him. By then Ralston had already unzipped his fly and pulled out his long, veined thing. He told Louis to touch it and he told him to put it in his mouth. Louis didn't like it, but he knew his mother would be mad if he made a fuss and caused her boyfriend to leave. Ralston did leave eventually, after an awful, drunken fight over money with Sharon Smalls. By then the damage had been done.

At fourteen Louis began to notice girls and desire them. He had been worried that he was gay, and his attraction to females proved to him that he was not. He was too young to know the difference between a homosexual and a pedophile. He had almost put Ralston out of his mind when his woodshop teacher kissed him on the mouth while Louis was working alone on a project after school one spring afternoon. Louis didn't tell on this one, either. He was embarrassed and scared of the potential ridicule and exposure. Why did men think that they could prey on him like this? It had to be his fault.

He began to hang with a crowd of misfits who were rejected by the cool heads, athletes, and scholars of the school. Louis didn't play sports; he was not particularly bright, and at six-foot-two, one hundred twenty-five pounds, he was scary skinny, a freak. He listened to metal and got piercings and tats. He rejected authority, particularly when it came from older men. He was suspended from school regularly and eventually expelled. He never did get a high school degree.

Years passed and Louis had accomplished exactly nothing. Whatever money he managed to make he spent on vehicles purchased at auctions. He favored big American sedans with V-8s. He moved from weed to crystal meth. He got a girlfriend with a habit, body odor, and brown teeth. Sex was drug-clumsy and quick, but she made him hard, and this told him he was straight. He left his mother's apartment and moved in with the girl and a bunch of other burnouts in a group house. One night Louis was wired and desperate for money, so he borrowed a .38 with cracked grips and knocked off a convenience store in Laurel. The man behind the counter had slicked-back hair and reminded him of Ralston, and when

Louis put the gun in his face, and he showed fear, Louis got excited and swollen. He robbed a couple of other stores the same way, chasing the same sensation. He would have robbed more, but he was only interested in places that were staffed by white men; these were few and far between. He found one in Burtonsville, on 198, but made the mistake of rolling up his sleeves before he went in. He got arrested, convicted by a video camera tape and the tattoo on his arm, and was sent to Hagerstown.

He did his full stretch, got clean of meth, and moved into a halfway house in east-of-16th-Street D.C. He found a job unloading trucks and stocking goods for a discount department store in the Maryland suburbs. It was the best he could do with a felony conviction and no GED. One day he struck up a conversation with a man named Billy King. He'd taken a television set out to the store's parking lot and put it in the man's car.

"You like your job?" said King, after he had handed Louis Smalls a five-dollar tip. Smalls, though still thin, had put on weight and grown a beard. His look said School of Hard Knocks, with a touch of shell shock.

"I guess," said Smalls, eyeing the big, blond-haired man with suspicion.

"Can't get too far up the ladder, though, after you've done time. Isn't that right?"

"How'd you know?"

"I can spot it," said King. In fact, he was guessing. What he saw was a damaged young man who seemed utterly lost and alone. "I'm not judging you."

"What do you want?"

"Why don't we grab a beer after you get off work?"

"I don't drink," said Smalls. He meant, I don't drink with older men.

"Relax, fella," said King, picking up on the vibe. "I like women. This is a business proposition."

"Tell me what it is."

King and Serge Bacalov had been planning to take off a check-cashing/payroll-advance operation in the District. It would be their first and only retail robbery, but they were missing a key player in the plan.

"Can you... What's your name, son?"

"Louis Smalls." He liked that the man had called him son.

"Can you drive a car, Louis?"

"I can drive the hell out of one," said Smalls.

"I got a partner, little Russian guy. We're about to embark on an adventure. But Serge never did learn how to drive."

Since that day, Smalls had been with King. Billy treated him right. Billy never once had anything in his eyes for Smalls except for friendship and respect. Billy was a father. So why had his father left him the night before, the same way his seed-father had left twenty-some years earlier, when Louis was nothing more than a baby? Billy had been carrying a full suitcase with a vague promise to return in a few days' time. Was he coming back? It seemed to Louis that all the men in his life had either abandoned him or tried to take him off for sex.

Once again, Louis thought: Is it me?

Disturbed and confused, Louis got up out of his chair and disconnected the speaker from his smartphone. He dropped it beside his earbuds on the bed. He wanted a cigarette, but he never smoked in his room, as Serge didn't like its smell. He decided to have a cigarette out on the porch, then drive to the nearest store for a fresh pack.

He put the phone in the right front pocket of his jeans. Beneath his underwear, in the top drawer of his dresser, he found the envelope of money that Billy had given him from the coin sale. He stuffed the envelope in his left pocket. It contained forty hundred-dollar bills wrapped in a rubber band. He always took his cash with him when he left the place. He didn't trust Serge.

He slipped his wallet into his back pocket. On his dresser he found his last cigarette. He fitted this behind his ear and threw the empty pack in the wastebasket. He swept his keys and matches off the top of the dresser and switched off the light before walking from the room.

He passed Billy's bedroom, now dark. As he came to Serge's room, he looked inside and stopped. Serge was seated on a chair, his feet up on his bed, his open laptop balanced on his thighs. Lying atop the bed was his Glock. Smalls knew that under the bed was an Ithaca pump. Serge liked his guns nearby. It made him feel tall.

The sound from the laptop, synthesized music and a conversation between a man and woman, was loud. From what Smalls could make out, the man in the video was trying to convince a woman that she needed to take off her clothes. "I can't cast you in the movie until I see what you have," said the man. "My panties, too?" said the woman, and the man said, "Yes, of course."

"Where you go?" said Bacalov.

"Out to get cigarettes. You want anything?"

"No. Wait a minute…We need milk."

"I'll bring back some milk," said Smalls.

He left Bacalov, turned the corner of the hall, and went down the stairs, his hand sliding down the wood banister as he descended. He walked through the living room, past the overstuffed couch and the cable-spool table, the chandelier and the dining room table, the stolen computer equipment heaped in a corner, and the paintings, wrapped in brown paper and leaning against the wall. He opened the front door, walked out, then closed it and checked that it was locked.

As he turned from the door, the motion detector triggered its lamp. His car, the white Crown Vic, was parked in the front yard, wholly visible in the pool of light. The remainder of the yard, the woods, and the gravel road that cut through them, was inked in black.

Louis Smalls stood on the porch and lit his cigarette. As he exhaled a stream of smoke, he heard something in the forest to his left. A rabbit or fox skittering through the brush.

To his right, Smalls heard the muted, heavy drum of feet on gravel and earth. He turned his head in that direction, took one step back, and froze.

A man was running toward him. Charging like an animal out of the night.

TWENTY

Lucas HAD humped the half mile through the woods wearing his night vision goggles while carrying a bag heavy with gear and iron. He was in superior shape, but still, by the time he reached the tree line bordering the house, he needed to rest. He peeled off his goggles, allowed his breathing to slow, and opened the bag that he'd dropped beside him. He then removed the Beretta .9 and S&W .38 from the bag and fitted them in the holster belt looped into the pistol vest. The vest held shotgun shells, an extra mag for the .9, and hollow point rounds. He took the Mossberg from the bag and placed that on the ground beside the NVGs.

Lucas looked at the yard, where a single car, the white Crown Victoria that had rammed Marquis, was parked. One car, one driver: the young man with the beard, the one called Louis. But this didn't mean there was only one person in the house. Maybe Bacalov didn't own a car. Maybe he didn't drive.

Lucas looked up at the house. One window had a light in it;

the others were dark. Dark windows had been a primary danger area in Iraq. So were doorways and doors.

The front door of the house opened. Louis closed it behind him, locked it, and stepped onto the porch. As he did, the motion detector came on and sent light out into the yard. Lucas remained still. He watched Louis stand there and light a cigarette.

Carefully, quietly, Lucas got two pairs of double-cuff restraints from the bag. Keeping his eyes on Louis, he put them in a pouch of his vest. He then retrieved the roll of duct tape and slipped that into the pouch holding the loose hollow points. He picked up the shotgun with his left hand; he needed his throwing arm now.

Lucas felt along the earth until he found a stone. He rose from his crouch and stepped out of the woods, into the portion of the yard still in darkness. He planned to use a box tactic; he would avoid the area exposed by light, move in the blackness, and stay inside its line. He got as close to the house as he could without crossing that line, then threw the stone, arcing it high into the woods on the other side of the house. Louis turned his head in that direction as the rock skittered through the branches of trees. Lucas moved the Mossberg to his right hand and broke into a run.

He was on the porch quickly, taking its steps while barely touching them, reaching Louis, startled and frozen, within seconds. Lucas swung the shotgun, putting his hips into the motion. The stock connected under Louis's jaw. He lost his legs, and Lucas hit him again in the temple as he was going down. Louis fell to the gallery floor. Lucas turned him over, flex-cuffed his hands and ankles, and wound duct tape around his head and mouth. He checked his breathing and searched his jeans pockets. Found a phone, a brown envelope holding money, a wallet, matches, and a ring holding keys. On the ring were the keys to the Ford. A house key, too.

Lucas moved to the door.

SERGE BACALOV heard a dull thud coming from outside. He turned the sound down on his laptop, closed its lid, dropped it on the bed, and got up out of his chair. He walked quickly from his lit bedroom and went into Billy's bedroom because the room was dark. He went to the window, pulled its curtain aside, and looked out into the front yard. The Crown Victoria was still there, and Louis was not. Okay, so he was smoking a cigarette out on the porch before he took off. But why the noise?

Bacalov returned to his room. He picked up his Glock, fully loaded with a seventeen-round magazine. He thumbed off its safety and holstered it under the belt line of his jeans at the small of his back. He then got down on the floor and pulled the Ithaca out from under the bed. In his dresser drawer he found a box of shells, and with fumbling excitement, he ripped open its thin cardboard top. He turned the shotgun over so that its bottom was facing up. He thumbed five shells into the ejection port, felt the stop, released the slide, and pushed it forward.

Bacalov heard the front door opening down in the living room. Perhaps Louis had forgotten something and was coming back inside. Perhaps.

Bacalov went down the hall but did not turn the corner at the stairs. He rested his back against the plaster wall.

"Louis," said Bacalov. "You come back, eh?"

There was no answer. Bacalov gripped the shotgun and smiled.

LUCAS ENTERED the house and shut the door behind him. He held the Mossberg ready, his finger inside the trigger guard, and stood still. He mentally cleared the room: an open living room/dining room area, a kitchen in the back. Old, cushiony furniture, a cable-spool table holding a bong, a chandelier over the dining room table. A stairway with a banister leading up to the second floor. Computer equipment heaped in a corner of the room. And square objects wrapped in brown paper, leaning against the right wall. His blood ticked.

As his eyes and shoulders moved, he moved the barrel of the shotgun. The index finger of his right hand brushed the trigger. His left hand cupped the pump.

He heard a voice from upstairs.

"Louis. You come back, eh?"

He heard the unmistakable *snick-snick* of a racking pump.

Lucas stepped toward the stairs and sighted the shotgun. He saw an elbow at the top of the stairs, a small triangle of flesh peeking out.

"All right," said Lucas softly.

Bacalov spun around the corner and fired as Lucas pumped off a shell. The banister exploded in splinters before him and Lucas stepped back, then moved forward and rapidly pumped out five more shots up the stairs, hammering the plaster at the top of the landing and tearing up the wall. The shotgun blasts shook the house.

"Fuck *you*," said Bacalov, and Lucas heard nervous laughter. He knew what that meant: relief. Bacalov had not been hit.

Lucas tossed the shotgun aside and drew his .38. He stepped out of the field of fire and walked backward, aiming the revolver at the stairs. He stopped and stood beside the couch.

"Take what you want," shouted Bacalov.

"I'm going to," said Lucas, blinking his gun eye against the sweat that was trickling into it.

"Who are you?"

"Come find out."

"I am going to lay down my gun."

Bacalov appeared on the stairway, shooting in descent. Lucas dropped behind the couch. Bacalov kept his finger locked on the Ithaca's trigger as he pumped, cycling rounds through the chamber, slam-firing into the buckling hardwood floor and cable-spool table. The room went sonic.

Lucas heard the thump of a shell hitting the back cushion, felt its impact, saw stuffing rise in the air above him.

Bacalov dropped his shotgun and ran across the room. At the sound of his footsteps Lucas came up firing. He squeezed off several rounds and saw red leap off Bacalov's shoulder. Bacalov fell behind the dining room table.

Lucas crouched back down behind the couch. He could hear Bacalov moving chairs. He holstered the .38 and drew the M-9, releasing the safety in the same motion. He pulled back on the receiver and let it go. Its recoil spring drove the slide home and chambered a round.

Bacalov, wounded but game, crouched on the floor behind the table and chairs he had pulled together. He drew his

Glock with a shaking hand, jacked in a round, and wiped at his face. He rested the barrel on one of the crossbars of a ladder-back chair and aimed it in the general direction of the couch.

"Rick Bell," said Bacalov. "Is this your name? Or is your name *pussy?*"

Lucas did not reply. He'd been talked to and taunted by insurgents in many of the houses he'd entered in Fallujah. It had unnerved him, but he'd fought on.

"I am not afraid," said Bacalov.

Yes, you are, thought Lucas. So am I.

"Show yourself," said Bacalov.

Lucas slid behind the couch and readied himself at its edge. With his left hand he pushed at the couch and moved it, and Bacalov let off several shots, punching lead into the cushions, and at that Lucas came up over the back of the couch and fired off many rounds at the chandelier. Glass and metal rained down on Bacalov and bit his face, and once again Lucas dropped behind cover.

"I am not hurt," said Bacalov, but now there was a quiver in his voice.

Lucas concentrated. The Beretta's mag held fifteen. He struggled to remember how many rounds he'd fired.

Recharge.

Lucas released the partially spent magazine and slipped it in his vest. From the same pouch he took a full-load magazine and palmed it home. He readied the gun and chambered a round.

"You are pussy," said Bacalov.

Lucas stood and fired. The dining room table splintered, and Bacalov came up out of his crouch and squeezed off a round. Lucas felt a bullet crease the air as he walked forward, focused, firing his weapon, and through the smoke and ejecting shells he saw Bacalov dance backward as blood misted from his chest. He dropped his Glock and fell to the floor.

Lucas kept his gun arm steady and aimed. He stepped to Bacalov, stood over him. Watched as he struggled for breath, saw his shirt flutter about the chest wound, listened to the rattle of his filling lungs. His eyes crossed and saw nothing. Lucas shot him twice more and walked away.

He went out to the porch and checked on Louis, now conscious, his eyes frightened, his wrists raw from struggle. There were no sirens in the distance, no headlights coming up the gravel road. Only the sound of crickets and a faint ringing in Lucas's ears.

He reentered the house and went up the stairs. He went bedroom to bedroom until he found the laptop on Serge's bed. The size of the shirts hung in the closet told him it was the little man's room. He'd corresponded with Serge via e-mail, and there'd be a record. He took the laptop off the bed.

Downstairs he went straight to the wrapped objects leaning against the wall. He tore off the brown wrapping of the top one and put it aside. He found what he was looking for when he unwrapped the second painting. Two men, bare-chested, one middle-aged, one young. In the right-hand corner was the artist's name: L. Browning. He'd found *The Double*.

He went back out to the porch, got his duct tape, and returned to the living room, where he re-wrapped Grace Kinkaid's painting. He then went around the room collecting ejected casings and shells, slipping them into his vest. He did the best he could.

He made two more trips outside and back again, carrying his shotgun, the painting, and the laptop to the edge of the woods. He left those items there and found his bolt cutters and a bottle of water in the bag. He was still wearing the .38 and .9 on his holster belt when he stepped back onto the porch.

"Serge is dead," said Lucas. "You can be dead, too. Blink hard if you understand."

Louis Smalls closed his eyes, paused, and opened them.

"I'm gonna free your hands and turn you over."

Lucas used the cutters to liberate Louis's hands. He removed the duct tape from his face, put him on his back, helped him sit up, then took him by the arm and moved him so that he was in a sitting position against the porch wall. He was still bound at the ankles. Lucas stood before him.

Smalls rubbed at his raw wrists and watched Lucas as he drank deeply from the plastic water bottle. Lucas capped the bottle and tossed it to Smalls. He had a long drink.

Lucas picked up the wallet off the floor, opened it, and examined the Maryland driver's license inside. The name said Louis McGinty. The photo matched, but the license's graphics were smudged and not quite right.

"What's your real name?"

"Louis Smalls."

"Billy's?"

"Billy King."

"Where is he?"

"With a woman, I expect."

"Where?"

"I don't know. I don't even know if he's coming back."

Lucas believed him. "How deep are you in with these guys?"

"Deep."

"Why?"

"I got no one else," said Smalls.

"You can do better."

"He's my partner."

"Not anymore."

Louis looked down at his hands. "What's gonna happen to me?"

"I'm giving you a chance. That depends on you." Lucas dropped the wallet in Louis's lap. "Take the envelope with you, too."

Lucas crouched down and cut the flex-cuffs from Louis's ankles.

"Why?" said Smalls.

"I got what I came for. It's done."

Smalls stood and gathered his things. He took the keys out of the door lock where they dangled.

"I need to get some things out of my room," he said.

"No. Keep the car keys and give me the key to the house. Get in your car and drive."

Smalls removed the house key from the ring and handed it to Lucas. Without further comment Smalls went to his car, fired up the ignition, and drove away.

Lucas locked the front door of the house. If King did come back, he'd find Bacalov rotting and ripe.

Lucas knew he'd never be able to carry his guns, gear, the painting, and the laptop back through the woods. He jogged the half mile to his truck unencumbered and drove the Jeep back to the house, where he loaded everything into its cargo area. He went down the gravel road with his headlights off, navigating by the light of the moon.

Lucas rode back to D.C. in quiet, with the radio off and the windows down. He thought of Bacalov and their battle, and he saw him dead on the dining room floor.

He would have killed me.

Lucas stared coolly at the road ahead.

TWENTY-ONE

LUCAS SLEPT peacefully and got up late. He'd disposed of Bacalov's laptop in a Dumpster the night before after breaking it into pieces on an alley floor. He'd built a compartment under a wood cutout in his bedroom closet, and there he'd stashed the guns. He'd return them to Bobby Waldron when he was certain that no heat had collected around the shooting.

He phoned Charlotte Rivers on her disposable and left a message. He read the *Post* out on his porch, did his prison workout, and had some lunch. Charlotte did not return his call.

He took a long bike ride, going north into Maryland, all the way out to Lake Needwood in Rockville. The trip took hours. When he returned to his apartment, he showered and phoned Grace Kinkaid. For straights, it was the end of the working day. She just gotten off work at her nonprofit and said she could be at her place in a half-hour's time. Lucas agreed to meet her there.

* * *

THEY SAT in the living room of her Champlain Street condo, the painting leaning against the coffee table. Grace had poured herself a large glass of white wine. Lucas was having water.

"I'm so happy," said Grace.

"I'm glad."

"I didn't think I'd ever see my painting again. It's not a reflection on you. I just thought, you know, that it had been sold and was somewhere out there in a collector's hidden room."

"I got after it," said Lucas.

"Indeed you did. Was it difficult?"

"Not very."

"Was there any connection to the car scam guy?"

"That was a blind alley."

"So you found Billy?"

"No."

"You spoke to him, though."

"Never had the pleasure."

"How'd you get the painting, then?"

"That's not important, is it?" Lucas looked into Grace's eyes. His message was clear.

"I suppose not," she said.

"As for my fee..."

"You took me by surprise. I have to call the buyer and make the deal. I could write you a check from my money market account right now, if you promise not to deposit it right away."

"I'd like it in cash, as we agreed. I can wait."

"Certainly."

"I know you're good for it."

"Of course." Grace looked to a space on the wall where a brass hook was nailed into a stud. "I'm going to put it right where it was."

"Would you like me to hang it for you?"

"No, I'll do that. I think I'm going to sit here and look at it for a while."

Lucas stood from his seat. "I better get on my way."

Grace placed her wineglass on the coffee table and stood. She came close to him, put her hand on his forearm, and kissed him, catching the side of his mouth. Her lips were wet and she smelled strongly of alcohol.

"Thank you so much, Spero."

"My pleasure."

"I'll probably have the money for you in a couple of days."

"Right," he said.

Lucas entered the elevator. In its polished steel interior he saw his reflection, refracted and dim.

HE MET his brother Leo at his neighborhood spot on Georgia Avenue, below Geranium, a nondescript, nonviolent bar with mostly middle-aged patrons and a jukebox stocked with soul, neo-soul, and funk. The room was filled with the voice of Anthony Hamilton, singing with gospel fervor.

"That's my man," said Leo, nodding toward the juke. "Anthony dogged his girl, now he's praying to God to bring her back."

"Maybe it'll work. He sounds convincing."

"That's no spiritual pose. Dude sings in church." Leo took a sip of his beer. They were drinking imports at a four-top in the center of the room. A woman at the bar had turned her head and was looking at Leo in a familiar way. "When's the last time you been to Saint Sophia?"

"Been a while. You?"

"I took Mom two Sundays back. Father Steve's still up there at the pulpit, preaching the good word."

"F.S. is the man," said Spero.

He needed to get to church and pray. Lately, he'd broken damn near every one of the commandments. But what good would it do? You couldn't unfuck another man's wife. You couldn't give life back to the dead.

Leo studied his brother's troubled eyes. "How'd that work thing go for you?"

"I took care of it."

"The job's done?"

"Yeah."

"What's up for you next?"

"Just keep doin what I'm doin, I guess."

"You don't seem too enthusiastic."

"What's your point?"

"You know what it means when someone wakes up in the morning and they don't see any promise in the day?"

"It means they've got a limp dick."

"I'm serious. You been feeling a little blue lately, right?"

"Shit..."

"You should talk to someone. Not to me. I'm sayin, you should take advantage of your VA benefits and see a professional."

"Please."

"I've been reading stuff, Spero. About all the veterans who've been committing suicide. It's up to one a day now. That's a higher rate than the combat deaths in Afghanistan this year."

"Screw you, Leo. You know me better than that."

"I'm not saying you're at risk. I'm saying, if those people had gotten help, they might not have done what they did. Ain't no shame in talking to a shrink."

"Screw *you*."

"Nice to see you have an open mind."

They changed the subject. They talked about the Nats and the Redskins, and the woman at the bar, whose head kept swiveling in Leo's direction.

"So you hear anything on the Cherise Roberts murder?" said Leo. "The law got any leads?"

"My attorney, Petersen, he put some feelers out down at the D.C. Jail. There's been no arrest as of yet." Spero killed the rest of his beer. "Let me ask you something, man. When you had Cherise as a student, was there anything off about her? Outside of the usual teenage, temporary madness stuff?"

"Cherise was funny and popular. Not much of a scholar, though. She wasn't headed to college or any place like it. She did the minimum, but she was pleasant, and she never disrupted my class."

"What about her home life?"

"No father in her world, but that's not unusual."

"Was she promiscuous?"

"No more than you or me at that age, from what I could tell."

Spero was carefully wading around the subject of Cherise's secret life. But maybe it wasn't a secret to her peers.

"Her friends ever call her by a nickname?" said Spero.

"Shoot, *all* the kids have nicknames."

"What was hers?"

Leo thought about it. "Cherry. Why?"

"I'm going to stay on this," said Spero. "I need to keep busy. To help me through this blue period I'm in."

"See, man, why you got to ridicule me? I'm concerned about you, is all. Always looking out for you, bro."

"The same way that minx at the bar has her eye on you. She's fine, too. You should talk to her."

"I got plans. I'm meeting a young lady tonight."

"Don't hurt her, Hammer."

"I gotta go. You coming out the door with me?"

"You go ahead," said Spero, holding up his empty bottle and signaling the waitress. "I'm gonna have one more beer."

LUCAS HAD three more. That made five, which for him was far too many.

He'd been thinking of Charlotte, and his inability to reach her, and his frustration welled up and crested, manifesting itself in a bad decision. He stood, left money on the table, and walked toward the door. On the way out he inadvertently bumped a patron, an older man, and Lucas said, "My bad, sir," and the man said, "That's quite all right, young man."

Out in his Jeep, Lucas put a guitar-heavy mix into his CD player and turned it up. As he drove west on Military Road he listened to Dinosaur Jr.'s "I Don't Wanna Go There," and the Hold Steady's "Most People Are DJs," two songs with long blister-bleed solos that made him more reckless. Soon he was in an upscale upper Northwest neighborhood, parked near a stately forest-green colonial. Lucas got out of his Jeep.

The first floor of the house, *her house,* was lit up. Many of its curtains and blinds were open, affording a view to the living and dining areas. He'd memorized her address. It had been easy to find, using one of the many programs on his laptop. He was good at what he did. After all, he'd found a group of lowlife criminals operating under false surnames. Stood to reason, he could come up with the residential address of a respectable citizen like Charlotte Rivers.

"'You're so respectable,'" sang Lucas, under his breath.

He thought of his father, listening to the cassette version of that record, *Some Girls,* in his Chevy Silverado work truck, Spero beside him on the bench, a boy happily going to a job site with his dad on a summer day, one of their many adopted Lab mixes back in the bed. Van's curly hair, salted with gray, was blowing about from the wind of the open window, and there was a smile on his face, because he was a man who was doing something very simple that he loved. He was headed to work in a pickup truck and hanging out with one of his sons.

"It's a great day," said Van.

"What are we gonna do, *Baba?*"

"Work. Family and work, boy *mou.* That's what matters. There's a lot to be said for leading the straight life. You'll see."

Lucas wondered what his father would think if he could see him now, drunk, creeping around outside the home of a married woman. Van Lucas would tell Spero to stop what he was doing. That he was all wrong. He'd tell him to get back in his car, go home, and sleep it off. And in the morning, he should ask himself what kind of man he wanted to be.

But Lucas did not go back to his truck. He walked on.

Past the house, Lucas turned into an alley. There, the home's screened-in porch shared space with a small side yard and a driveway leading into a freestanding garage. Along the porch was a series of windows, and through them Lucas could see a modern kitchen with a built-in refrigerator, wall oven, and island. Charlotte and her husband were standing next to the island. They were talking and drinking red wine.

Lucas wondered if it was that Barolo she liked.

The husband was not what Lucas had envisioned. In his head, Lucas had seen a smallish guy wearing glasses, with a receding hairline, a man who lived the life of the mind rather than the physical. But in the flesh he was on the tall side, well built, with a full head of hair. A handsome guy, still in his dress shirt and tie, having a glass of wine and a conversation with his wife after an honest day's work. Straight.

Family and work, boy mou. *That's what matters.*

The husband said something, and Charlotte smiled shyly, then sipped at her wine.

They looked content to him. Comfortable with each other. At the moment, happy.

Soon they'd be upstairs in their master bedroom. Maybe they'd just go to sleep. Or maybe he'd undress her, spread her out on their bed, and make love to her. She'd enjoy it, if only in a familiar, reassuring way. She'd told Lucas that her sex life was the insufficient piece of her marriage, and that he, Lucas, filled a void. So this was what he was to her in the end: a piece in a puzzle. Something that made *her* complete.

But on his own, Lucas wasn't enough for her. He wasn't

even in the ballpark. She'd never leave this man, her security, this house.

Charlotte's husband stepped forward and touched her forearm, and both of them smiled.

Don't do that, thought Lucas.

She's mine.

TWENTY-TWO

BILLY KING had been shacking up with Lois Wilson for a few days in her waterfront house, a brick two-story on Dyer Road in Newberg, Maryland. Courtesy of her ex-husband, the home was furnished handsomely, with new appliances and an up-to-the-minute home entertainment center. A hundred yards from its back porch sat a dock, complete with boathouse, on a brackish deepwater creek leading out to the Wicomico River. In the boathouse was a nearly new twenty-two-foot Whaler powered by a big Merc engine. King figured he could spend some quality time in this place and live princely like the stud he was. But he was restless.

Not that he wasn't wanted here. Lois was hungry, and he gave it to her until it seemed she couldn't take any more. Then, when he hinted he might go, she begged him not to leave. He had her where he wanted her, but he'd gotten tired of her quick. Old stuff was all right in a low-lit bar, but when you got it home under stark incandescence it sure did look its age, and some things couldn't be hid. Lois's cans had been worked on, and her crow's feet had been erased, but her thighs were oatmeal, and when the Spanx came off there was that dreaded roll around her waist. Still, she had some nice jewelry lying about on her bedroom dresser, a pearl necklace, diamond earrings and such, and a sweet emerald-and-diamond ring.

King was about to leave her for a while, but he'd return. For now, he had business in D.C.

The unsold paintings were bothering him. He'd worked hard to get them, two from the crinkle-bunny who lived at the Wyoming, and the last one from that juicer on Champlain Street. Jobs like those were an investment in time and effort. Now the paintings were sitting there at the house in Croom, wrapped in brown paper. That was real money, gathering dust. Charles Lumley needed to do his job and move the goods.

But Lumley wasn't returning his calls. This disturbed King and made him suspicious. He didn't like to be ignored. Worse, his phone calls to Serge had gone unanswered and unreturned as well. And now Louis had become unreachable. This was Louis, who followed King around like a broke-dick dog. Something was wrong.

King walked out of the house carrying his bag. He opened the rear lid of his Monte Carlo SS and stashed the bag in its trunk.

Lois followed him from the house wearing a bathrobe, cigarette in hand.

"Billy," she said, reaching him as he opened his driver's-side door. "Where you going, hon?"

Hon. Lois liked to brag that she hailed from Baltimore, and King gave a fuck.

"Work, doll."

"You're coming back, right?" She clutched at her robe, let it fall open slightly to give him a look at her retooled globes. She was going for sexy, but the sunlight did her no favors.

"Oh, yeah," said King. "I wouldn't leave a dish like you alone for too long."

She moved to kiss his mouth. He let her, but held his breath. She smelled like an ashtray.

King fired up the SS.

HE DROVE right into Washington and parked near Lumley's shop. Going to the door, he felt the heat well up in him as he read the note taped inside the glass.

> *To my loyal patrons:*
>
> *After several years here as a merchant in Dupont Circle I have made the difficult decision to close my business and move on. I'd like to thank you for your loyal patronage and friendship, and hope that our paths cross again.*
>
> *Best,*
>
> *Charles Lumley*

King looked into the nearly empty shop. No paintings on the walls, no easels, no goods for sale. Only a desk and a chair remained. Even the landline had been removed.

King drew his cell and phoned Lumley. Once again, he got dead air, not even a recording.

Lumley owed him no money. In fact, he had stood to make a hefty commission on the sale of the paintings. Maybe the fit young man in the Oxon Hill parking lot, the one who'd stood

228 • George Pelecanos

down Serge, had come back to Lumley's shop and persuaded him to leave town. Maybe Lumley had given up the location of the paintings to this private heat before he skipped.

With growing dread, King got back into his Chevy and drove out to the house in Croom.

LOUIS'S CROWN Vic wasn't in the yard.

King approached the house with care and used his key to open its front door. He smelled death and heard the buzz of insects as soon as he walked inside.

Serge was lying near the dining room table, dotted with flies. He'd been shot several times.

King went to the paintings. *The Double* was gone. The other paintings had been left behind, and the computer equipment had gone untouched.

The couch, tables, and floor had been shot to hell. Up on the landing, a large portion of the plaster wall was gone.

In King's bedroom, not one item was missing. Even the Bushmaster with the folding stock was where he'd left it.

In Serge's room, King found a cell and put it in his pocket.

In Louis's room, his earbuds and the small speaker he attached to his smartphone lay on the bed. His clothing still hung in his closet. Louis would have taken these things if he had intended to leave for good. Unless he had escaped in a rush or been forced to leave against his will.

King went back downstairs. In the kitchen he wet a towel and wrapped it around his nose and mouth. Returning to the living room and dining room area, he found a couple of nine-millimeter shell casings on the floor. Serge's Ithaca and Glock lay on the floor as well. King checked under a couch cushion and found a semiautomatic pistol he'd stashed there.

The thief had left hastily and had taken only the painting King had lifted off of Grace Kinkaid's wall. So the raider was some kind of professional. At the very least, he was a man with focus.

King sat down on the shredded couch. He'd paid rent to the home's owner several months in advance, in cash, along with a cash security deposit. The man had asked for no ID after King had given him the money and one of his assumed names. He hadn't even glanced at the license plate on King's car. As usual, greed had trumped good sense.

King was going to lose his security deposit, but he'd clean the place up the best he could. Gather up the rest of Louis's things, and Serge's things, and all of their identification, false and otherwise, and take everything out to the county landfill. Do same with the guns he didn't want and the computer equipment, which wasn't worth the trouble it would take to sell. Call Arthur Spiegel and see if he could middle the remaining paintings through an art specialist. Stay here until he finished that bit of business, then get out, because the landlord dropped in unannounced from time to time. Move back into Lois's place for a few more days. Get his hands on her jewelry and leave town.

He'd ridden alone his entire adult life. Partnering up with Serge and Louis had been a one-time deal, and it had been a mistake. It was time to get back on a familiar path.

But first he had to take care of the Kinkaid woman and draw out her rented man. Also, put Serge underground. His corpse was stinking up the house.

*   *   *

IT WAS dusk when King finished burying Serge in a shallow grave, deep in the woods. King had found an animal feed and farm supply store down 301, and there he'd purchased a fifty-pound bag of hydrated lime. He would have preferred quicklime, which burned the body as well. But it was difficult to buy without a commercial account, even if you could find a tractor supply company or masonry material house. The hydrated variety didn't do the burn job like quicklime, but it worked just fine for the smell. Man behind the counter said, "You got a Jiffy John, or somethin?" and King said, "Just a big old dog."

King bought a large tarp, shovel, mask, and tube of Vaseline at a regular hardware store. He put on the mask, dabbed the petroleum jelly inside his nostrils, and laid Serge in the tarp. Dragged him out to the woods, found some soft earth, and dug a hole. It felt good for King to work his back, put some of his anger and muscle into the job. He dumped Serge into the hole, shrouded him with lime, filled the hole back up with dirt, and covered the spot with brush and a log. When he was done he was still agitated, but his vision was clear.

It was full dark as he walked back into the house. He showered and had himself a beer, and as he drank it he called Arthur Spiegel and got the ball in motion. Then he found the phone number that Serge had given him in the bar of the Russia House on the first night they'd met. Serge had bragged that he knew a man who'd do certain jobs for money. King made the call and, when it connected, was surprised that the number was still good and pleased that the voice on the other end of the line was that of a black man. After a short conversation, they agreed to meet the next day.

AROUND NOON, Billy King walked down Minnesota Avenue in Northeast. He had parked his car, locked the glove box, and made sure to lock the Chevy's doors, taking note of the many blacks, the Korean and Chinese merchants, and varieties of brown that were on the street. From what he could see, he was the sole white in the area, but he was not concerned. King had never lacked confidence.

He found the man he was looking for in a Laundromat, seated in a plastic chair. The place was warm and loud, with the sound of washing machines, tumbling drums, and women alternately talking on cell phones and raising their voices at children who were going about the business of being kids.

King took a seat beside the man and said, "I'm Billy Hunter."

"Jabari Jones." His last name was Alston, not Jones. He was about forty, with an unstylish modified Afro, salted gray, and a full beard interrupted by bare spots he couldn't "get." He wore a blue chambray shirt and black slacks. His eyes were crafty but not hard. He looked like a custodian or liquor store clerk. He didn't look like someone who would do violence for cash.

"Thanks for seeing me," said King.

"You wearing a wire?"

"No."

"Let me see."

King raised his polo shirt, then dropped it.

"How's my friend Serge?" said Alston.

"Resting."

"Would've liked to have seen him."

"He's not available."

"Is he with a woman?"

"That would shock me."

Alston's eyes smiled with recognition. "Getting his hair cut, then. Those blond locks of his do get unruly."

"Serge has black hair. And one eyebrow."

"That's my boy."

"Any other questions?"

"No," said Alston. "I believe we're straight."

"Let's get to it, then."

"What'd you have in mind?"

King told him and said, "It's half a job, for you."

"That don't mean I take half the pay."

"If you want to rape the bitch, go ahead and do that, too."

"I don't think so."

"That's extra?"

"It's not on the menu."

"How much for what I asked?"

"Seven thousand, three hundred dollars," said Alston. "Cash, today."

"Why seven and change? Why not six, or five? Or ten, for that matter?"

"I was born in seventy-three." Alston shrugged sleepily. "That's my quote."

"I give you the cash right now, how do I know you'll complete the job?"

"'Cause I *took* the job. I get my work from referrals. If I don't maintain a rep, I don't get paid."

They walked to the Monte Carlo and got inside. King unlocked the glove box and took out cash. He turned the key in the ignition and kicked on the AC. King and Alston completed the deal.

"Don't try to tail-gun me," said King, handing Alston the money and giving him a meaningful smile.

Alston counted out the bills, folded them neatly, and put them in the right pocket of his slacks.

"Did you hear me?" said King.

"My ears work fine."

"If you fuck me, I'll find you."

"I believe you would."

"Take care of this right away. And make sure she sees you."

"Assault by a deadly nigger," said Alston wryly.

"Something like that."

"Just so there's no misunderstanding…you don't want me to dead her, right?"

"I'm just sending her a message."

"But it should be something she remembers."

"Leave scars," said King.

TWENTY-THREE

LUCAS HAD his stitches removed in the small white room of an urgent care clinic in Manor Park. He sat in a wooden chair as a Dr. Nikolic snipped and pulled the sutures using a set of clippers. It stung a little when the threads passed through his skin, but he didn't let it show on his face. The doctor was a knockout, and he was going for tough.

Tanya Nikolic was tall and on the cusp of thirty, a black-haired beauty descended from Eastern European stock. She examined his wound closely and then poured hydrogen peroxide over it. Lucas watched it bubble over the raised crescent mark. When his hand was dry she affixed a butterfly bandage to the cut.

"That ER doctor did a good job," said Nikolic. "It healed nicely."

"What about that scar?" said Lucas.

"It's real. You'll have it for life."

"Is that it for us?"

"What else would you like me to do?"

"You could take my blood pressure. I think it's up right now."

"Why's that?"

"It always happens to me when a good-looking woman walks into a room."

"You're the first patient that's ever said that to me."

"Really?"

"No." Dr. Nikolic smiled a little as she removed her gloves. "Just let that bandage fall off naturally. You're good to go."

Lucas left the clinic and headed downtown. Petersen had asked him to come in. Something to do with Calvin Bates.

TWENTY MINUTES later, Lucas sat before Petersen's desk in the offices at 5th and D. Petersen, in Western drag, wearing a shirt with a yoked back and snap buttons, reached into a drawer and produced a deck of playing cards in a cardboard case. He dropped the case on the desk in front of Lucas.

"Do you know what these are?" said Petersen.

Lucas opened the pack and inspected the top card. The back of it read, "District of Columbia," and the next line read, "Cold Case Homicides and Missing Persons," and had a phone number and phone code printed below it. In the center of the card was a rendering of the D.C. flag overlaid with a small map of the District.

"Turn it over," said Petersen.

Lucas looked at its flip side. It was the four of hearts, with the words "Unsolved Homicide" and "Up to $25,000 Reward" under the heart. Below that, a photo of a deceased woman named Sharmell "Mella" Hall, her age, the location of where her body had been found, a brief description of the crime, and its case number. She had been shot to death in 1989.

"I've heard of these," said Lucas.

"The company that manufactures the cards distributes them in prisons and jails via various law enforcement agencies. They make them for about thirty different states and cities. Inmates love to play cards. The idea is, while they're playing, a prisoner could see a missing person or murder victim, and they might know something about the perpetrator."

"You mean, they'd roll on a killer? That doesn't happen too often."

"But it does happen. They do it for the reward, or just because they don't like someone. Or for consideration at a later date. People who cooperate with the law do better at parole hearings. Of course, it's often a false lead. But there've been a number of arrests and convictions off these tips."

"How does this connect to Calvin Bates?" said Lucas.

"Apparently, a friend of his was playing poker in the common room of the jail and he recognized a name on one of the cards. Calvin asked to speak to you."

"Why?"

"I don't know," said Petersen, and Lucas tried to read Petersen's face for the lie. For legal reasons, and to preserve their relationship, Petersen made it a point to stay out of Lucas's side work and private affairs.

"That a fact," said Lucas.

"You'll have to ask him. You should do it quickly, though. His case has gone to the jury. If he's convicted, he's going to be moved to a federal facility. That means he'll be incarcerated somewhere far away."

"What are his chances of an acquittal?"

"I did the best I could," said Petersen gravely.

Lucas looked at the cards. Petersen watched him intently as he began to slowly go through them. When Lucas came to the ace of spades and saw the photo and murder description of Cherise Roberts, and her nickname, his eyes registered surprise. Petersen saw this, too.

"They're not all cold cases, strictly speaking," said Petersen. "They've recently produced a new series for D.C. The deck you have is the latest."

"What was Bates's friend holding?" said Lucas.

Petersen grinned. "I thought you'd want to know. You do like your details."

"What was it?"

"Bates said it was eights and aces," said Petersen. "The dead man's hand."

"I thought that hand was known as aces and eights?"

"It scans better the other way," said Petersen. "It's more poetic. Bob Seger thought so, too. He changed the order in 'Fire Lake.' 'Who wants to play those eights and aces'? Do you know that song?"

"My father liked it. He said that Seger was Springsteen for the authentic workingman."

"Indeed."

"When can I see Bates? I know they schedule visitation days by the first letter of the last name."

"I already put in a letter to the DOC. You can see him today. Actually, you'll be seeing him on a video screen in a building alongside the old D.C. General. They've got a new policy down there."

Lucas got up out of his chair, slipped the deck of cards in a pocket of his jeans.

"You okay, Spero?"

"I'm fine."

"You seem stressed."

"Tired, is all. Thanks for this."

"Don't be a stranger," said Petersen.

Lucas didn't comment. He was already walking away.

LUCAS CHECKED in to a room holding rows of chairs and screens in the shuttered hospital's grounds, near RFK Stadium and close to the D.C. Jail. In the jail, which held prisoners awaiting trial, convicted detainees transitioning to federal prisons, or those serving less than one-year sentences, men sat in common rooms in front of similar screens and spoke to loved ones, relatives, priests, nuns, or attorneys. Face-to-face visits had recently been stopped, a money-saving measure that eliminated the humiliating, time-consuming search-and-frisk procedure that all visitors to the facility had once endured. The shift in policy and procedure had also taken away the needed human contact that came from two people sitting across from each other and looking into each other's eyes. Even if there had been glass between them, and armed security in the room, most found that closeness preferable to the coldness of video visitation.

"My man," said Calvin Bates, his face and shoulders filling the screen. "I appreciate you stopping by, Mr. Lucas."

"Make it Spero."

"I know what you did for me. Finding that dirt on Brian Dodson, and all that. Putting the possibility out there that it could have been his truck in that field. I'm thinking maybe it's gonna help me with the jury. Least, I hope it does."

"If you get a break, it's probably because of Petersen."

"You went beyond, though. You did."

Lucas studied Bates. He was older than Lucas had expected him to be. His eyes were baggy, moist as a hound's, and not unkind. It was hard to imagine him planning the murder of his girlfriend, Edwina Christian. But Lucas had seen all kinds of killers. Quiet men, fathers, educated men who'd grown up in stable, loving homes. Men who wore crucifixes, and men who killed in the name of Allah.

"Petersen said your buddy recognized someone on one of the playing cards they hand out in the jail."

"That's right. My friend's name is Josh Brown. He's in on a manslaughter thing."

"Josh recognized this person when he saw the victim's photo?"

"No. It was when he saw her name. Also, how the card said her body got found."

"Just to be clear, we're talking about…?"

"Cherise Roberts. Petersen had put the bug in my ear, told me to ask around the jail. I told Josh, and he remembered. He was holding eights and aces in a poker game he was havin one day right here in this room."

"What happened?"

"I guess he was looking real hard at one of the aces he had, and he saw her name. Not Cherise, but her nickname. *Cherry.* The card said how she got found in a Dumpster in Columbia Heights. And something went off in his head. Wasn't but a few days earlier that some low-ass inmate, dude called Percy, was braggin to him on killing a young girl name Cherry and putting her body in a trash can."

"Why would he do that?" said Lucas.

"Dude was high. Just Josh and him at a table, talking. He didn't even want to be there with Percy, but wasn't anyplace to walk away to. Shit, ain't none of us even *like* the man. And I guess Percy sensed it, 'cause he started to braggin about who he was on the outside, how he made more money in one day than a pockets-turned-out dude like Josh made in a year. The shit he was up on made him bold."

"What was he on?"

"He was dippin. All you got to do is drop a Newport into that juice, if you can find a bottle. Ain't too hard to get in here if you pay the right CO."

"What did he say?" said Lucas.

"Said he ran girls. High school girls who sold their licorice on the Internet. Said he got them in the fold by offering them blow, and then offered them more drugs and protection if they'd bring him the money they earned and let him hold it. Said most of these girls had no fathers, so he acted like one and moved right in. Said it was easy. Said these girls got to lovin on him and fearing him at the same time."

Lucas looked around the room and lowered his voice. "What about Cherry?"

"Josh got tired of all his talking, see? He asked Percy, Who'd believe anyone, even a high school girl, would fear a no-ass, skinny-ass Bama like you? And then Percy got all puffed up in that bony chest of his and said they feared him plenty. Matter of fact, he'd had to make an example of this one girl he had named Cherry, after she lipped off and threatened to walk away. Said he got a nut in her backside and rubbed his jam on her face, and then he broke her neck. Put her in a trash can and left her for the rats. Dude was so goddamned ripped on boat he probably don't even remember telling Josh this bull-shit. But Josh remembered."

"Is Percy still in the jail?"

Bates shook his head. "He's out."

"Sent to a federal joint?"

"On the street. He was up on charges for distribution, a major violation for him, and he was looking at years. But someone on the jury refused to convict. He got freed on a nul-lification thing. Man went right back to his neighborhood, I expect. He lives in the area where he said he dumped that girl."

"What's his full name?" said Lucas.

"Percy Malone. Goes by 'P.'"

"He stays in the Heights? Where?"

"I don't know the numbers on his door. But he shouldn't be too hard to find for a guy like you."

"Right," said Lucas. *It'll be easy.*

"I hope this helps."

"Would Josh Brown repeat what he said to the law?"

"You mean, will he testify? Sure."

"Even if it could come back on him?"

"He's not afraid. Neither am I." Bates looked deeply at Lucas. "You want to know why I'm comin forward with this, right?"

"It crossed my mind."

"I'm about to get my verdict," said Bates. "Whatever the decision, I accept it. But no twelve can judge me. Only God can. If I can do something right in His eyes..."

"Understood."

"I'm tired," said Bates.

"Thank you," said Lucas.

TWENTY-FOUR

GRACE KINKAID had a light day of work at her nonprofit and could have gone home early, but she usually stuck around till after five. She enjoyed the company of her coworkers. Also, if she went back to her condo too early, she'd start drinking, and the night would be too blurry and long. She was aware of her problem with alcohol and was making an effort to cut back. She'd heard that drink-counting was a warning sign of dependence, but she'd taken to doing just that, looking to keep her intake to three, four glasses of wine per day. Her intention was to get it down to two. As of yet, she'd not come close to achieving that goal. But she was trying.

Her office was on the sketchy side of the Hill, on one of the low-numbered streets in Northeast, between Constitution and H, but closer to H. She was an attorney but she earned a modest salary, not much more than the younger folks she worked with, who only had undergraduate degrees or no degree at all. The organization was called Food for Children, which was good for fund-raising and solicitation. People saw those words on a mailer, it was hard to throw away.

Grace didn't have the high salary that came with a law firm, or its politics and rigidity. She liked the fact that she was doing something positive for her native city. Her work was mostly administrative, but in her mind she was helping to feed hungry kids.

"Good night, Neecie," said Grace, to an overweight, pretty-faced woman with red lipstick, who sat at a nearby desk.

"Have a good one, Grace."

Grace walked from the offices out to the street. There were neighborhood folks around but not too many, as most had not come home from work yet. Her car, a late-model Jetta, was parked down the block.

Grace had not yet gotten the money she owed Spero Lucas. Her intent was to close the deal with the painting's buyer soon. She'd blown it off in part because he'd not reminded her, though she realized the responsibility was not his. It was funny about Spero. He didn't even seem to *want* the money when he'd returned the painting. It was like it wasn't important to him.

As she walked down the sidewalk, her purse in hand, she idly noticed a man get out of a nondescript sedan. In fact, it was an old Ford Taurus, a hack with stolen plates that the man had rented for one day from a resident of Lincoln Heights. The man wore a multicolored knit tam that normally covered dreads, but today covered wads of paper resting atop a modified Afro. His face had been shaven clean hours earlier, except for a thin Vandyke missing spots he couldn't "get." He wore aviator sunglasses with large lenses.

To some, he went by Jabari Jones, but his surname was Alston. He was in disguise.

Grace did not pay much attention as the man approached her, and paid little more attention when he reached under the tail of his shirt. As he neared her, she saw his hand come out with a knife. It was long and serrated, and as he raised it, late-afternoon sun winked off its blade. Grace dropped her handbag to the sidewalk and turned her head, as if by looking away she could stop this. Alston grabbed Grace by the throat, came down with the knife, and stabbed her deeply in her right breast. Grace said, "Oh," and felt the air go out of her as her knees buckled. Alston held her up and again plunged the knife into her chest. He released his hand from her throat, and as she fell, she felt blood leave her. Then a great deal of pain, but only for a moment, because she was going into shock. One leg twitched in spasm as she lay on the ground. Alston picked up her handbag and walked away.

A witness later described the assailant as "a Rasta dude with shades." She said he'd gotten into an old blue "Ford or Chevy" and drove away. She noted that he'd looked "sick" as he'd quick-stepped to his car.

LUCAS SPENT the latter part of the day in his apartment. Using the Intelius program on his laptop, he background-checked Percy Malone, found his record of multiple arrests and convictions, and brought up his photograph. Over a twenty-year period, since the age of fourteen, Malone had been into everything from drug distribution to felonious assault to pandering. His incarcerations had begun at the old Oak Hill facility for juveniles. He'd done a stretch at the now-shuttered Lorton

Reformatory and one out-of-state facility as well. He was a career criminal, a poster child for those who were anti-rehabilitation or -reform. Lucas was all for redemption. He also knew that some men couldn't be saved.

Next, Lucas ran Malone's name and DOB into the People Finder program and came up with a current residential address. Calvin Bates had been mistaken. Malone did not live in Columbia Heights, but rather in a house on Princeton Place, Northwest, in Park View. Lucas was familiar with the 700 block and knew it held smallish row homes on the south side. The "First Floor" designation told Lucas that Malone stayed in an apartment or rented a room in a house. Bates had been right about one thing: Malone was easy to find.

LUCAS DROVE his Jeep down to Park View.

He parked on Princeton, the nose of his truck pointed east. Lucas knew that at the top of the grade was Warder Street and Park View Recreation Center, and one block beyond, the grounds of the U.S. Soldiers' and Airmen's Home, which most folks called the Old Soldiers' Home. Just five years earlier, Lucas would have stood out if he were parked on this street. Since the sixties, and for many years after the riots, the neighborhood had been almost entirely black. Park View also was home to the once-infamous Park Morton Complex and the Black Hole go-go club on Georgia, a trouble spot for police in 4D. But Park View's demographics and amenities, like those citywide, were changing. There were whites, blacks, and Hispanics now on the streets, and new coffee shops, bars, restaurants, and condos opening on the Avenue. Lucas couldn't decide if the changes were positive. Maybe it was just a cultural and economic evolution. Neither good nor bad, just different.

He waited in the car for a couple of hours, keeping an eye on Percy Malone's residence, a two-story row home painted gray. He listened to music from his iPhone and peed once into an old water bottle. He was about to go home when Malone emerged from the house. Lucas mentally recorded the time.

Malone looked like his photograph. Average height, spidery, with skinny arms and legs, and gangly wrists. Malone glanced around the street. His eyes, even from this distance, had the alert but deadened look of an abused child.

Lucas had expected Malone to go down the block to Georgia, but instead he walked up Princeton toward Warder Place. Then Lucas saw him stop, cup his hands around a match, and light something thinly rolled. So Malone was smoking a little weed on the way to wherever he was going next. Lucas waited until he was out of sight, then started the Jeep and drove east, slowly following Malone's path.

At the Warder intersection, Lucas looked right and saw Malone turn the corner on the other side of the rec center, onto Otis. Warder was one way heading north. Lucas took a chance and drove against traffic, and when he came to Otis and turned right, Malone had vanished.

Lucas pulled over and put the transmission into Park. As always, the map of the city was in his head. It helped that he'd done surveillance work in this neighborhood many times. He guessed that Malone had cut into the alley past the rec center field, at 6th, then made a left into the alley that ran between the backyards of Princeton and Otis. This would take him down to a sharp left turn and another short alley that would open back up to Otis, close to Georgia Avenue. Malone was "walking his smoke." There was no need to follow in his Jeep, as the alley was narrow, sometimes clogged with trash cans, and hard to navigate by vehicle. Next time, Lucas would bring his bike.

Malone soon appeared at the bottom of Otis and headed for Georgia, where he crossed to the west side of the Avenue. Lucas drove down there and watched him enter a surprisingly upscale liquor and wine store.

Lucas waited. Malone reappeared ten minutes later with a long brown bag in hand and walked up Georgia toward Princeton. He was headed back to his spot. Lucas had seen enough. He drove home.

Back at his crib, Lucas smoked a joint, drank a couple of beers, and listened to some dub. He phoned Charlotte Rivers and fell asleep on his couch, waiting for her to return his call.

EARLY THE next morning, he was woken by a phone call from Amanda Brand, his bartender friend, telling him that Grace Kinkaid had been stabbed in a street assault the previous day. Lucas fired down a cup of coffee and drove over to the Washington Hospital Center on Irving Street, where Grace had been taken for treatment. Amanda had said she'd meet him there.

He talked his way into the ER. Amanda was sitting in a chair outside one of the recovery rooms. Her eyes were shadowed, but she looked like she'd recently freshened up. She stood as Lucas came into the space. Standing nearby was a man in a suit and tie who had the look of MPD. He eyed Lucas as he and Amanda hugged.

"How is she?" said Lucas.

"Unconscious right now. Two deep cuts, one that severely damaged her breast. The blade collapsed her lung. They've catheterized her chest."

"Is she going to make it?"

"They're trying to reinflate her lung. They've done the irrigation and suturing, but there's the risk of infection. Spero, I saw what that knife did to her…"

"Amanda," he said, holding her shoulders, looking straight into her eyes, trying to get her to focus.

"I'm okay. I've been here all night. I'm just tired."

"What did she say? Did she talk to the police?"

"No, not yet. There was a witness. She gave a description of the guy. Black man, wearing one of those knit hats, like a dread cap. He took her purse. Why would he do this if he only wanted to rob her?"

"I don't know."

"She called me a couple of days ago. Said you'd found her painting and brought it back."

"I did."

"This doesn't have anything to do with that, does it?"

"No," said Lucas, cutting his eyes away. "Take a walk, Amanda. Get something to eat. I'll sit out here for a while."

"You can't go in there."

He didn't want to go in. He pushed her arm gently and said, "Go."

Lucas watched her punch a wall button and walk through the swinging ER doors. He went to the doorway of Grace's room and past a mobile curtain that partly obstructed his view. He saw her lying on the bed. A clear tube snaked out of her robe and there were thick bandages at the top of her chest. In the tube, blood and brown material flowed back and forth with each labored breath. A morphine drip led to her arm.

"You a friend of hers?" said a voice, and Lucas turned. The man in the suit, a guy in his thirties with broad shoulders, had approached him from behind.

"Yes," said Lucas. "Actually, more of a friend to the woman who just left. I'm here because Amanda asked me to stop by."

"Your name?"

"Spero Lucas."

"Spell Spero," said the man, and Lucas did. The man wrote this in a small notebook.

"You're a detective?"

"Detective Paul Strong. Homicide and Violent Crimes. What do you do, Mr. Lucas?"

"I'm an investigator for a criminal defense attorney here in town."

"One of those guys," said Strong, without malice. "Ex-military?"

"Yeah. What happened here?"

"Are you working right now?"

"No."

"Then allow *me*."

"Okay."

"Do *you* have any idea who would have perpetrated this crime on Miss Kinkaid?"

"None," said Lucas. "Amanda told me what the witness saw. A guy with dreads stabbed her, then took her purse."

"*Black* guy," said Strong, who was black. "It's okay to say it."

"Kind of an extreme way to rob someone, isn't it?"

"Homicides are way down in the city. We like to brag on that. But violent robberies and assaults are pretty much up citywide. East of the river, but also on the Hill. It can get pretty rough."

"Why stab her, though? Why not just hit her on the head or push her to the ground?"

"That's a good question."

"Maybe he wanted to hurt her because she was white."

"That's your theory?" said Strong.

They looked at each other without speaking. It was perfectly comfortable, in the way that silence can be between men.

"Let me ask you something," said Lucas. "You ever hear of the Ammidown killing, happened in D.C. around nineteen seventy-one?"

"You weren't even born in seventy-one. Neither was I."

"My father told me about it many times. He was a Washingtoniana freak. Loved his local history."

"Go ahead."

"Short version is, a white woman named Linda Ammidown was raped and murdered under the East Capitol Street Bridge. A black guy, a local pool player, was arrested and convicted of the crime, and sentenced to the chair by a Judge Sirica...the same Judge Sirica who would later get famous during the Watergate trials. A little more than a week later the Supreme Court threw out the death penalty, so the killer didn't fry. Eventually, it came to light that Robert Ammidown, the victim's husband, had hired the guy to kill his wife. It was a contract hit."

"Black dude rapes and murders a white woman, it deflects the suspicion away from her husband."

"Exactly."

"What happened to those two gentlemen?"

"Ammidown pled to second-degree murder. Word is, the guy who did the killing is now out on the street. Friend of mine said he saw him recently in a pool hall on Central Avenue."

"And the point of that story is what?"

"Something to think on, is all."

"What do you know, exactly?"

"I'm making a suggestion, Detective. If you ever arrest this so-called Rasta and get him in the box, I'd ask him who paid him to do the job."

"Thanks for the tip."

"Just doing my civic duty."

"Fuck you and give me your phone number," said Strong.

Lucas gave him the number to one of his disposables. Detective Strong drifted, and Lucas had a seat.

When Amanda Brand returned, he went home. There was nothing else for him to do.

NOT LONG after he entered his apartment, he picked up one of several disposables he owned and dialed the number for Billy King that Charles Lumley had given up the day they'd tortured him and run him out of town.

King answered.

"Hello."

"This is Spero Lucas. Is this Billy King?"

"Do I know you?"

"You know what I've done."

After a silence, King said, "Are you on a clean line?"

"Yes. You?"

"Uh-huh. So you're the one who stole my painting and murdered Serge. The guy in the parking lot, right? It's good to put a name to the face. How'd you get this number?"

"Charles Lumley," said Lucas. "We should talk."

"I'm listening."

"Face-to-face."

"Call it," said King.

They agreed on a place and time.

TWENTY-FIVE

Bᴵˡˡʸ ᴷᴵᴺᴳ wore a faded red polo shirt, frayed khaki shorts, and Sperry topsiders with no socks. His sunglasses hung on a leash over his broad chest. He was seated at a two-top across from Lucas, in a new Ethiopian-owned coffee shop on Georgia Avenue, in Petworth, located on the second floor of a house.

Lucas had arrived a half hour early and found a seat with its back to a wall. When King had walked in, moving with a jaunty strut, he made an impression. Close up, he was even larger than Lucas had remembered. Below the waist, he was an animal. Freakishly flanked, a full-on beast. He'd be hard to take down.

The morning rush was over, but there were still several patrons seated at tables and on couches, killing time, working on their laptops, using the free Wi-Fi. Others stood by the go-counter, picking up stirring sticks and napkins, glancing at their phones before hurriedly leaving the shop.

"Suckers," said King, pointing his chin in the direction of

two young go-getters who were heading out the door. "Where they going that's so important?"

"I imagine they've got jobs."

"*I* work. So do you. But you and me, we don't have to be anywhere at a certain time. We don't walk fast unless we want to." King brushed blond hair off his forehead. "So you're an independent contractor?"

"Something like that."

"Like one of those Blackwater guys."

"No, not like them."

"You find things."

"Sometimes."

"I'm curious. How'd Grace Kinkaid pay you? A flat fee or a commission?"

"Aren't you gonna ask me how she's doing?"

"I don't know what you're talking about."

"She's going to recover," said Lucas. "I'm not sure if that bothers you or makes you happy."

"Oh, has she been ill?" King furrowed his brow in a comic manifestation of concern.

"Cut the bullshit. You didn't have to do that to her. This was between you and me."

"She hired you, didn't she?"

"Yes."

"Then she brought this on herself."

"You're a coward, Billy."

"Careful." King smiled pleasantly, showing Lucas his white teeth.

"Your man gave you your money's worth. He almost cut off one of her breasts."

"That's a damn shame. Grace had nice tits. A little smaller than I normally like, but nice. And she had a real tight pussy, Lucas. For her age, I mean. Fit me like a glove."

"Fucking degenerate."

"I'm supposed to be ashamed? Of *what?* I got a big pipe and I like to use it. I make women come. I don't buy 'em flowers or expensive dinners or any of that bullshit, because that's all smoke and a waste of time. I take them straight to the bedroom and I give them what they want. It's as simple as that. You know damn well what I'm talking about. You're a healthy young man. You're the same way."

Lucas thought of Charlotte, naked beneath him, her mouth open, her face contorted in climax.

Lucas said, "No."

"Sure you are. You ever fuck a woman against her will, Lucas?"

"Never."

"Not even in high school, in the backseat of a car? Girl says no, but you keep trying, right? You talk her into it, or she gets tired of fighting and lets you in. Your cock's so hard a cat can't scratch it, and all you can think of is *you.* You're not concerned with that girl's feelings anymore. You just need to bust. Isn't that *right?*"

Lucas said nothing.

"Don't be so high and mighty," said King. "It's the same for you as it is for me. Once you get inside that box, your conscience goes out the window."

"How would you know?" said Lucas.

"What's that?"

"I hear you can't get there unless you put it in a woman's mouth."

King sat back. For the first time Lucas saw the infinite nothing in his blue eyes.

"Let's get to it," said King.

"Fine."

"What are we doing here?"

"You're all alone now. Your crew is gone. Think about that."

"I have. But I don't need 'em, see? I'm stronger when I go solo."

"Then go elsewhere," said Lucas.

"You're in no position to threaten me."

"You paid someone to put a woman in the ER. You're as guilty as the man who used the knife."

"And you're a murderer. You can't go to the police."

"I don't plan to," said Lucas.

They looked at each other across the table.

"I'll leave," said King. "But not without the money Grace paid you. How much was that?"

"Eighty thousand dollars," said Lucas.

"That'll get me started in another town. That'll be just fine."

"What if I say no?"

"If I have to stick around and wait for my money, there's no telling what could happen to your friend Grace when she gets out of the hospital. That would be awful, seeing as how she's so traumatized. You know what I mean?"

"I think so."

"You do have the money, right?"

"I can get it," said Lucas, without hesitation.

"Well, then. You know what to do. But don't even think about bringing a newspaper in a backpack, like you did to Serge. I won't like that."

"I'll bring what you need," said Lucas.

King's eyes assessed Lucas. "Serge said you lectured him about impersonating a marine. Is that what you are?"

Lucas did not reply.

"Tough guy," said King.

"Just a guy," said Lucas. "I'll be in touch."

King got up and walked from the coffee shop, a spring in his step.

LUCAS SPENT the rest of the day planning his next move. He took a long bike ride. He phoned Winston Dupree and explained himself, apologized for not calling sooner, and assured him that he would be paid for the time he'd put in on the job. He made a similar call to Marquis.

In the evening he drove out to Silver Spring, stopped at the Safeway for flowers, and handed the bouquet to his mother as she greeted him at the door of the bungalow. She'd made *macaronia* with burnt butter, and a country salad of cucumbers, onions, and tomatoes from the backyard. They sat together in candlelight on the screened porch. Eleni Lucas sipped from a large glass of Chardonnay. Spero nursed a Stella. He'd just taken his last bite.

"Work going okay, honey?"

"It's good, Ma."

"Any thought of going back to school?"

"No."

"Your father would have wanted you to get your degree."

"I know," said Spero. "But that's not how things worked out."

"The government will pay your tuition."

"They'd pay for some of it. That's not the issue."

"What is?"

"I'm not going to college."

Eleni stood up. "Would you like anything from the kitchen?"

"Nothing for me," said Spero.

She returned with a full glass of white and a photograph in a frame. Eleni set the photo on the table before him.

He'd seen it before. His mother had taken it the day Spero had been brought home from the adoption agency. In the photograph, Spero sat on the floor of their family room, strapped in a car seat. Leo sat beside him, his arm around his new kid brother. Apart from them sat Irene, their oldest and sole biological child, and Dimetrius, the Lucases' first adopted son. In the middle of this group kneeled Van Lucas, curly haired and black of beard, smiling broadly, looking somewhat shocked but happy. Shilo, one of their dogs, sniffed at Spero's feet.

"I always liked this one," said Spero.

"It was a tradition for us," said Eleni. "Soon as we brought each of you kids home we'd take a family photo. The day Leonidas came home with us? It snowed like crazy. Your *baba* had sandbags in the back of the Silverado to weigh it down. We almost didn't make it up our hill, but we were giggling all the way. We were just so excited. Dad had snow in his hair and beard when he carried Leo inside. He was holding him like a football."

"I've heard that story," said Spero. In fact, he'd heard it many times.

"You know, Leonidas was supposed to be adopted by another couple, but when they saw the most recent baby photo of him, they turned him down. They thought he was too dark."

"They wanted a *white* black baby," said Spero. "I know."

"And then you. The couple that was in line to get you said they weren't quite ready when you became available. They needed to paint the nursery or something first. Can you believe it?"

"Our gain," said Spero. "Leo and I scored."

"No, honey. It was your father and me who scored." Eleni picked up the photograph and held it out to Spero. "This is why I brought this out. Look at the family room window, right there."

Spero examined it. Through the window, in the gray winter sky, was a wink of light.

"What is that? It looks like a star."

"Your father said it was the reflection from the camera flash. But I always believed it was something else. Like an eye, looking after us."

"That's nice," said Spero, because he didn't know what else to say.

"After he passed, Dad became that light. He's the eye. Do you see what I'm saying?"

"I do."

"You're skeptical."

"Just trying to get my head around it."

"Your father's here, right now, and he's thinking of us. Thinking of *you*."

"Okay."

"You've always been on his mind, Spero. When you went overseas, he was troubled. Not just about your safety. We were all concerned about that. He was worried about what the experience was going to do to you, mentally, moving forward into your life. How you were going to react to everything you'd seen and done after you returned."

"I make do," said Spero.

"Because of the mess in Vietnam, our generation distrusted the military. In the seventies, to go into the service was just about the most uncool thing a young guy could do. Your dad never even considered it. And then, when you enlisted…"

"What?"

"He was proud of you, of course. Among other things, Nine-Eleven made many people look at military service in a positive way again. He understood why you felt you had to go and do your part. But he was still angry that we'd gone to war. He didn't support the decision. He wasn't fond of politicians who send young men and women to fight and die for an ideological experiment."

"I fought for my brothers."

"Even so. Your dad wondered how a man like you could be trained and ordered to kill, and then be expected to simply turn that switch off when you came home. He said it was like telling a lion to become a vegetarian."

"Most of the guys I served with manage to deal with it."

"How about you?"

"I'm fine."

"Are you?"

"Is this about college again? 'Cause I'm still not going."

His mother's gaze was unyielding, but there was a hint of a smile on her face. "You always were stubborn."

"Family trait."

"Change the subject?"

"Please."

"How'd you like the *fayito* tonight?"

"The food was great, Ma. Thank you."

"How 'bout a little ice cream or something, for dessert?"

"I've got a big day tomorrow," said Spero. "I better go."

Eleni's eyes softened. *"Se agapo, agori mou."*

"I love you, too."

AT HIS apartment, late that night, Lucas phoned Billy King.

"Yeah."

"It's Spero Lucas."

"Lucas."

"Are you still at the house in Croom?"

"Yes, I'm here."

"And tomorrow?"

"I'll be here all day."

"I was thinking I'd stop by tomorrow night."

"You're coming with what we discussed?"

"I'm gonna bring it," said Lucas.

"Now you're talking," said King.

"Say, just after sundown."

"I'll be waiting."

Lucas ended the call and set his phone alarm. He stripped to his briefs and got into bed. Staring at the ceiling, he thought of the coming day.

You hit us, we hit you.

TWENTY-SIX

SINCE HE'D been staying out in the Croom house, Billy King had gotten into a morning routine. He'd wake up early, down a cup of coffee in the kitchen, drive to a diner on 301, and load up with a full-on breakfast. After, he'd head over to the boat launch at Jug Bay, bullshit with the fishermen, talk bait, hulls, and engines. There wasn't much marina action to speak of down there, which meant few loose women, but the Patuxent River area would have to do for sport until he could get himself to a livelier place. Deep water, powerboats, trim, and drink. It was what he was made for.

King had never owned a boat, but he had ambition. As of yet, he hadn't amassed the kind of cash a man needed to afford even a used runabout, let alone a Parker or Shamrock. The maintenance, the slip fees, winter storage, hell, the cost of gas alone…You had to have bank, or be born with it.

The eighty thousand that Lucas was going to deliver would get King closer to his goal. He'd never had that kind of money, all at once, in his life. Now he was about to score.

He'd grown up with only the bare essentials. Food on the table, little more. His old man was career military. Glenn King turned a wrench for the air force, and in Billy's early years, the family moved quite a bit. It was a stretch to call it a family; there was little warmth in the dynamic, and Billy was an only child. His mother was a plain, quiet woman, submissive, obedient to the father, fearful of him when he drank. The father was a beer man who went for quantity, cans, and price over taste. Rheingold, Hamm's, or Schlitz, depending on where they lived. At the end of the night, the father would sometimes go into his bedroom and wake up the mother, and Billy would hear the creak of the bedsprings and the father's grunts. But never a sound from his mom.

The father didn't praise him or notice him much at all. Glenn was a big man, so Billy, who already had some bulk on him by the time he was thirteen, vowed to get bigger and started throwing weights as soon as he could get into a gym. By the time they moved to Florida, where Glenn was stationed at Eglin AFB, on the Emerald Coast, Billy had grown huge and was recruited to play high school football. In the off-season he wrestled as a heavyweight, and because of his strength and athleticism, he dominated the mats. But football was his sport. Being an accomplished football player meant something in Florida; he was known. He partied with kids who had money, sometimes on big, beautiful powerboats docked at exclusive marinas in the Gulf. The rich kids told him, in subtle ways, that he wasn't one of them, which only made him more determined to gain entrance to their club. In the locker room, the other guys joked with him about his big pipe, and the word got out, which made him very popular with the girls.

Billy banged them in cars, under the mangroves, on the beach at night, and in bathrooms at parties. He got a rep as a guy who could last. He liked to hear the noises the girls made when he was fucking them, and chuckled low when their faces changed as they were about to come. He laughed out loud when they begged and said please. He took little pleasure in the act himself. He'd never loved any of them, or even liked them. Females were whores to him, nothing more than holes.

The important thing was, he'd outmanned his father. He knew how to cause a girl to make those sounds. He was bigger than his old man, and stronger. He drank bottled Heineken, not piss water in cans. He had a future. He'd never wear a military uniform or have a boss. Billy was going to own a boat.

But he didn't get to tell the old man any of this or shove it in his face. Glenn King died of a massive heart attack on base one day while Billy was at school.

The way it turned out, high school was the highlight of Billy's life. A torn ACL ended his football career. His grades were shit, so college was out of the question. He was slick but not smart. All he had left was his good looks and size. That got him out of town, and a long way further, for a while.

Now he was an aging stud nearing his expiration date. He knew this. The sun had wrinkled him prematurely, and though he was as muscled up as ever, he was carrying too much weight. Time seemed to be moving fast. There'd come a day, not too far off, when women would stop wanting Billy King.

But he had a plan. Secure the money from Lucas, take care of him, and get out of this house. Head back down toward Cobb Island and shack up with Lois. Use her till she was dry, pinch her for her jewelry, and get gone. Move to the South, where life had been good for him. He'd heard the Flora-Bama coast was real nice. Settle somewhere down there, maybe even get a job. Buy himself a boat.

King went to his bedroom dresser and opened its top drawer. There he kept his cash and a shoe box that had once held his first pair of Chuck Taylors. In it were the things that meant the most to him since his childhood. A baseball signed by an Atlanta Brave, a buffalo nickel coin collection, a pen with multicolored ink that he'd saved up for as a kid, and a cardboard crown. The crown had been made just for him and put on his head at a homecoming dance, when they'd named him Senior of the Year. In sloppy, glittered letters, someone had written "King Billy" on the front of it. King looked at the crown and issued a small smile. This faded as a familiar feeling dropped through him like a black curtain, an emptiness that could never be filled.

He reached under his socks, took some cash from a roll, and closed the dresser drawer.

Billy walked downstairs to the living area of the house. He'd cleaned it up as best he could. In a closet he found an aluminum bat he'd purchased the previous day. He leaned this against the couch. The couch back had been shot to hell. A .45 with a full magazine was wedged beneath one of the cushions. He'd placed it there himself. Though King wasn't good with guns, it was there for insurance. He could overpower Lucas. He'd do it with his hands. Or use the bat.

Billy went to the kitchen in the back of the first floor and made himself a cup of instant coffee. When he was done drinking it, he locked up the house, got into his Monte Carlo, and headed for the diner and a full breakfast. He was going to fortify himself with some food. Come back and dig a hole in the woods. Wait for night, and Lucas.

BY THE time King returned it was close to noon. The sun was overhead and the trees from the surrounding forest threw no shadows in the yard. He unlocked the front door of the house, stepped inside, and closed the door behind him.

He walked up the stairs and turned the corner, where the plaster wall had been decimated by buckshot. He was going to change into a T-shirt, jeans, and steel-shank work boots, so he could start digging that grave. He moved through the hallway, a large, empty space.

As he neared the entrance to his bedroom he heard something behind him. His blood jumped as he turned around.

Lucas was standing in the open doorway of Serge's old room. He was holding a revolver in his hand, his finger inside the trigger guard. It was a .38, and it was pointed at King's middle.

"You came early," said King calmly.

"Yep."

"How'd you get in?"

"Louis gave me a key."

"And all you brought was one measly revolver?"

"It's all I need. I've been out on the edge of those woods since six A.M. When you went out, you made this easy."

"I don't see my money."

"I didn't bring it."

"You plan to shoot me?"

"That depends on you. If you leave right now, we won't

have a problem. That is, if you leave and don't come back to D.C."

"Just like that."

"Right."

"And if I come back?"

"Then this is gonna go on."

"Why don't we just settle it right now, then?" said King.

"We probably should."

"You're not the type to murder me in cold blood."

"No."

"You want to try me. *Don't* you?"

"I'd say the same thing right now if I was you."

"You *are* me, fella. You're as close to me as I've come across in a long while." King smiled and pointed his chin at Lucas's gun. "Now why don't you throw that gun away and let's get started."

Lucas tossed the .38 onto the bed in Serge's room. He stepped out of the doorway and into the hall.

King barked a laugh. "God, you're stupid. You just made the last mistake of your life."

"Come on."

"I'm gonna break your fuckin neck."

Like rams, they charged. Lucas bounced off King as if he'd hit concrete.

"How'd *that* feel?" said King.

Lucas came in again, tried to wrap up King's arms, but King windmilled and broke free. King moved forward, backed up Lucas, and got him in a hug. He picked him up off his feet and threw him into a wall. The plaster cracked and Lucas felt a sting. As he turned his head he came into a punch that split his ear. Lucas righted himself, got square, and covered up, his elbows tucked into his chest. King, close in, threw a roundhouse and got nothing, then went high and hit Lucas square in the jaw, and Lucas saw white explode in his head. He felt a tooth loosen; his mouth filled with blood. King faked a right, and when Lucas brought up his arms to cover, King threw a left into his ribs and a right that stood Lucas up.

King dipped and went low for Lucas's legs. Lucas threw his legs back and pancaked against the shot, but King was too strong, and he drove Lucas back to the wall and put him up against it. Lucas smelled sour breath as King squeezed him in a crushing hug. He fought for air, and in a panic he drove his forehead into King's face. Lucas did it again, this time with fury, and he felt the cartilage give way on King's nose; King released him and put a hand to his face. A great deal of blood leaked through his fingers.

"Okay," said King. He dropped his hand.

They circled each other in the center of the hall.

King was in a stagger stance, his right leg farther forward than the left. Lucas circled to the trail leg. King came forward and grabbed Lucas by the shoulders, and Lucas cross-faced, pushing on King's cheek with his right biceps. King grunted in frustration and broke free, and as he did his hand raked Lucas's face.

King came in strong, faked a shot, and charged bull-like, his massive legs propelling him forward in a steamroller rush. He danced Lucas back toward the stairwell. At its opening Lucas dragged King's right arm at the same time he dropped and held on, pulling King with momentum, and they both tumbled down the stairs.

For a few seconds, maybe longer, Lucas blacked out. He was lying at the foot of the stairs. He came to and got to his feet. The room spun. He shook the spin from his head. His left shoulder felt wrong. Blood covered his T-shirt. He swallowed blood and coughed.

King was standing, cradling his right hand. It was bent unnaturally at the wrist. Bone pushed out against bluing skin. He willed the pain from his face when he saw Lucas staring. He stood straight and smiled. His teeth were pink. His nose was a stew of smashed bone and blood.

Lucas walked toward King. He knew that King had only his left hand. But the left came fast, and he couldn't stop it. Lucas's head snapped back. The tooth that had loosened was now free, and Lucas spit it out onto the hardwood floor. King wheezed in laughter.

Lucas came back in, threw a wild right that missed and carried him too far, and King hit him with his left fist, once, and again, a granite head blow and a glancing punch to the split ear. Lucas staggered and righted himself, and got back into a straight stance, his weight on his back foot. He balled his fists and touched the thumb of each hand to his nose, his eyes dead on King. Lucas was finding his hands.

King jabbed with his left, and Lucas stepped away from it. He moved in quickly, grabbed King's left triceps in a monkey grip, and with his free hand got hold of King's broken wrist and twisted it. King screamed. Lucas dropped to one knee, shot one arm behind King's leg, and hooked him there. In one motion he put his good shoulder into King's torso and exploded up, and with rage and adrenaline he lifted King and tripped him. They both tumbled back to the floor, with Lucas on top. He punched through King's nose, aiming for the back of his head. He punched him again and again until his hand was slick with blood.

Lucas rolled off of him and stood. He looked down at King, lying still on his back. His face was unrecognizable, his breathing ragged and labored.

Lucas turned and went up the stairs, gripping the handrail for support. He found his .38 on Serge's bed, hefted it, and held it by his side. He rested for a moment, then walked back down to the ground floor.

Billy King was standing in the center of the room, a .45 in his right hand, an aluminum baseball bat held loosely in his left. One of the cushions of the couch had been pushed aside.

Lucas raised the S&W and pointed it at King.

"Fucker," said King, a hint of regard in his voice.

"It's over."

King winced and let go of the bat. It dropped and rolled across the floor.

"Almost," said King.

"Drop the gun, Billy."

"I can't do that, fella," said King, and his gun hand went up.

Lucas squeezed the trigger of the .38. The slug entered King's chest. He stumbled and fell. Lucas walked forward and fired, the cylinder of the revolver advancing with each shot. When the hammer clicked on an empty chamber, Lucas lowered his gun.

King sat with his back against the couch, blood flowing down his shredded polo shirt and into the lap of his shorts. He stared at Lucas as he took short, desperate breaths and the light leaked from his eyes. King stopped breathing. Lucas kicked him viciously between his legs and there was no reaction at all.

Lucas picked up King's Colt, turned it on its side, and racked the slide several times. There had been no chambered round. With only one good hand, King hadn't managed to ready the gun.

Lucas holstered the Colt in the small of his back and dropped his .38 in the pocket of his Dickies. He searched the living room floor and found his tooth, and pocketed that as well. There was nothing else he could fix or do. From the kitchen's refrigerator he liberated a plastic bottle of water, drank half of it down, refilled it with tap water, and walked from the house.

He entered the woods, short of breath and in pain, and slowly navigated his way back to his Jeep. An hour later, he found his vehicle, parked in the lot of the shuttered gas station, a half mile away.

TWENTY-SEVEN

LUCAS STOOD before the bathroom mirror of his apartment. One ear was torn and bloody, and several knuckles were raw and skinned. His face had sustained scratches from the close-in fight. His jaw was swollen and bruised. It was difficult to fully bite down. When he raised his arms to remove his T-shirt, his left shoulder pained him greatly, telling him that his rotator cuff had been strained or torn in the fall down the stairs. It hurt to take deep breaths. When he smiled he could see the space where his incisor had been. He looked like a hillbilly meth dealer who'd taken a beat-down at the hands of police.

Lucas took a long shower. After he'd dried off, he phoned Marquis Rollins.

"I could use some help," said Lucas. "I'm at my apartment."

"What do you need?"

Lucas gave him a list. "No questions, Marquis."

Marquis said, "Right."

274 • George Pelecanos

LUCAS WAS in bed when Marquis knocked on the door. He got up with effort and let him in. Marquis took a look at him and shook his head. But he asked him nothing.

Straightaway, Lucas ate a couple of the Vicodin that Marquis had been given at the VA Hospital. They went into the bathroom, where Lucas sat on the edge of his tub while Marquis worked on his friend. He poured hydrogen peroxide on his cuts, his torn earlobe, and knuckles, applied Neosporin to the same areas, and gauzed and taped him where it was needed. Lucas himself rubbed Anbesol on the bloody gap where his tooth had been, and Orajel on the cuts inside his mouth. Marquis wrapped Lucas's chest with tape. He could do nothing for Lucas's shoulder.

"I'm no doctor," said Marquis.

"For real?"

"Sayin, you need to *see* one."

"This is going to have to do me for now."

"You start pissin blood..."

"I know."

"I don't like that your chest hurts, man. If that rib broke and pierced your lung..."

"I *know*. Help me up."

Marquis reached his hand out and Lucas took it. They moved to the living room, and Lucas sat on his couch.

"Couple of cold ones would be nice," said Lucas.

By the time Marquis returned with two beers, Lucas was in the process of rolling a joint. They smoked it down to a roach, and Lucas lay back on the couch. Marquis went to the stereo and put on an Ernest Ranglin CD that he knew Lucas liked. That was what Lucas was listening to when the Vicodin, alcohol, and weed kicked in and gave him a nice slow kiss.

When Lucas next woke it was the middle of the night. Marquis was still with him, sleeping in a chair.

HE SPENT the next several days in relative quiet. When his phone rang he checked the ID, but didn't pick up. Every morning, Lucas went outside to get his morning *Post* off the front lawn, and once hit the Safeway on Piney Branch Road for beer and essentials, but pretty much stayed inside his apartment. He read, watched movies, and allowed himself time to recover.

It no longer hurt when he breathed. He threw the rest of the Vicodin away. Marquis didn't use them, and Lucas didn't want them anymore.

He scoured his laptop for any up-to-the-minute news. The first hit came on the Crime Scene blog of the *Washington Post*'s Internet site. A body had been discovered in a house in Croom, Maryland, when the home's owner had stopped by to check on his tenants. The item said only that local police were treating the death as a homicide.

In the following day's print edition of the *Post*, a longer, more detailed article appeared inside Metro. The piece did not give the victim's name but simply described Billy King as an adult white male, the victim of multiple gunshot wounds.

Lucas knew that the crime scene, a forensic professional's nightmare, would pose a great challenge to investigators. Three bedrooms, three men wearing different-size clothing, two men missing. The house contained stolen paintings, other burgled goods, guns, and probably drugs. Its furnishings were riddled with rounds, and sections of the walls had been torn away with buckshot. King had been both beaten and shot. Police would surmise that the victim had been involved in some sort of criminal enterprise. That he was murdered in a home invasion. A retaliation, or a turf war, or a message kill. He was in the business and he'd paid a price.

The story deepened the next day, when uniformed police and dogs, combing the surrounding woods, came upon a shallow grave. In it was a lime-covered body in a state of decomposition. Again, the victim went unidentified in print. But the unfolding event had now made the television news, and the column inches grew in the *Washington Post*. DEA agents were said to be on the scene. A spokesman said that they had been investigating drug rings and bikers in the largely rural area, and were exploring a possible connection to this crime in which two men had violently died.

Lucas put down the newspaper.

Two dead.

They were trying to kill me.

But he'd made the first move. *He'd* gone out to the house, twice, and sought out conflict with Bacalov and King.

You want to try me. Don't *you?*

It was true. He'd wanted to test himself with King.

You are *me, fella.*

No, thought Lucas. *I'm not.*

At first, he'd paced the apartment, pulled back curtains, and eyed the street. But soon he willed himself to put the outcome of his raids out of his mind. Short of Louis Smalls coming forward with information, the police had no concrete way to connect him to Bacalov and King. If the law came, he'd lawyer up with Petersen. Make do the best he could.

A week passed, and the law didn't come.

WHEN HE finally reentered the world, he spent the first two days with various doctors and medical technicians. He started with Dr. Tanya Nikolic at the clinic in Manor Park. Lucas stripped to his boxer briefs and waited for her in the small white room.

"How did you sustain these injuries, Mr. Lucas?" she said, as she examined him. "You fall down in a bunch of glass again?"

He was lying on his back on a papered table. She was poking around his stomach.

"Car accident," he said.

"Okay. That's possible, I guess. But these abrasions and ecchymoses are not new."

"Ecky what?"

"Your bruises. The nature of their coloration suggests you've had them for some time."

"The accident happened over a week ago."

"You waited a week to come in?"

"I'm shy."

"Open your mouth."

"Aaah," said Lucas.

She shined a penlight there. "See your dentist. As for today, let's get some chest X-rays. We can do that here. For your shoulder I'm going to have to send you to an orthopedist. He'll probably want an MRI. You might need therapy or just a shot of cortisone. That'll be up to Dr. Abend. He's up in Wheaton."

"But I don't want to go to Wheaton," said Lucas. "I want to stay here with you."

Dr. Nikolic smirked. "Who told you to take your pants off?"

"Was that presumptuous of me?"

"Put 'em back on. A nurse will be in to take care of your X-rays. I'll talk to you in a little bit."

She returned a while later. She told him he'd cracked a rib. It hadn't punctured his lung. It would hurt for a while and it would heal itself. The ear was gnarly, and he'd have a scar, but that would heal, too. The shoulder injury was going to be stubborn.

The next day, he got an MRI at an open-air facility in Silver Spring. In Wheaton, he saw Dr. Abend, who studied the pictures and told him that they revealed inflammation and strain. The doctor administered a cortisone injection there in the office. A few hours later, back at his apartment, Lucas began to have more mobility in his shoulder as the steroid did its work.

He was beginning to feel whole again. He went to bed early that night and slept soundly till morning.

While he'd been asleep, he'd gotten a message from Tom Petersen, asking him to stop by. Lucas phoned to check that he was in, dressed, and drove downtown.

LUCAS SAT in a rickety chair in the offices at 5th and D. Petersen was in non-court attire, a mix of jeans, cowboy boots, and a flowery shirt imported from the U.K. His feet, and the boots, were up on his desk.

"Calvin Bates got twenty-five years," said Petersen. "The jury convicted him of second-degree murder."

"It's a win, in a way. Right?"

"It's better than life. I would have preferred a dismissal. You were instrumental in getting the sentence reduced. The information you dug up on Brian Dodson and his vehicle changed the tenor of the trial."

"I planted a seed of doubt."

"Yes, Mr. McCoy."

"Where's Calvin going?"

"They'll ship him to the Federal Transfer Center in Oklahoma City. Then he's headed for Leavenworth. When Lorton was open, a special Metrobus ran out there from the city every day. Inmates could visit with family and loved ones. Now, the convicts are spread out all over the country."

"Could he get parole?"

"He's eligible, sure."

"If Calvin was to come forward with information related to a homicide…"

"That might help," said Petersen, and left it at that. He was honoring the unspoken contract he had with Lucas. "I've been calling you."

"Been layin low this past week."

"What happened to you?"

"I got in a street fight," said Lucas, with a sheepish shrug.

"Looks like you caught the worst of it."

"You should see the other guy."

Petersen folded his hands on his belly. "'Some men like to hear a cannonball a roarin'.'"

"'Whiskey in the Jar,'" said Lucas. "Thin Lizzy. My dad loved their live record."

"Phil and the gang did a version of it, yes. The definitive version, I'd say." Petersen eyed Lucas curiously. "So now you're rested."

"I'm coming around."

"That's good. I just picked up a case. It could use your special talents."

"Give me a little time," said Lucas, and he got up out of his chair.

"You look different, Spero."

"I took some punches."

"I don't mean that."

"See you around, Counselor."

Petersen watched Lucas walk away.

WHEN LUCAS returned to his apartment, he got on the website Homicide Watch D.C., founded by journalist Laura Amico. Amico and her staff kept the victims of violent crimes in the public eye, no matter what part of the city they hailed from, long after the traditional media had stopped writing about them. He typed in Cherise Roberts and reread the details of her murder, the location of the Dumpster in a Fairmont Street alley where she'd been found, and looked for any updates on the investigation. No progress had been made on the case. He studied her photo, a smiling, magnetic young woman standing in front of the Cardozo High School sign, HOME OF THE CLERKS, at the top of the 13th Street hill.

At dusk, Lucas rode his bike down to Park View and swung off the saddle at Georgia and Princeton. It was his first ride since he'd been injured. He felt the bumps and potholes in his shoulder and rib cage, but it was bearable and close to fine.

He checked his watch. September had arrived and the sun was setting earlier now. If Percy Malone was still in his usual routine, this would be the time for him to leave his place for his evening walk.

Percy, dressed in a wrinkled, long-sleeved shirt, emerged unkempt and spidery from the gray row house where he stayed and walked up Princeton toward the rec center. He stopped to light his weed. Lucas kept far back and walked his bike up the hill. At Warder he looked right and saw Malone turning the corner at Otis, and Lucas followed, and watched Malone cut right into the short alley at 6th. He'd then go down the alley that ran behind Princeton, reappear at the bottom of Otis, and cross Georgia to visit his liquor store.

Lucas didn't need to see the rest. He pedaled home in the night.

He'd gotten a call from Amanda Brand, so he phoned her back. Grace Kinkaid had been released from the hospital and was convalescing in her condo in Adams Morgan. She'd asked to see him. She wanted to settle up her debt.

Lucas said he'd drop by.

THE PAINTING hung on the pale green wall in its original spot. Grace Kinkaid sat on her couch, a large glass of Chardonnay in hand, her legs folded under her. She wore green slacks and a white blouse buttoned to the neck. Through the sheer material of the shirt, bandages of some kind were visible. Grace's face was drawn; she'd lost more weight.

Lucas sat in a chair, nursing a bottle of beer. WPFW came softly from the living room stereo.

"I know you visited me in the ER," said Grace. "I appreciate it."

"I'm just happy you're coming along," said Lucas.

"After they reinflated my lung, the main danger was infection. But my doctor is pleased with my progress. There's some reconstruction to be done. I'm not afraid of surgery. I'm grateful to be alive." She cocked her head oddly. "Do you think they'll get the man who did this to me?"

"Hard to tell."

Lucas watched her empty half of her wineglass. She licked her lips and placed the glass on the table before her. She looked up at the painting on the wall and her eyes grew bright.

"My painting's back home, thanks to you, but not for long. After the buyer paid me, I persuaded him to let me keep it for a few more days. Don't you think it looks nice?"

"It does."

"Do you know why it's called *The Double?*"

"Because of the two men," said Lucas, lamely.

"But it's not a painting of two men. Not really. The dark and the light colors in the background represent a man's complex nature. It's *one* man. Don't you see?"

Lucas studied the painting.

"Yes," he said. But he wasn't sure.

"Would you like another beer?"

"No. I should be on my way."

"Let me get you your money."

She left the room and returned with an envelope thick with cash. Lucas had stood and had no intention of sitting back down. As was his custom, he counted the money to ensure that there would be no misunderstanding later on. He told her that it looked fine.

"Thanks again," she said. She hugged him carefully and kissed him on the side of his mouth.

Lucas nodded, looking into her unfocused eyes. She walked him to the door.

On the elevator ride down, he looked inside the envelope again.

Eighty thousand dollars, less ten each for Marquis and Winston, less expenses. He'd walk with fifty-five, fifty-six thousand. Tax-free.

Lucas slid the goddamned money into his jeans.

THE NEXT morning, Lucas took the guns, armor, and gear back to Bobby Waldron in Rockville. In his basement bedroom, Waldron inventoried his goods and got a look at Billy King's Colt, which Lucas had brought along.

Waldron inspected the .45. "I like this."

"It's clean," said Lucas.

"Why'd you bring it?"

"I was thinking I'd keep the Beretta."

"What's the deal?"

"How 'bout I straight trade you the Colt for the nine."

"I could do that," said Waldron. "What about the silencer?"

"I'll take that, too."

TWENTY-EIGHT

THE DAYS remained warm as summer turned to autumn, even as the nights grew markedly cooler. Lucas slept with the windows open and woke at dawn to scores of blackbirds calling from the trees of 16th Street Heights. He recommenced his prison regimen of sit-ups and push-ups, and rode his bike daily. He kayaked several times a week. He was busy with his rehabilitation and flush with money. He didn't need to work, but he was restless.

He twice phoned Detective Paul Strong, of Homicide and Violent Crimes, to get an update on the investigation of the Grace Kinkaid assault. The first time, Strong reminded Lucas that he was not police, and added that only immediate family could expect to get the information he was looking for. The second time Lucas called, Strong told him to piss up a rope, then informed him that the perpetrator, most likely, would never be found. Lucas told himself that he was merely curious. He had simply wanted to know the suspect's name.

One night he rode his bike down to Park View and followed Percy Malone once again as he made the loop from home to liquor store and back. Lucas had now committed Malone's route to memory. He knew why he was tailing him and where this was headed.

ONE DAY, at the end of the month, he got a call from Charlotte Rivers. She apologized for being out of touch for so long, and wondered if he would like to meet her for a drink.

"Just a drink," she said, sensing his hesitation on the other end of the line. "Tonight, at our usual spot. I'd like to see you again."

"One last time?"

"We should talk face-to-face."

"I don't know if I can make it," said Lucas.

"I'll be at the bar," she said. "Try to come."

Lucas told himself he shouldn't meet her, that it was better not to. But as the day went on, and he thought of her more and more, he knew that he would. It wasn't just curiosity. She was still in his head.

Around 6:30, he dropped off his Jeep at the door of the boutique hotel, four blocks north of the White House, and went inside. Walked the checkerboard marble floor of the hall that led to the bar, and found her there, seated at the turn, on a high-backed stool. She was wearing the orange dress with the low neckline that she'd worn the first night they'd met, and she was every bit as lovely. He kissed her cheek and took the empty seat beside her.

"Would you like some of this?" she said, pointing to the bottle of Barolo on the bar. "It's nice."

"You know, I'm not much of a wine man, to tell you the truth. I'd rather have a beer."

The quiet, attentive bartender heard this, asked Lucas for his preference, and returned with something in a green bottle. Lucas had a pull as Charlotte looked him over. He was healed, more or less, but not entirely. His ear was scabbed, and the scratch marks on his forehead and nose, where the blood flowed less freely, still faintly showed.

"You've been in a fight," she said.

"I had a little trouble," said Lucas. "But not too much." He gave her a reassuring smile and revealed the gap in his row of incisors.

Her eyes flickered. "Spero, what happened to you?"

"It's fine. I just haven't got around to the dentist yet."

"You stopped phoning me. Were you in the hospital or something?"

"I stopped because you weren't calling me back."

"I apologize for that. I do."

"I figured you were sending me a message. I took the hint and stepped back."

"It wasn't that, exactly."

"*What* was it?"

"I needed some time away from you."

"Because, what, we weren't getting along?"

"We got along fine."

"I don't recall any complaints."

"We were perfect," said Charlotte, and she touched his arm. He drew it back.

"Tell me," said Lucas.

Charlotte took a sip of wine and set the glass on the bar. "You're a little intense."

"I know it."

"You don't give up much."

"That's true."

"When we started seeing each other, I couldn't foresee that it was going to get as deep as it did. In the beginning, I was looking for a break from my routine, not more complication. After a while, you were all I thought about. I thought about you at work, I thought about you when I was with my husband… You were taking up too much space in my head. What was happening between us scared me."

"And you felt you had to end it. Why didn't you talk to me about it?"

"I didn't know how you'd react."

"*Shit,*" said Lucas.

"No, listen. You want me to be honest with you, so let me say it."

"Go ahead."

"My husband is a steady guy. Maddeningly so. I told you this from day one. But with that came a stability I could rely on. I started to think, I should meet him halfway. Initiate more intimacy instead of just waiting for him to make a move. Make him go out on dates, or book weekends out of town. Talk to him more. Try to recapture what we had when we first met. *Try.* Because I wasn't going to leave him."

"Leave him for me, you mean."

"For anyone. I didn't mislead you about that."

"No, you didn't."

"Truthfully, I never stopped caring for him. And if I was going to stay with him, I knew I was in for a long world of hurt and frustration if I just allowed things to stay the way they were."

"So my intensity made you appreciate your husband's steady personality. Is that it? You're saying being with me drove you back to him?"

"In a way. You were a bridge."

"Glad to be of service."

"Please, don't be that way."

"Charlotte, what's going on? For real."

"My husband and I are taking small steps. That's all I know for now. As for you and me…" She wrapped her fingers around his biceps and this time he let her. "Spero, I'm sorry."

In his movie, he saw her asking him if he'd like to go up to her room, one last time. He'd consider it, because she was beautiful, and he knew how it would be between them, and he loved her. She'd ask, and he'd turn her down. *He'd* be the one to drive the final nail in, not her. Walk from the bar unscathed, with his head up.

But Charlotte didn't ask him. Instead, she told him that she needed to get home. She reached for her wallet, but he stopped her and paid the tab in cash.

Out by the valet stand, waiting for his Jeep, he looked down at the palm of his hand. The wormy, crescent-shaped mark, pale red and pronounced, had settled into the shape of a C.

Lucas laughed.

C for Charlotte. He'd wear her scar for the rest of his life.

ONE EVENING in October, as the sun began to set, Lucas dressed in black shorts, a black T-shirt, and bike shoes, and put some items into a backpack. His face was grim as he worked.

Lucas had checked D.C. Homicide Watch daily to see if

there had been any movement on the Cherise Roberts case. There had been none.

On three occasions, Lucas had surveilled Percy Malone, who always left his apartment at the same time for his walk and liquor store run. Lucas had waited weeks for nightfall to coincide with Percy's habitual behavior. In August, when Lucas had first followed him, there had still been daylight as Percy had stepped out his front door. Now Percy left at night.

There was no internal debate. Lucas put his bike on his shoulder and carried it downstairs. With his bag slung over his back, he pedaled down to Park View in the gathering dark.

PERCY MALONE stepped out of his apartment at the usual time. He stood on his stoop and eyed the street like a sick, hungry animal emerging from the woods. Lucas was at the bottom of Princeton Place, leaning on his bike. He watched Percy go east on foot toward Warder. He watched him stop to light his weed, and then he waited as the spidery man moved on. Percy was walking his smoke.

Lucas followed, granny-gearing up the hill. At Princeton and Warder he saw Malone turn right past the rec center, onto Otis. Lucas took his daypack off and from it removed his lead-filled sap, wrapped in black electrician's tape. He slung the pack over his shoulder and held the sap loosely in his right hand. He got back on his saddle and pedaled to Otis, where he cut right and went down to 6th. There he made another right into the short stretch of alley. It was full dark.

Lucas waited. Percy Malone would now be walking south on the alley that ran behind Princeton. Lucas heard the deep bark of a large dog coming from a yard. He proceeded to ride. He took the short stretch and turned left at Princeton's alley. He coasted now and let his momentum take him down the hill. Percy was halfway down the alley, walking. He turned his head at the sound of Lucas's bike, turned his head back, and stepped slightly to the right to let the whiteboy biker pass, and as the bike came alongside him, its rider swung the sap violently. It made a wet sound as it connected to the back of Percy's head. Percy fell forward, unconscious on his way to the alley floor. The dog, a dark figure moving about excitedly in a nearby yard, continued to bark, but no one came outside.

Lucas leaned his bike against a chain-link fence and slid the sap into his shorts. From his pack, he quickly removed his Berretta, the silencer screwed into its threaded barrel. He released the safety, chambered a round, and stood over Percy, who was lying facedown. His tightly curled hair was matted with blood. A lit joint was lying beside him, its ember glowing orange.

Lucas crouched down and rolled Percy over on his back. He was breathing through his open mouth. Lucas slipped the suppressor into Percy's mouth and put his finger inside the trigger guard of the gun.

Lucas eyed him clinically.

The gas jolt would bug his eyes. A little barrel-smoke would curl out of his mouth. Funny. It would look like Percy was smoking a cigarette.

You are *me, fella.*

Lucas's finger slipped on the trigger. His hand felt slick. He was dizzy. He stood up. There was sweat on his forehead and he wiped it off.

Lucas put the gun in his daypack and walked to his bike. He swung onto its saddle and rode uptown.

IN HIS apartment he had a shower, then took a seat in his favorite chair. Next to the chair sat a lamp and a small side table that held books. The Berretta and its silencer lay there, atop a thick biography. Lucas intended to unload and disassemble the weapon, and put it back in the toolbox under the false floor of his closet. But there was something he needed to do first.

He phoned Tim McCarthy, his contact at the MPD. He got a recording, left a message, and waited for Tim to return his call. He didn't have to wait long.

"What's going on, Marine?"

"I've got something for you, Tim. It's a homicide case. The Cherise Roberts murder."

"You mentioned that one before."

"I know you're IA. It's not your department, but I have no one else to call."

"Whatever you give me, I'll pass it along."

"A guy named Percy Malone killed Cherise. In effect, he was her pimp. Percy confessed to a fellow named Josh Brown when both of them were incarcerated in the D.C. Jail. Brown's still in. Percy's out on the street."

"A jailhouse confession."

"Hear me out."

"What's Brown in for?"

"Manslaughter."

"Lovely."

"He'll testify. A guy named Calvin Bates will back him up."

"That's all you got?"

"The killer left semen in Cherise's rectum and on her face. You pick up Percy and DNA him, you're gonna get a match."

"Spell all those names for me."

Lucas did it, and gave up Malone's address.

"I'll let you know if this pans out."

"It will."

"You doin all right?" said McCarthy.

Lucas said, "I'm fine."

He ended the call.

He sat in his chair and thought of the dead. He looked at the gun lying on the table beside him. He picked up the gun and held it in his hand. He pulled back on the receiver and eased a round into its chamber. He turned the gun in the light.

I've killed. I'll kill again.

To what end? What good has it done?

Lucas stared at the gun.

I could stop this now.

"Fuck it," he said. He put the gun back on the table.

Lucas got up, walked into the kitchen, and opened the refrigerator door. He grabbed a Stella and uncapped it. Standing in the dim light of a forty-watt bulb, he drank the shoulders off the bottle. The beer was good.

I'm all right, thought Lucas.

I'm fine.

ACKNOWLEDGMENTS

This novel references and honors the work of John D. MacDonald, Charles Willeford, and Don Carpenter. Those authors, and many others, were influential in the creation of Spero Lucas and *The Double*. Many thanks to Jon Norris, Joe Aronstamn, Andy Moursund, and Natalie Hopkinson for their help during the research phase. Thanks go out as well to Michael Pietsch, Marlena Bittner, Tracy Williams, Betsy Uhrig, Keith Hayes, Heather Fain, Karen Torres, and all at Little, Brown. My editor and friend, Reagan Arthur, worked this into shape. I'm blessed to have her on my side. Sloan Harris, gentleman lit agent, raconteur, and sportsman, did what he does best. Alicia Gordon and Greg Hodes represented on the film and TV side. Finally, my sincere thanks to the readers. Long live traditional publishing, long live books.

READING GROUP GUIDE

THE
DOUBLE

BY

GEORGE
PELECANOS

An online version of this Reading Group Guide is
available at littlebrown.com.

A CONVERSATION WITH GEORGE PELECANOS

What was your inspiration for The Double?

There is a painting, *Double Portrait,* by the American impressionist Minerva Chapman, that has been hanging on a wall in my house for many years. It depicts two men standing beside each other against slightly different backgrounds. To me, it represents the dual nature of one man. I have always been fascinated by the painting and wanted to write about it. In *The Double,* Spero Lucas attempts to retrieve a painting stolen by a sexual predator named Billy King. King represents the dark side of Spero Lucas. King is his doppelgänger, his double. So there you go. It all dovetails. In fact, the book practically wrote itself. Don't tell my editor.

What, if anything, does Spero Lucas have in common with George Pelecanos?

Like Lucas, I like the physical side of life and the natural world. I'm out on my bike nearly every day and frequently out on the water in my kayak. My daily driver is a black-over-black, old-school Jeep Cherokee with the Inline 6, which I use for my street research. Lucas drives the same vehicle for the same purpose. I'm about twenty-five years older than Lucas. So the similarities end there.

*Billy King is an unusual and disturbing villain, with his "marina rat"
vibe and his habit of preying on older women. How did the idea for
Billy come to you?*

The Spero Lucas setup (a recovery expert who takes a per-
centage of what he retrieves) is a direct nod to the central idea
of John D. MacDonald's Travis McGee series. The first crime
novel I ever read was MacDonald's *The Deep Blue Good-by,* and I
named one of my dogs Travis, even though she was a bitch. Obviously, the character had a big influence on me. Billy King is
a direct descendant of Junior Allen, the infamous antagonist of
The Deep Blue Good-by. The wharf-rat thing is a nod to McGee
and Allen. Both of them were into boats. You see guys like Billy
King in beach towns and marinas, hanging around past their
prime, hustling older women and free drinks. He's not a good
guy. But I have empathy for him. Monsters are created.

*Winston Dupree says at one point, "A man only feels like a man when
he gets a paycheck." What did you do for paychecks before you became a
writer? At what point did you commit to writing as your full-time job?*

I grew up working in my father's diner, starting at the age of
eleven. I then worked in various dining rooms, kitchens, bars,
and retail sales floors, hawking stereos, appliances, and ladies'
shoes. Worked construction, drove a truck, managed a chain of
appliance stores. Ran a film production and distribution outfit
here in D.C. I was forty-two when I went out on my own as a
full-time writer. At that point I had published eight novels. So
I was working two jobs for many years. But I didn't mind it at
all. It's a blessing to have work.

Who is your favorite author? Why?

That's difficult to answer. I'm a pretty voracious reader. Who do I exclude? I reread Elmore Leonard frequently to remind myself how it's done, but I don't read a whole lot of crime fiction these days, because I'm catching up on all the other kinds of books I didn't read in my youth. I go on jags. For example, I discovered James Salter last year and have been steadily enjoying his incredible body of work. Lately, I've also been into the literature of veterans who've come out of the Middle East wars. *Redeployment* by Phil Klay was stunning, as was *The Yellow Birds* by Kevin Powers. I read *The New Yorker* cover to cover each week and am always amazed at the consistent quality of the writing. I was recently published in that magazine, which was on my "list" (I was also published in *Playboy*, which was on the same list). Every morning I walk out to my driveway and pick up my *Washington Post*, which I have been reading for almost fifty years. The morning newspaper is like a miracle to me. I still don't know how they do it.

What's a typical writing day schedule like for you? Can you share with us any routines or rituals that help you through the writing process?

I front-load all of my research so that when I'm ready to begin a book, I have no excuse for leaving the house. When working on a novel, I typically write two shifts a day, seven days a week. The continuity is important to me because I don't outline and have to stay in the zone. In between shifts I do something physical to blow the cobwebs out of my head. At night I rewrite what I did in the morning so I'm ready to move forward the next day. It's how I've always done it, and it works for me.

You write such believable and dynamic dialogue. How did you develop your skill for it, and how do you stay current with slang?

I've been into the poetry of language my entire life. Even when I was a kid riding the D.C. Transit buses down Georgia Avenue to the F Street line, I loved listening to people talk. Being a bartender and shoe salesman didn't hurt either. Short answer: I was interested and I had an ear for it. As for the slang, here's a secret: Sometimes I make it up. That's what fiction writers do. They make stuff up.

How much research was required for The Double, *and how did you conduct it?*

For many years, and many books, I've gone along on jobs with a private investigator who works criminal cases, and gathers evidence, for defense attorneys here in D.C. I have sources in the police department, in the underworld, and in local jails and prisons. And I get out there by myself and just try to figure out what's going on. You can fake this, but I don't want to. The research and discovery is half the fun.

You rarely miss an opportunity to note what clothes a character is wearing. What's your attire of choice on a typical workday?

501 Levi's, a wife-beater, and a pair of Nike Pegasus or Doc Martens on my feet.

Spero often remembers his father, Van, when he hears songs Van liked. What music did your father listen to? And what are you listening to these days?

When I was very young my father worked in a soul-food diner on 14th Street. He'd often come home with records that I'm pretty sure were bought on the black market. So we had a lot of jazz circa the fifties and sixties, Miles Davis on the Prestige label, like that. My dad loved Sinatra and listened to him in our house on the weekends. We still have my father's collection of Sinatra on vinyl, the original Columbia recordings. My tastes are all over the place. Anthony Hamilton and the Stax/Volt catalog for soul, Galactic for funk, DBT and the Hold Steady for rock, Massive Attack and the xx for background, Morricone and Lalo Schifrin, Lee "Scratch" Perry, Gregory Isaacs…I like the quiet country songs of Garrett Hedlund and Ashley Monroe. Nick Cave. Silver Jews. Barry White. New Orleans rock and roll from the sixties, surf guitar instrumentals from the same period. Willy Vlautin's latest record, *Colfax*, is pretty beautiful. So is a guitar solo by J Mascis or Nels Cline. Local heroes Fugazi, Nation of Ulysses, Chuck Brown, the Nighthawks, and Backyard Band…Their music is all good.

Spero covers a lot of ground on his Greg LeMond. What kind of bike do you have and what's your favorite route?

I own a black Greg LeMond road bike, too. I also have a Trek that I use off-road. Don't worry, I don't wear the outfits. I just like to ride. My Jeep has a big cargo area, so I can throw my bike back there and go anywhere. I do Sligo Creek Park every day. There's a twenty-six-mile ride out to Lake Artemesia that I hit when I'm ambitious, and my weekend route takes me down to Carter Barron Amphitheatre in Rock Creek Park, where I once saw Funkadelic and the Manhattans on the same bill.

What's next for you? For Spero?

I have a new novella called *The Martini Shot,* which will be published in a single volume along with my short stories in January of 2015. This year I am focusing on television and film. I've got a couple of pilots in development, have done some script doctoring, and am hoping to produce a feature film in the fall based on one of my early books. I'm thinking about the next Spero Lucas novel. But don't tell my editor.

QUESTIONS AND TOPICS FOR DISCUSSION

1. Tom Petersen says, "Spero, sometimes you work too hard at being an aw-shucks kind of guy." When else do we see Spero working to appear as a certain kind of person, and how does it serve him? Is he ever truly himself, and if so, when?

2. Why do you think Spero takes the job to retrieve *The Double* for Grace Kinkaid? Is it just for the money, or are there other motives and sympathies at work here? What details do you notice about their first meeting?

3. Dr. Olivia O'Leary points out that Spero seems to have adjusted to civilian life much better than many of his fellow veterans. What's his secret? Do you ever see the cracks showing? And why do you think he dismisses the idea of therapy?

4. Why does Spero ask Marquis and Winston, both war-injured veterans, to help him on the Grace Kinkaid job? Is his enlisting of his friends charitable, strategic, manipulative, or all of the above?

5. "Do I get to be the good guy or the bad guy?" Dupree asks Spero at one point. Discuss the relationship between

"good" and "bad" in this novel. Is anyone completely in-nocent? Are any of the characters irredeemable or beyond sympathy? How and where do you draw the line between moral and immoral—or do we draw it at all?

6. After the two men scope out Billy King's house for the first time, Spero decides to leave Dupree out of the rest of the job, observing that his friend had left his "warrior nature" behind in Iraq. How does Spero make this call? And based on what evidence? Do you agree with him?

7. Washington, D.C., emerges vividly in this novel, almost as though the city itself were a character. What strikes you as distinctive in Pelecanos's D.C.? Could Spero Lucas just as easily be a creature of New York or Los Angeles? Why or why not?

8. Pelecanos rarely introduces a character without pausing to describe his or her clothes—in fact the novel opens with a description of a man's outfit. What do you make of this focus on fashion? What do clothes (along with ac-cessories, tattoos, and other physical features) tell you about the characters, about Spero, about the world of the novel?

9. Why do you think Pelecanos chose to give the novel the same title as the painting that the characters are seeking? Does it have a greater significance than the painting?

10. Do you think Spero does right in leaving Percy Malone to the professionals rather than dealing with the killer himself? Why do you think he makes this choice?

11. Does Spero change over the course of the novel? If so, how? Are the changes you see in him permanent? Why, or why not?

ABOUT THE AUTHOR

George Pelecanos is the author of several highly praised and bestselling novels, including *The Cut, What It Was, The Way Home, The Turnaround,* and *The Night Gardener.* He is also an independent-film producer, an essayist, and the recipient of numerous international writing awards. He was a producer and Emmy-nominated writer for *The Wire* and currently writes for the acclaimed HBO series *Treme.*

... AND *THE MARTINI SHOT*

Gritty, sexy, fast-paced, and humane, this collection of short stories delves deeper inside the world of some of Pelecanos's most popular characters while introducing new stories he has yet to tell.

Following is an excerpt from the opening pages of *The Martini Shot,* the title novella, which takes readers behind the scenes of a cable TV cop show where the writer gets caught up in a drama more real than anything in his script.

I WAS UP in my suite in a residence hotel, where the production housed out-of-town talent and department heads, when I heard a knock on my door. It was late, around two in the morning, but we had wrapped less than an hour earlier, and crew kept different hours than straights. Few of us went to sleep as soon as we got home. We had to have a snack, or a couple of drinks, or some smoke, a little television, sex if we could get it. Anything to make us feel normal at the end of the day. Anything that would make us feel that we led normal lives.

I looked through the peephole. Annette was standing out in the carpeted hall. She'd called me minutes earlier on the house phone and asked if I wanted some company. I was expecting her, but still, I liked to watch her out there, waiting for me to open the door. It made my pulse run. Both of us had been single for a long while, but our relationship was private.

I let Annette in and closed the door.

"Hi," she said, her mouth curved up in a sweet smile. She stepped out of her sandals.

"Hi."

I kissed her soft lips, held her, and stroked her bare arms. She was warm to the touch. She wore tailored velour sweats and a cut-off T, and her copper-and-brown hair was up and back in a soft band. She was in her early forties, a large-featured woman with green eyes. She was curvy, big-breasted, thick in the thighs, and generously built in back. She was olive-skinned and exotic, a Mediterranean girl built like a black woman. She was exactly what I like.

"Good day?" she said.

"Fourteen hours. The director shot too much stuff we'll never use. Anyway, we got the pages. You?"

"A little rough." It was all she needed to say. I knew she was under the gun. "I could use a glass of wine."

I opened a bottle of Rodney Strong, a good everyday merlot that Annette liked, poured it into two short, hotel-issue glasses, and took it over to the living room couch, where we had a seat. I lit a couple of candles in glass and programmed my phone to play some tunes through a Bluetooth speaker I took from job to job. The phone-and-speaker arrangement was my portable stereo, similar to the portable push-up stands I traveled with, the contents of my shaving kit, my fold-up Beats, my Swiss Army knife. Everything portable. I owned a condo in a Mid-Atlantic city, but I lived in hotels.

Annette and I drank wine and talked about our day. We laughed about the bosses, though she was a department head, and technically I was management, too. Typically, I was on set call to wrap, and she popped in at various locations before rehearsal, to check out the work of her crew. Then she'd go off to prep the next episode. Seeing her arrive on set wearing one of her many cool, understated outfits was always the highlight of my day. Hats were her trademark. She walked like a cat. She was smart and talented, a true artist. Annette was our art director and she had style.

"You mind if I take this off?" she said, her hands going up under her shirt. "It's too tight."

"I like tight things."

"Stop."

She unfastened her bra, produced it like a magician, and dropped it on the carpet beside the couch.

"Don't forget this." I took liberties and pulled her T-shirt up over her head.

"You too, buster."

"Don't call me Buster. That's a name for a dog."

"Come on."

I removed my shirt. We embraced and kissed, both of us naked above the waist, skin to skin. I caressed her and squeezed one of her dark nipples, rolling it between my thumb and forefinger until it was a pebble.

Our tongues mingled. I felt a catch in her breath and heard her moan. She gently pushed me away and chuckled.

"Who's this?" she said, nodding at my speaker.

"The new XX," I said, and shrugged sheepishly. "Not very original of me, I know."

"Wine, candles, and make-out music."

"I'm not as creative as you."

"It's perfect."

We kissed some more and had a few laughs. While we talked, I slid my hand beneath her sweats, pushed the crotch of her damp lace panties aside, slipped my longest finger inside her, and stroked her clit. It got warm in the room. She lay back on the couch and arched her back and I peeled off her pants and thong. Now she was nude. I stripped down to my boxer briefs and crouched over her. I let her pull me free because I knew she liked to. She stroked my pole and took off my briefs, and I got between her and spread her muscular thighs with my knees and rubbed myself against her until she was wet as a waterslide, and then I split her. We fucked for a while, slow and deep, with my feet against the scrolled arm of the couch for leverage. Neither of us allowed ourselves to come. It was too good to end.

"Let's go to my bed," I said. We were pretty sweaty by then. I brought the candles, the speaker, and my phone with me. Annette followed with the glasses and the bottle of wine. Entering my bedroom, I switched the music over to an Anthony Hamilton mix and let that ride. Anthony was our favorite, spiritual and secular, authentic and sublime.

My room was large, with a four-poster bed and floor-to-ceiling windows that gave a view of the street below and the city skyline. Because it was on the top floor of the hotel, and because there were no nearby buildings as high as mine, it was completely private. Moonlight and candlelight are a heady aphrodisiac, and I kept the curtains open at all times.

I pulled her to me. I took her band off and her hair fell free about her shoulders. I cupped my hand around the back of her neck and we made out standing beside my bed. It felt good to both of us, pressed together, her body lush, soft, and hot against mine. She was a good kisser; our mouths fit.

She got onto the bed, atop the blankets, and I spread her out. I held her hands and raised them above her, and I kissed her. I kissed her chest and her inner thighs and everywhere. Her pussy was clean, with a five o'clock shadow and just a hint of smell. I penetrated her with my thumb while I licked and kissed and pressed my tongue into her swollen button. She talked to me and told me what to do. "There," she said, and "Yeah," and she said my name, and then her thighs tensed and shuddered. She spasmed and pushed my head away. I lay back and left her alone to enjoy her last rippling throes. But I only left her for a minute. She was ripe, and I pulled her to the edge of the mattress and stood beside the bed and spread her legs. I fucked her like that, me looking down and watching myself, thick, plunging into her velvet, standing on the carpet with great purchase, her lying there, her knees bent, taking me in. I turned her face to lick inside her ear and kiss her neck, and then her mouth, and she said, "God," and said it louder, and I controlled it, and she bucked as she came, this time harder than the last.

When her heart had slowed down, I withdrew from her and handed her a short glass. I took mine off the dresser and both of us drank some wine.

"Now you," she said.

I lay on my back and Annette put a pillow under my head. She spread my legs as I had done for her before, and got between me and played with my dick. She knocked the head of it against the nipples of her pendulous breasts and hit it on her tongue like a hammer to a bell.

"I love your cock," she said.

"It loves *you*."

"What do you want me to do?"

"Touch my ass."

She tickled my anus as she licked my balls and shaft, and slathered her tongue on my helmet. I laced my fingers through her hair and closed my eyes.

"Go," I said.

I stopped breathing and, like her, invoked a higher power. My orgasm was eye-popping as I blew a hot load into her mouth. It seemed to last forever, and she took it all.

"Thank you," I said, my hand still in her hair. I must have been twisting it. It was a mess.

"My pleasure."

"Sorry. I know that it was a lot. It felt like a lot."

"You could help me out and empty that thing once in a while."

"I don't care to spill my seed. I like to save it all for you."

She moved up and came beside and rested her head on my chest. It was quiet now, with just the soul music playing in the room. She blinked slowly and shut her eyes, and I listened and waited for her breathing to slow down. Soon, with each of her inhales, I heard a small click. That was the sound of her in sleep. In the candlelight, I watched her.

I checked my wristwatch. It was nearly four a.m. We had a short turnaround, a nine o'clock call, which meant I had to be up at eight. Four hours of sleep for both of us, but that was workable, and not unusual. It was late in the shoot and all of us were running on fumes.

A little while later, I touched her shoulder and said, "Annette." Her eyes fluttered open. I hated to rouse her, but I knew she liked to wake up in her own bed.

"Hey," she said.

"Hey."

She looked up at me without raising her head. The moon had dropped and its light came full into the room and it was in her eyes.

"That was nice," she said.

"Yes."

"I love you, Vic."

I made no comment. I studied her face, a mix of affection and disappointment, and felt a rush of emotion. When production wrapped we'd go our separate ways. "If it happened on location, it didn't happen." That's what was said in our line of work. Maybe it would be like that with me and Annette, too. She'd move on, and so would I. But I knew that she'd always be deep in my head.

OUR DRIVER, a teamster named Louise, picked us up in a white Ford window van at 8:15. There were five of us standing on the sidewalk as she pulled to the curb. This episode's director, Alan Lomax, out of LA; our DP, a Danish cinematographer, Eigil, now spelled Eagle for marketing purposes; the camera operator, Van "Go" Cummings, from Venice, California; the gaffer, Skylar Branson, a young Texan who ran the electric crew; and me, Victor Ohanian, writer-producer. We got into the van.

As was decorum, the director rode in the shotgun bucket beside Louise, a religious woman with kinky blond hair. Van plugged his iPhone into the auxiliary jack of the stereo and programmed some Laurel Canyon singer-songwriter jive into the system. The deal was, Van commandeered the music in the mornings, Skylar (college radio) had the middle of the day, Eagle (jazz) took the post-lunch DJ spot, and I (all over the place) had the ride home. The director listened to whatever we played and was at our mercy.

Skylar handed me the latest *New Yorker*. When he was finished with magazines and novels, he passed them on to me.

He was wearing a STIHL chainsaw ball cap and a trumpeter's triangle below his lower lip. He was improbably young for a department head, and very bright. He also sold marijuana to the crew. His girlfriend, Laura, a wardrobe assistant, was in on it, too. It wasn't as if he needed the money. He was a pothead, and felt that he was selling happiness to his friends.

"Thanks, buddy." I slid the magazine into my book bag.

"My pleasure," he said.

There was no hint of pleasure on his face. He was troubled about something. I knew him well enough to see it. But it was his business, and I didn't push it.

Skylar was a good soul. We'd been friends since the first day of production, though I was practically old enough to be his wayward uncle. I had his back and he had mine.

"You all right?"

"Fine," he said. "I just need to work."

We'd been at it for six months. The shoot was a cop drama for one of the cable networks, based in a southern port city, in a state that offered significant tax credits to film productions. It was a good long gig. It paid enough to set most of us up for the year. When the money ran out, we'd get on something else. That was what we did.

Our morning ride to the first location was usually quiet. Some read the *USA Today* provided by the hotel, others made phone calls to family. Eagle, Van, and Skylar often discussed the first shot and how it would be lit. Or they discussed their golf game. If any of them or the director had a question about the content or tone of the day's scenes, I tried to answer it. It was business, but not as defined by the straight world. We were playing with many million dollars of studio money, but we dressed as we wanted to and wore our hair and facial hair as we desired. We thought of ourselves as handsomely compensated rebels. No conventions, no uniforms.

I studied the landscape as we made our way across town. Often, the crew sees more of a city than the locals do, because we have access and security. The low-end neighborhoods, the seedier bars, rat- and needle-infested alleys, the mayor's office, police stations, prison and jails, private mansions, back-of-the-house kitchens, the homeless camps under the freeways. I was the curious type, so that aspect of the job suited me well.

As we neared our destination, we glanced at our call sheets, which detailed our daily shooting schedule. The director was on his cell, talking to his daughter and telling her to have a good day at school. It was six a.m. in Los Angeles and she had just woken up.

"Three moves today," said Eagle, in his heavy Scandi accent. It sounded like "moofs." He was tall and lean, with long flowing hair, and he was bearded. He looked like a showered Viking.

"Four scenes," said Van, youthful in his fifties, now on his third marriage. Van was a connoisseur of women and a bit of a philosopher. He sometimes entertained us with his ruminations on romance and the fleeting aspect of life.

"A lot of dialogue in scene thirty-eight," I said. "Two pages, four people at table. And then the secretary comes in from the B-G and drops the file on the table. She's got a line, too. We'll have to cover that."

"Why'd you give her a line?" said Van playfully.

I'd cast the secretary, a young would-be actress, as a day

player after seeing her audition. I was just giving her a break. She'd get an extra eight hundred bucks for that one line, and residuals. Maybe someone would notice her and she'd get more work. Plus, she was hot as balls. Van knew me well.

"Lots of coverage, is all I'm saying."

"It'll be fine," said the director, turning his head to us in the back rows of bench seats, interrupting his call to his kid. Lomax was wearing a black Patagonia vest under a black Marmot shell, Merrell shoes. He was overdressed for the weather, a walking billboard for REI. "I storyboarded it and I know what I need. Two hours, tops."

He was telling us that he was prepared, that the scene wouldn't take long, and that he wouldn't overshoot. But we knew Lomax's MO. He leaned toward artsy, with shots that made no sense in terms of POV, angles and footage we'd never use when it came time to cut. The secretary's arrival, easily accomplished by a walk into frame, would be complicated by his insistence on bringing her in with a dolly shot, which meant laying down track and more lighting, which meant time. We'd get behind, and the rest of the day we'd be playing catch-up, and consequently the last scene or two would suffer. We'd worked with Lomax before. He made the days longer than they had to be, but he was all right.

Louise dropped Eagle off at catering, so he could get his usual hearty breakfast, and drove the rest of us to the location. The company trucks were parked on a street in the business district of town, and crew members were milling about, waiting for the AD to call out that we were "in." First up was a scene in a bank (INT: BANK, DOWNTOWN—DAY), where our protagonist would interview some board members about the death of a teller, whose body had been found in the teaser, a scene we had yet to get in the can. We rarely shot in sequence.

Louise told us to have a blessed day as we exited the van. The lead set PA, waiting on the sidewalk, handed me my sides, which were the day's scenes, complete with dialogue, collated into one stapled set of pages. I folded the sides and slipped them into the back pocket of my Levi's, and asked the PA to order me a breakfast burrito and a coffee from catering.

"You got it, sir," he said.

I thanked him and said good morning to crew as I walked down the street toward the bank.

This was my favorite time of the day. Stepping out of the van in the morning and walking onto a set among a hundred other crew members gathering in one place to build something together gave me a feeling of great anticipation and promise. Costumers, hair and makeup people, props, set dressers, scenic, light and camera crew, sound recordists, all of these people, in their own way, were artists. Unlike a painting, signed by one person, or a book, with one author's name on its spine, the tail credits on a movie or television show carried hundreds of signatures. I *liked* that. I had no illusions that what I did as a television writer had weight or permanence. But, because of my comrades, I was proud to have my name on that scroll.

Inside the bank, the first AD called for a private rehearsal as the actors arrived on set. Eagle had come in with his breakfast and was shoveling it down. The lead actor, supporting actors, day players, and director stood in a circle and read their lines.

I stood nearby with Lillie, the script supervisor out of New York, wearing New York black. She was by necessity a hyper, detail-oriented person who had one of the most demanding and important jobs in the production. Lillie watched every take in the monitors for continuity and matching issues; she was a pain in the ass, in a good way.

As the actors rehearsed the lines, I looked for trouble spots. Often the written word seems fine on the page but when spoken can lose its luster. Occasionally, what I thought was a great scene didn't work in practice, and I was there to adjust lines. The actor might not like something I'd written, and I had the authority to change the words if I felt the objection was warranted, or stand my ground if it was not. An actor could misinterpret my writing and not do it justice, and an actor could also elevate what I'd done. Sometimes the words or sentences were just too much of a mouthful, or there was a redundancy I had not seen before, and I'd subtract. All of this came out on set.

"Scene," said Lomax, when the actors were done. He then blocked the action, putting the actors through their movements and stops. We were to shoot this one with two cameras, A and B. During the second rehearsal, the B camera assistant laid down the actors' marks with pieces of colored tape. Lomax discussed the various shots with Eagle and Van, Skylar standing close by. Master, medium shot, then the singles, tighter, tighter, tighter, three sizes. Lomax expressed his desire to bring the secretary in with a dolly shot. Van wiggled his eyebrows at Eagle: *I knew it.*

"Crew has the set," said the first AD.

The actors went to their trailers as the crew flooded the

set and prepped the first shot. Stand-ins took the marks of the actors so that they could be properly lit. It would be about forty-five minutes before the cameras rolled. My breakfast arrived and I ate it while Brandon, the on-set prop master, set up the cast chairs around the monitors, an arrangement called Video Village. I had my own chair with my name printed on the canvas backing, as well as the name of the series: *Tanner's Team*.

The show was a serialized cop drama. It detailed the exploits of an elite homicide squad headed by a handsome middle-aged lieutenant named Jeremiah Tanner, a semi-clairvoyant father figure whose detectives, his children in effect (Tanner's Team), consisted of various attractive, youngish men and women, a mix of blacks (but not *too* many blacks), whites, and Hispanics, cast to hit all the demographic buttons. The lead was Brad Slaughter, a former film actor who had briefly flirted with cinema stardom and was now highly compensated for his work on the small screen. His co-lead was Meaghan O'Toole, an actress who had come from the stage originally and had won an Emmy for her work in an HBO original. She played McKenzie Hart, the "hard-charging" assistant district attorney who prosecuted the criminals the squad arrested. Mainly, to the actress's chagrin, she was written as the love interest for the lieutenant.

As we neared the start of the first shot, the executive producers arrived and immediately the tenor of the crew changed. People stood straighter and worked faster. There was less joking around and grab-assing than there was when I was in charge of the set. The big guns were in the house.

Bruce Kaplan was the show's creator, head writer, and show

runner. His partner was Ellen Stern. Ellen was not a writer but rather a general of sorts who hired and fired crew, kept the trains running on time, negotiated with the vendors, and brought the show in on budget. They complemented each other and made a good, efficient team. The credits listed five executive producers, but Bruce and Ellen were the only two who actually worked on the day-to-day of the production. To-day they looked very tired, with black circles under their eyes, ill-fitting clothing, and uncombed hair. The hours and craft services were a killer for everyone, and they had the added pressure of bringing the show in on budget and taking the calls of the cable execs.

I had no desire to do or learn Ellen's job, and no ambition to become an EP, so there was little friction between us. I had a decent relationship with both of them, though I was "just" a writer-producer and was kept out of the loop on major deci-sions. As for Bruce, he was respectful to the writing team but tended to rewrite our scripts in a rather mercenary fashion. I was good with that, for the most part; I knew that there had to be one voice for the show and uniformity from episode to episode. But my ego was such that I felt he cut some of my best stuff at random. On the other hand, he sometimes made my writing better, and unlike other show runners who put their name on scripts they reworked, he always gave me sole credit. After a while I learned to beat the game and began to write in Bruce's voice rather than my own. It was another thing I'd given up. I was a long way from my youth, when I'd wandered the stacks of the county libraries and dreamed of someday be-ing a published novelist. I *had* become a writer, in a manner of speaking. But mainly I was a well-paid hack.

I said hello to Bruce and updated him on our progress. "We're just about to shoot."

"You have a laptop?" he said.

"There's one in my trailer."

"I'm gonna need you to do a little rewrite on scene forty-two."

"Hold up." I fished my blue script (the Blues) out of my book bag and turned the pages. It was a restaurant scene (INT. CAFÉ, UPTOWN—DAY) where Tanner and Hart discuss a case in dialogue overripe with lame double entendres. Brad Slaughter was a pro and would read the lines. Meaghan O'Toole would be the problem.

"Meaghan called me first thing this morning," said Bruce. "She thinks the scene makes her out to be a slut rather than a professional."

"What's her beef, exactly?" I asked disingenuously.

"I'm guessing it's the part about the in-box."

I pretended to study the lines, but I already knew the trouble spot. In the scene, McKenzie tells Tanner that she needs the arrest report "A-SAP" so she can get started on the prosecution of the case.

TANNER
Where do you want the report?
McKENZIE
Just put it in my in-box.
TANNER
It'll be my pleasure.

"Oh," I said. "*That*. How about if I just have her say, 'Shove it in my box'?"

"Asshole. And what's that bit about what he's gonna have for lunch?"

"*What?* All he says is, 'I'm partial to fish.'"

"And then the action says, 'She smiles demurely.'"

"I'll change it, boss."

"Get it done. We're publishing pinks today, and the scene's up this afternoon."

"Right."

"Crazy fucker." Bruce smirked a little and went off to craft services for a Slim Jim and some peanut butter crackers.

We were ready to shoot. The second second called "last looks," and the hair-and-makeup crew went in to touch up the actors. Lomax and Lillie were in the first row of chairs, right in front of the monitors. I was in the second row, behind them. The second AD slated the scene on camera by slapping the sticks.

"Camera."

"Speed."

"Action!"

We rolled. I watched the first take to make sure Lomax was getting what we needed. Among the actors, there was one dreaded ham.

"Anything, Victor?" said Lillie, after Lomax had cut it.

"Tell Board Member One to say his lines as I wrote them," I said, referring to a day player who was being far too creative.

"I'll do that," she said, and went in to give him the note.

"He's playing it too defensive, right?" said Lomax, turning to me.

"Well, he did kill the teller," I said. "But we don't want him to telegraph it. It's a reveal for later on."

"He's making a meal out of it."

"Yeah, guy thinks he's Larry fucking Olivier."

"I'll tell him to bring it down," said Lomax.

When Lillie returned to the village, I told her I was going to my trailer for a little while. She said she'd call me if anything came up.

Out on the street, I saw Annette showing Ellen something she had drawn in a sketchbook. Ellen was nodding her head in encouragement while giving Annette some suggestions. Ellen's cell rang and she walked down the block to take the call. I approached Annette, who was wearing brown velvet pants tucked into dark-brown buckled boots, and a tan newsboy cap with tiny mirrors across the bill.

"Hi," she said.

"Hey. What are you up to?"

"Just showing Ellen how I plan to dress the nightclub in one thirteen." She opened the spiral book and showed me some sketches. "What do you think of these?"

"They're beautiful," I said, looking at her breasts, standing up firm in her scoop-necked shirt.

"Stop it," she said. She had instantly blushed.

I lowered my voice. Crew was walking by us, standing about.

"I can't help it," I said.

"People are looking at us."

"No, they're not. Remember last night?"

"I'm not an amnesiac."

"It was good, wasn't it?"

"Yes."

"I'm hard as a two-by-four right now."

"Victor."

"And thick as a can of Coke."

"Vic."

"Okay, I'll stop. But damn, girl, you were hot."

"*We* were."

"Will I see you later?"

"I'll be around. Where you off to?"

"I've got to rewrite a scene for Number Two." We were supposed to call Meaghan O'Toole "Number One," since she was the lead actress in our show. But we often called her Number Two. As in doo-doo.

"Good luck."

"Check you later, beautiful."

I watched her walk toward her car.

My trailer was around the corner. I went there and rewrote the scene.